Underground Connection

Underground Connection

MARC **E**LLIOT

UNDERGROUND CONNECTION

This is a work of fiction. All of the characters, names, incidents, organizations, and dialogue in this novel are either the products of the author's imagination or are used fictitiously.

iUniverse books may be ordered through booksellers or by contacting:

iUniverse
1663 Liberty Drive
Bloomington, IN 47403
www.iuniverse.com
1-800-Authors (1-800-288-4677)

Because of the dynamic nature of the Internet, any web addresses or links contained in this book may have changed since publication and may no longer be valid. The views expressed in this work are solely those of the author and do not necessarily reflect the views of the publisher, and the publisher hereby disclaims any responsibility for them.

Any people depicted in stock imagery provided by Thinkstock are models, and such images are being used for illustrative purposes only. Certain stock imagery © Thinkstock.

ISBN: 978-1-4917-5220-3 (sc)
ISBN: 978-1-4917-5221-0 (e)

Library of Congress Control Number: 2014919553

Printed in the United States of America.

iUniverse rev. date: 12/27/2014

Chapter 1

Thursday

———————>>◆◆<<———————

*D*awn comes early at the marina, where I live. Even as the blue/black night fades to the gray false dawn, shrill-voiced gulls begin their feeding routine, scavenging residue on the marina's breakwater. Rigging clinks softly against the masts of a hundred boats snugly secure inside the marina, rocking gently, in contrast to the greater bay motion. Ropes and canvass flutter and snap as breezes tug at loose ends. On very still mornings the chugging engines of commercial fishing boats drift across the bay as the fishing fleet heads for coastal fishing grounds. Living in the Small Craft Harbor at Gas House Cove, I can hear the pounding feet of joggers performing their masochistic ritual, headed into the Marina Greens in the gray light of early dawn. I feel a part of nature during this early morning cacophony, my senses alive to the nuances of the budding day, delighting in being a part of the Bay.

But right now I am missing it. Instead, I am standing in a sewer, holding back a strong urge to vomit. The stench, even empty, is overpowering. The odor is like a weight pressing on me. It feels as if it is penetrating right through my clothing against the pores of my skin. All I want right now is to be back in my bunk asleep, awakening to the morning symphony.

But the body, propped grotesquely against the gray tunnel wall, was why I was there. He must have been dead for a while…at least two or three days, I guessed. Fully clothed in suit and rain coat, there were no visible marks to show how he died. But, by now it would be hard to tell from my observations in the dim light of electric lanterns.

He was past being stiff from rigor mortise, lying on his side, bent like he was just rising from a chair. His skin is gray-green and his face was bloated to the point of almost being unrecognizable.

I hate being called out of bed at three-thirty in the morning, especially for this. Someone flipped on the police flood lights which now made surrealistic shadows on the wall as the light faded off into the tunnel darkness. The stark white light made his skin appear even greener.

The sewer, where we stood, was large enough to drive a full-sized panel truck through. There was no water in it now, only a little dribble running down a foot-wide channel in the bottom. The lab crew, meticulously going over the area around the body, wore face masks against the odor. A young uniformed officer near the manhole ladder, twenty feet away, bent over the channel, vomiting. I tried hard not to notice him. If I thought very much about it, I'd soon be joining him. The police homicide lieutenant walked me through the crime scene. He pointed out why they knew the body was moved after death. "Maybe from another point in the tunnel, though I doubt it. I think it was from someplace else. But there is no evidence they brought him down this manhole. I'm sure there are other entrances."

"It's him, isn't it? I knew you were looking for him, and I owed you, so I thought I'd let you see for yourself just how he was found him." I don't know if it was his perverse humor, or a way of turning me off from my predilection to investigate crimes on my own. On the other hand, it could be that he sincerely believed I enjoyed being called out at odd hours to see a body in a sewer tunnel. I had written about Lt. Andy Sullivan when he worked a series of Chinatown killings. He was a sergeant then and attributed his promotion, in part, to the positive publicity he had received. Since he had more coverage from the Clarion than the two major dailies, he credited, or blamed, me the most.

I nodded. "It's awful, but it looks like him. Who found him, Lieutenant?"

"A couple of the sewer workers doing their monthly maintenance checks. They have to check the line and outfalls to make sure there are no obstructions. There's an outfall about a hundred feet down that way." He pointed the opposite way from the manhole and ladder I had come down.

I showed my flashlight up and down the walls and toward the outfall. "Really strange, Lieutenant. Last Saturday I'll bet this sewer was nearly full."

"Why do you say that?"

"There was sewer water coming out of that outfall. We were sailing and saw it. He even took pictures of it. There must be some residual marks of how deep the water was in here to cause an overflow. We ran some of those pictures after his disappearance."

"Interesting. Let's see how deep it would have to be for water to overflow." We walked the hundred feet to the intersecting tube, about three feet in diameter and shoulder height on the tunnel wall. The bottom of the tube was just below my shoulder. "So it had to be at least this full." He indicated the bottom of the tube.

"Fuller. It had a pretty good flow. I'll get you some pictures." We walked back to the body.

The lieutenant shook his head. "Whoever put him here, like this had a rather macabre sense of humor, putting him in a sewer and leaning him against the wall that way. It looks like he had been tied up and left that way after he died. See the way his arms are positioned?"

"So you're calling it murder? Any idea how he was killed?"

"I won't say its murder yet, but it is a felony to move a body. And it's clear that someone moved the body here. We won't know cause of death until the autopsy, but it doesn't appear like he was shot or stabbed. However, with the condition of the body we can't tell about blows yet." He must have seen me starting to waver. "Hey, let's go get some air. I could use a cigarette." He asked the lab crew to determine, if they could, what the most recent high water level had been.

The fresh air was delicious, but I could still taste the sewer air and the rest of me felt slimy, like the sewer vapors that enveloped me and had seeped through my clothing and coated my skin.

"Boy, I was starting to turn green down there. I don't know how those sewer guys can take it." The Lieutenant pulled an unfiltered cigarette from a pack and stuck it between his lips. He started to put the pack back in his pocket, stopped, and offered me one as an afterthought.

"Thanks, I don't smoke."

"What was it, Monday or Tuesday you were looking for this missing persons report?"

"Tuesday. They released it the next day. Lieutenant, if you were going to guess how long he had been dead, what would you say."

"Off the record?"

"Off the record."

"I'd say at least three days. If he was in the sewer all the time, it could have been longer because they don't deteriorate very rapidly when it's cool. But with the bloat and discoloration, I doubt he had been in a sewer all the time. So tell me about the guy. You know him, well?"

"Not well. I was acquainted with him, but I didn't know him well. His name is Simon Blare and he was the City's senior engineer on the big sewer project. Good position, lots of responsibility, comes from an old San Francisco family."

"So tell me about this sailing episode."

Although I only outlined the day generally for Lt. Sullivan, I remembered it vividly. I should have been suspicious because it hadn't started well, at all.

Last Saturday:

Normally I awaken early, but the sun was well above the horizon as I struggled for consciousness. The sunlight streaming through the portholes of my boat sent darts of pain to the frontal lobes of my head. The alarm clock seemed to be clanging as loud as a fire truck and quit when I hit it. I squinted at the ships clock on the bulkhead. My stomach churned, competing with my head for attention. I knew there was a reason to wake up, but my foggy mind refused to focus on anything but my throbbing temples and burning belly. Oh, dear god, I promise never to drink like that again. The evening started to come back to me.

Damn that woman. Just when I started to feel comfortable in the relationship, she began punching buttons on the traits she wanted to change. I guess it wasn't her fault, though. She just said what she felt, and there was truth to what she said. If there hadn't been, it wouldn't have bothered me. I am self-centered. I can be moody and don't mind being alone. Matter of fact I have been called a loner on more than one occasion. I focus on my work, often to the exclusion of my friends. And I never talk about what

I do. All these traits are true, I admit it. But some of that goes with the beat, when you're a journalist. A news story never waits for you. You never know when you'll have to work late, or when you'll be called out. And no, I don't get very close to people. I say it's because people want to talk about what I wrote last week, to disagree when they don't know the facts, or have some wonderful story idea I ought to write. Besides, everyone has a bias and I don't want their baggage to influence me.

But I'm beginning to suspect that the truth is, we - all of us news people - are more observers than participants in life. We'd rather watch and comment or criticize than take an active role, to present events as an instruction in morality. Bad news we present as bad, horrible, awful or evil, and we delight in telling stories about those who make a difference, touting their works with praising adjectives. This is how we see our contribution to society.

In truth, all of us are afraid of getting too close, of actually having to take a personal moral position, or of taking an action, and especially of getting hurt by people, people we start to trust. So we tell stories of others that present the good, the bad, the sordid, and the sublime.

Last night, lovely, petite Angelina Denucci held this mirror in front of my face before she terminated our relationship. I will miss her laughing eyes and bouncing dark curls. She was fun to be with, stimulating, witty, intelligent, and an enthusiastic lover.

"Ohhh." I groaned as I sat up. My head ached and my tongue tasted awful. Got to get some coffee in me. Then I remembered why I had to get up. The Blares were coming to go sailing at nine. It's what time? Eight forty. Oh, shit! I grabbed a pair of jeans and a shirt, clumsily banging into the bulkhead and dinette. There are many delights to living on a sailboat. But moving about quickly in a thirty-six footer requires sober dexterity. With a hangover it's a nightmare. I put the fixings in the coffee pot and lit the stove under it. Opening the hatch to freshen the cabin air, I cringed from the sunlight.

I was mad that she dumped me, but what angered me more was how she did it. And after I had conned an invitation for her to the Foreign Ministers reception that I had to attend. The reception was hosted by the City's Chief Administrative Officer, Brian Elliston, and all the City's elite were invited. I had just finished dressing in my only suit when I felt the motion of someone boarding the boat and there was a knock on the hatch. Appearing in jeans and a pull-over, she was obviously not going to the reception.

"We need to talk," she launched without a preamble. "Don't go to the reception. Let's go for a sail, or out to dinner." She paused, waiting for my response. It seems that most women like to appear mysterious to men, but usually there is some little sign, a signal that reveals the essence of the mystery. Sometimes it is so subtle one doesn't even know he is picking it up. But last night there was nothing I could read. It was like she was wearing a mask.

"Angie, are your being spontaneous? This isn't like you. You always have everything planned and prioritized. What's up?"

Angie was not a typical San Francisco Italian Catholic woman. She had rebelled. Shunning the traditional Italian Catholic woman's life style of child-rearing and home-maker, of her San Francisco fishing family traditions, she graduated from San Francisco University with honors. She went on to the University of California Law School, where she also graduated with honors. Since then she had been working for one of the City's prestigious law firms and the rumor was that she would be offered a junior partnership the end of the year.

"Look, you are always dragging me to some function or another, and I'm tired of it."

"I thought you enjoyed these things, a chance to mix and mingle with some of the City's high flyers. Besides, this way we can be together. Anyway, it is part of my job. I really have to go tonight." It was the reward and penalty, depending upon how you look at it, of my job as a reporter for the San Francisco Clarion.

"That's the whole problem. You don't care what anyone else wants, only your job."

We argued, and finally she said, "I just think it would be better if we didn't see each other anymore." Her matter-of-fact tone stopped me.

Know how, sometimes, you have a feeling down in your gut that something isn't quite right? That's how I had been feeling. I think she was planning to dump me. I think she even planned the timing for when I couldn't drop everything to go sailing or out to dinner. I had been feeling our relationship starting to drift. I even had suggested that. "I think what you really want is a husband and children, not a prestigious career." She denied it at the time, but maybe she had been thinking it over and decided I was right.

Perhaps her interest in me was an intrigue with my free life style, membership in the media, and living on a sailboat. And when she saw this was the real me, that I didn't have an ambitious drive beyond what I was doing, and that I was not going to change -- not the life style, not the media, and not living on a sailboat -- she lost interest.

She left and I finished dressing. My interest in the reception was gone, but I went, fulfilling my responsibilities. However, my heart wasn't in it. A bruised pride and smarting psyche interfered with my full involvement. It was as if I were watching the reception scene through someone else's eyes. But I did my job, mingling with the crowd and collecting story leads. As the reception wore down, I found myself flirting with the host's twenty-three-year-old daughter, Margaret Elliston, and was pleasantly surprised when she flirted back. She was tall and gangly, serious competition for models like Twiggy, if that was still the style. Her evening gown was meant for someone with more cleavage, or maybe it was just that the style was 10 years too old for her. But she had a cute personality and I enjoyed her banter.

Women seem to enjoy my company, and pleasant as that is, I am usually surprised. I have been compared to a woolly brown bear. Hirsute, five-foot-eight-inch, stocky, one hundred-ninety pound, forty-four-year-old, bearded males, with slightly flattened noses are not usually considered the Adonis type. Perhaps woolly brown bears are in fashion, or maybe it is that I don't appear threatening. Either way, feminine company is usually available. As a balm to my wounded pride, I invite Margaret to go sailing and to a barbecue on Sunday. She accepted.

Following the reception some journalists gathered for drinks at a nearby bar, and I tagged along. I had been sipping scotch all evening, so when we got down to serious drinking it didn't take much for me to get smashed. Angie wasn't forgotten, but at the time the pain was numbed.

There were footsteps on the dock. The steps stopped at my boat and someone tapped on the boat railing. I grabbed the loose clothes lying about and threw them in a locker. "David! David Montgomery! Are you in there?" It was Simon Blare. I heard the soft giggle of a woman's voice and I knew he had brought Barbara, his wife, along.

"Coming," I croaked my voice raspy from the booze.

"Barbara, I think there's something alive in there." Simon's humor was lost on me this morning.

"I hope it's not a wild animal." Barbara's voice was full of laughter. I emerged from the hatch to the deck. "Oh, it is a wild animal. It's a bear coming out of hibernation." Barbara laughed at my appearance. Lange, my neighbor on the cruiser in the next slip, looked up from polishing his bright work when I emerged. He and I have gotten to be friends, frequently sharing meals, coffee or a drink, and swapping yarns. He recognized my discomfort, and was grinning in amusement.

"No, but I'm just as gruff. Grrrrr. I eat pretty young things like you just for an appetizer." Barbara giggled at my response.

"God, David. You look awful. Are you well?"

"Thanks, Simon. Great confidence building," I grunted. "I just got up and I'm a little hung-over."

"Look, if you don't feel up to it..."

"Hell." I interrupted, "A cup of coffee and I'll be good as new. My latest flame dumped me just before I went to Brian Elliston's reception last night. Then after the reception I went out with a bunch of those rowdy press types for drinks." Lange gave me a knowing look and turned back to his polishing.

"I heard Elliston was throwing quite a party. We were supposed to go, but we had this Saturday morning sailing date we didn't want to miss..."

"Oh, shut up and come on aboard. I will tell you that you missed some great food. This city's Chief Administrator goes first cabin."

Barbara handed over a grocery bag as I gave her a hand to climb over the side. Her hands were stronger than I expected. She was more agile than her well-proportioned body would indicate. "Here are some sandwiches and beer we thought we'd contribute to the day's excursion. My, this is nice. Not as large as I thought it would be." Her gaze took in the cockpit and deck, as she stepped into the cockpit. Her movements were those of one who was very physically fit.

She had a finished look; flaxen hair that could have been natural was tucked neatly under a variegated red scarf.

"The boat is 36 feet long and about 12 feet wide."

"And you live on it?" Her voice rang of incredulity.

"Sure. I have simple tastes. You're on the patio, now come below into the cabin and I'll give you the grand tour." I guided them down the four-step ladder into the cabin. "It has a large bunk in the forw'd stateroom, that's sailor talk for up front in that cubby hole. Here is a dinette, a galley with a stove, oven, refrigerator and sink; and a head, err... that's a bathroom, with a shower, and back here under the cockpit is another large queen-sized bunk. All the necessities. What more does one need?" The designer had made excellent use of space and it felt larger than its actual size.

"What's this desk, with all the electronic dials and knobs?"

"It's a navigation station, with radio, directional finder, satellite navigation, depth finder and weather equipment, all the goodies one needs to get from here to there without billboards or road signs. But I don't yet have radar."

As Barbara and Simon inspected the cabin, exclaiming at all the little comforts tucked into niches and crevices, I stowed the sandwiches and beer in the refrigerator and poured coffee for the three of us. "Do either of you take milk or sugar in your coffee? I'll feel much more alive once I get a cup of coffee inside." I put out bagels, cream cheese and jam. We sat at the dinette, ate, drank coffee and mostly talked of trivial things, like the San Francisco's parties and social life. They were polite and didn't intrude on my ruined love life, though I caught Barbara surreptitiously appraising me. She returned my look and smiled.

Being fairly new to San Francisco, I was interested in who they thought were the important people and who were in the social pecking order. Hired as an investigative reporter, I also covered for any of the beat reporters who were ill or on vacation, which is how I met Simon, filling in for Ernie Stahl, our public works reporter.

We were finished with our coffee and Barbara excused herself to try out the head. She stood in the doorway looking at the toilet for a moment. "My, this is a small bathroom. Should I back in? How does this thing work?"

"There is a knob on the side that you turn like a faucet to open the water line. Then you push and pull the other handle to bring water into the bowl. When you are finished, close the knob and push and pull the handle to take the water out of the bowl."

"Oh. That sounds complicated."

"Want me to help you, honey?"

"Of course not. I'm quite capable."

A week ago, I had run into the Blares at a city function. During the conversation I mention I lived on a sailboat. They were fascinated about what it was like to live on a sailboat. So I invited them to go sailing -- today.

Barbara was out of the head and I rounded up the coffee mugs. "What do you say we go sailing now? We have a few things to do before we cast off -- that means untie the ropes from the dock."

I asked Barbara to make sure anything that could roll around and get broken was placed somewhere safe. Meanwhile, I disconnected the electrical, telephone, and water lines. Simon unfastened and folded the sail covers. In a few minutes we were ready to sail.

"There, in about five minutes we've converted from a live-aboard to a sea-going sailboat." I prided myself on keeping everything ready for sailing at a moment's notice. To me, the whole reason to live on a sailboat is to have the bay and ocean immediately accessible. Unwinding from the day's work with an hour or two of sailing was almost as refreshing as a night's sleep for me. A lot of people that live on boats just like to be near the water, to have the feel of the soft motion while drifting off to sleep. I live on the boat to have that, but also to be able to get out on the water easily. That means keeping everything organized and shipshape.

"All right, lady and gent, we are about to cast off for parts unknown." I used my tour guide voice reserved for first-time passengers. "As your tour guide, I'm obligated to tell you, just like in the airlines, about certain safety regulations. This orange horseshoe-shaped float I am placing in this holder on the stern -- back of the boat -- is to be used in in case someone falls overboard by accident or stupidity. Be sure to throw it to the person, and try not to hit them on the head."

I handed each a life jacket. "These are your personal floatation devices, and must be no farther from you than the end of your arm, if you choose not to wear it. The water is fairly quiet today, so the skipper has decided that wearing a life jacket is optional, as long as it is easily available."

I turned on the bilge blowers in preparation to starting the engine.

"What's that noise? What are you doing? Tell me. I've never been sailing on a boat with all this...this stuff." Barbara gestured to the dials, gauges, buttons, and jungle of ropes and wires.

As I started the engine, I said it was necessary to blow any vapor that might have built up near the engine so we would not explode when the engine was started. I described what everything was, and what we would be doing next. "We'll actually motor out of the marina before hoisting our sails." The little diesel engine settled into an even chugging beat, we cast off, and backed out of the slip. Moving slowly between the rows of boats and empty berths, whose boats were already on the bay, Barbara read the names of the boats from their sterns.

"Oh! I didn't look. What's your boat's name?"

"It doesn't have a name. We're still getting acquainted. And, like every writer, I'm looking for the perfect name. Since I haven't found it yet, I just call it 'Boat'."

Barbara and Simon were both sitting on top of the cabin. As we hit the small waves at the end of breakwater, Barbara squealed at the increased motion, grabbed the life line and slid into the cockpit. Simon laughed and continued to sit on top of the cabin riding with the motion. I steered into the wind.

"Here, Barbara, take the wheel. Just keep it going in this direction. See that number on the compass?"

"Wait! Where are you going?"

"I'm going to raise the sails. Just steer it like a car. It won't react as quickly as a car, but it steers the same way." I could have locked the wheel to hold us into the wind for the short time it took to raise the sails, but people enjoy sailing more if they get to participate. I stepped up onto the cabin and hoisted the main sail, while Simon hoisted the jib sail. As we tied off the halyards, the sails flapped noisily.

Barbara shrieked, startled by the noise. "What's wrong? What do I do now?" Her eyes and mouth were as round as a ball. Simon laughed at the expression on her face.

I shouted back. "You're doing fine. Just hold it right where it is." Back in the cockpit I tightened in on the sails a bit, then turned toward the Golden Gate Bridge. As we turned, the wind filled the sails and in one motion the boat leaned and lifted in the water. This is one of the more exhilarating moments of sailing, for me, to feel wind born. It's similar to the sensation of flying, I think. I saw the effects of the sensation in Barbara's and Simon's faces, too.

Killing the engine, we were now under sail. With the engine sound gone, the rush and gurgle of water was audible.

The motion of a sailboat running under sail is very different than running under power. It's an easier, smoother motion, at one with the water.

"Lady and Gent, we are now under sail. You can feel the difference from when we were motoring. Today, we'll give you an ocean view of the Marin coastline, a seal's-eye view of tourists at the Cliff House and see what Mile Light really looks like." I said in my tour guide voice again.

"Will we get to see the Faralone Islands?" Barbara's enthusiasm rang in her voice.

"Not today. The Faralones are about twenty-six miles off the coast, and that's a three or four hour sail under the best conditions. Then, of course, we'd have to sail back. We'll have an easy sail. There's about a twelve-knot breeze, and I don't think there'll be any fog."

"Do you sail much, Simon?" He seemed to know his way around a boat.

"Not as much as I'd like. I think I'd like to buy a sailboat, but berthing is so difficult to find these days, I'm hesitant to even look.

"How'd you ever decide to live on a sailboat? And what brought you to San Francisco, anyway?" Barbara was watching me, not the view. It was like she wanted to see my reaction as I answered. I decided then and there she was really a nosy broad. There was something else that bothered me about how she was pumping me for information, but I couldn't put my finger on it.

I thought for a moment about how to answer, and then decided on the canned version. "It's kind of a long story, but in a nut shell I had been working for U.P., Universal Press, and I was tired of traveling. I was looking for a city to call home. I love sailing, so it had to be near open water--San Diego, San Francisco, Seattle. I had always liked San Francisco best, and when I was able to land a job with the Clarion I knew it was a perfect fit. I arrived with two suitcases and a computer."

"But the boat?"

"Yes, the boat. Have you tried finding an apartment, or have you priced one in the city recently?" Both shook their heads. "Well, let me tell you, with what you have to pay and what you get..." I shrugged. "It just wasn't worth it. Since I was going to buy a boat anyway, a friend suggested I just buy one I could live on. I didn't have to buy any furniture. Slip fees and boat payments are about the same as I would pay for an apartment, and I'm where I want to be. So, here I am, living on a boat and I love it."

"Oh, look! A big ship!" Barbara pointed to a large container ship entering under Golden Gate Bridge. We trimmed sails and steered a course to keep us well clear of the ship and it's wake. The wake from ships like that can swamp boats, even ones my size, if we get too close. As we narrowed the distance between us and the ship, Barbara exclaimed at its size.

"It is a large ship, but when we are sitting here nearly at water level, it looks much larger than it really is." Simon, being the engineer, explained the rules of perspective and how things appear to be different from different angles.

His point was interesting, for even in news writing a story can appear to have a particular perspective, or slant. Unless the reporter is very careful to include views from other angles the reader only sees the perspective the reporter projects.

"Now lady and gent, this is your tour guide, again. We are about to pass under the Golden Gate Bridge, built in 1937. It is the longest single-span suspension bridge in the world."

"On your port, excuse me, the left side of the boat, is Fort Point, one of the oldest structures in the entire Bay

Area. It was built to defend the entrance to the Bay, but has never fired a hostile shot. And on the starboard, that's opposite of left, is Fort Baker. A few Army personnel are still stationed there."

"This sparkling monologue is designed to take your mind off the increase in turbulence as we go through the channel to the ocean. This is commonly called the potato patch, and is where the flow of the Sacramento and San Joaquin Rivers meet the ocean currents and tidal movement at the narrowest point on the bay. So if you've ever seen a potato patch after harvest you'll remember it is all lumpy and bumpy. We may bounce a little as we go over the bumps."

I was feeling pretty good now. The hangover had worn off, and I was sailing. Sailing always clears my head and gives me a lift. And the company was enjoyable. We cleared Point Bonita well before noon and were off the Marin headlands. We changed course to the Northwest so we could run parallel to the Marin coastline, about two miles off shore. The sea was running four to five foot swells with small waves, just enough motion for a pleasant easy sail.

"Well, I believe its lunch time. I think I remember someone saying there were sandwiches, beer and chips." I turned the wheel over to Simon and went below to get the lunch. As I emerged from the cabin, I heard Simon telling Barbara a little of what I did for the Clarion, how I did investigative reporting.

"Oooh, that sounds so exciting. It must be very interesting." Barbara practically gushed.

I'm always embarrassed when people call me an investigative reporter, although that is the title. While some of the work is a little like that of a detective, mostly it is research, pouring over old records and documents, looking for pieces of information or contradictions in information. So I usually play it lightly when people comment on the title. "That's right. I just get right down in the slimy gutters and dig up all that lovely dirt and scandal, so our readers can know what sordid pleasures they are missing." Barbara's response was a little titter and a weak smile. That didn't work, so I shifted gears.

"Actually I spend a tremendous amount of time reading old documents, checking whether all the "i's" are dotted and "t's" crossed; all very routine. I actually get more excitement filling in for one of the regular beat reporters. That's how I met Simon, you know." I didn't tell her I rather preferred the routine over the excitement, having already experienced all the excitement I cared for in life.

"Now, who'd like a sandwich?" I passed them around and unwrapped mine. "Oh! Fantastic! Crab sandwiches. You certainly know your way into this old scandal monger's heart." Barbara and Simon giggled at my exclamation.

After lunch we just settled back, relaxed and enjoyed the day. The boat, with the sails properly trimmed, will sail itself. However, I let Simon continue handling the wheel because he seemed to be enjoying it so much. As we sailed along I pointed out landmarks along the Marin coast. We went nearly as far as Bolinas before coming about and setting a course for Mile Light and Seal Rocks.

"How'd you get into journalism? Did you go to journalism school?" Barbara popped a question out of the blue.

"Oh, it's a question game? I like question games, but as I remember the rules I get one for each one of yours. I only play is if it goes both ways." This brought a giggle from Barbara and a knowing smile from Simon. "Actually, I majored in business and minored in English literature and government in college." I also had four years of ROTC and spent eight years in the Army, part of it with the Special Forces in Vietnam. But even though I had been promoted to Captain, eight years of military life was enough. At the time I was released from the Army, the U.P. was looking for someone to replace their reporter who had been killed in Vietnam. Since I had been in 'Nam and supposedly knew what was going on, they hired me.

After 'Nam, I bounced around the world, Paris one day and Tokyo the next. It was interesting. I learned a lot, and for a while it was exciting. However, it was hell on my marriage, and after ten years of missed anniversaries and birthdays we divorced.

"Do you have any children?"

"No"

"So how long have you been divorced?" Barbara had that glint in her eye that said she knew a woman who would be a perfect match for me.

"Three years. And I have to tell you I really enjoy being single. I don't think I'll ever remarry."

"He's on to you, Barb." Simon was grinning at her transparency.

"You just haven't met the right one, David." She said it with the conviction of one who believes that every man should be married and tamed.

"I've met lots of 'right' ones. I'm very self-centered, devoted to my work that I love, and I work crazy hours. Besides, I'll never leave the boat, and two of us would never fit."

"You may have a point. It could be difficult for two people to live on a boat this size."

"Now that you have my life story, how long have you been married? How'd you meet?"

"Two years, three months, and five, no six days. We met in Las Vegas." Simon answered instead of Barbara and anticipated my next question. "She was a show girl, and I was there for the annual engineering convention. I saw her in a show, and ran into her later. I don't know where I got the courage, but I told her how much I liked the show and asked if I could buy her a cup of coffee." He looked at Barbara to continue.

"Actually, I was trying to become a dancer, but the best I ever got was some of the duo routines and the chorus line. Then Simon stole me away from the glitter and bright lights of show business." That explained her physical fitness, but her answer came out glibly, like an explanation that had been rehearsed too many times.

While her story was that of the typical Midwestern girl with some talent who goes to Hollywood to become a star, it seemed incomplete. She had grown up in a small Iowa town, and like all little girls there, took ballet and tap dancing classes at the one and only local dance studio. As encouragement, her friends and family kept telling her she had real talent and should become a ballerina.

"I grew up hearing this constantly, so of course I believed it. As soon as I graduated from high school I headed straight for Hollywood. Ballet is stuffy. What I really wanted was to get into movies."

Like so many other young ladies who arrive in Hollywood with a dream, Barbara thought she'd be a star in a couple of years--three at the most. "But it doesn't work that way. For more than five years I got just enough work for me to keep chasing the dream. I waited tables to survive."

"One day a friend told me about Las Vegas. There was a demand for chorus girls and background people. There was a lot of action and more exposure there than in Hollywood. She told me that you could make real money, even if you weren't a star."

"That weekend I threw everything I owned into a suitcase and grabbed a bus to Las Vegas. That was ten years ago. It didn't take very long for me to know that I was just one of a crowd; that I was never going to become a star. But the work was steady and it paid well. Then Simon...walked into my life." She had liked Simon's quiet self-assurance, his awareness and knowledge about many different things. He enjoyed her lack of inhibitions, bubbliness and happiness with life. It was nearly instant love.

"By the time I met Simon, I had gotten all the show biz out of my system. He represents everything a little girl from Iowa should have been thinking about all the time, home, family and most of all - love." Simon, watching her as she talked, was literally drooling love. They married six months after they met, a year ago.

Barbara adapted to San Francisco quickly, and plunged headlong into the city's social scene. In spite of being a newcomer, with her looks and Simon's family name, she had her pick of social events. And she dragged Simon to every one they could make. Simon, the student and scholar, found the whirling social circuit a dizzying experience. But he enjoyed the attention that was paid to him and Barbara, and he rationalized that it would help his career.

It was a little after three in the afternoon when we crossed the San Francisco Bay channel on our approach to Seal Rocks and the Cliff House. I took the helm and asked Simon to get my binoculars from the cabin so he and Barbara could better see the sea lions and seals. "We're now south of the entrance to the Bay. The light on the rock to your left is the south entrance light for entrance to the Bay, called Mile Light. When we get closer to Seal Rock you should be able to see some sea lions and seals through that horde of pelicans on the rocks. And if you want to see some really interesting animal life, watch the people near the Cliff House."

The currents around there are pretty tricky, so I didn't get too close. Each year a number of small craft get washed onto these rocks, I've been told, and I didn't want to become one of the statistics.

But that was before Simon discovered water coming from a sewage outfall.

Chapter 2

Saturday – Sunday

———⟫◆◆◆⟪———

It was a delightful sail, really nice until we got to the Cliff House and Mile Light. Both of them were enjoying themselves, acting a little like typical newly-weds, only they weren't, not real newly-weds. Simon said they had been married about a little over a year. Barbara was excited as she scanned the Cliff House promenade.

"Oh my God! Those people up there look so funny, and they are looking at us and pointing. They do look funny from out here. Now, the seals . . . Oh, there they are."

"The seals are up at the Cliff House? This, I've got to see." Simon's sense of humor was a little strange, but he was fun. He took the binoculars as we entered the Bay channel at Lands End and headed for San Francisco. He studied the shoreline. "There is supposed to be a nude beach along here somewhere, but I don't see anyone."

"Oh, give me those." Barbara made a grab for the binoculars. "The only nude you look at is me." She looked at me as she said it, as if to test for a reaction.

"Why, do you want to see a nude too?" He was still staring through the binoculars. "Wait a minute. David, how close can you get to the shore?"

"Not too much closer. Why?"

"Look up there on the cliff, about a third of the way down. See the large pipe? Does it look like it has water running out?" He handed me the binoculars.

I scanned the cliff until I was aimed at where he had been pointing. "Yeah. There is. It looks like a fair amount of water. Why?"

"There shouldn't be any. That's a sewer outfall, an overflow for when the rains overflow the system. Only, it hasn't rained. I wish I'd have brought a camera."

"I think we can get a little closer than this." The tide was flowing out of the bay, so we should have pretty good control against the current. I paused for a moment as I brought the boat around and headed back toward Seal Rocks. We had been more than a quarter of a mile off the shore. If I was going to get closer, I wanted to ease in slowly, taking full advantage of the current -- like landing a light plane into a head wind.

"I left my digital camera at the office. But, I have an old 35mm film camera. It's in the same locker where you found the binoculars. There's also a 200mm telephoto lens there as well." We turned back toward the Bay, this time easing closer and closer to Lands' End. I was trusting that the tidal current would counteract the effects of the undertow and turbulence of the waves hitting the base of the cliff. I tested the rudder constantly to ensure we could turn sharply in case we saw a submerged rock.

"Hey, Uhhh, guys. Do we have to get this close? I can already see us smashing into one of those rocks. I really don't want to go for a swim. It'll ruin my hair." Her knuckles were white as she clenched the up-wind rail.

Simon emerged from the cabin with the camera, telephoto lens attached. "This is great. It's a good vantage point." I told him the camera had automatic metering, if he set the meter on the green dot. It was already loaded with black and white film.

The water was rough here, as we approached the best shooting point. "Barbara, we're going to bounce a little, and you may catch a little spray."

"Oh, I wish we weren't doing this." Barbara was now clinging to the rail with both hands. "Simon, why'd you have to ask him to do this crazy thing?"

We worked for position, but it was awkward. We were parallel to the waves. One moment we were in a trough between waves. The next moment the bow crashed into the side of another wave, and we'd roll sideways over the top. I concentrated on holding the boat as steady as possible for Simon, and I almost missed seeing a half-submerged rock dead ahead. I swung the wheel hard to port, but the undertow sucked us directly for the rock. In my imagination already I could feel the grinding jolt and sickening lurch that was sure to happen in seconds. But the rudder caught the current and we cleared the rock with a full ten feet of water between us. Neither of them saw how close we had come. Barbara was looking away from the shore, as if she felt safer by not looking. Throughout the heart-pounding moments that our fate hung on those precarious wave tops, Simon fired off frame after frame oblivious to the danger. After giving him a good three or four minutes, I turned us back toward the channel. The wind was nearly behind us so it was much smoother, and it seemed like we were flying. But with the current against us we were making only about three or four knots.

As Barbara regained her composure, she released her anxiety with real anger. "I don't know what you had to do such a damn, dumb, fool thing for, just to take a damn picture of some dumb pipe with some stupid water running out of it." It wasn't hysterics, it was pure anger and she bellowed it like she was ready for a street brawl. What a different image from the sweet, cutesy show girl of half-an-hour ago. "God damn it, Simon, your stupid engineering curiosity almost got the three of us killed."

"Oh, Hon, there was nothing to worry about. David is an excellent boat handler, and we were never in that much danger, were we David?" Simon cajoled, trying to calm her.

"Not really." But I sure was glad to be out of there. Neither of them knew how close we had come to that rock. I tried to bring us back to a lighter mood. "Besides, you can bet I'm not going to chance smashing my boat with a damn, dumb, fool thing, just to take damn picture of some dumb pipe with some stupid water running out of it."

Barbara giggled nervously at my parroting her words. "I'm sorry. But that really scared me. Those were really big rocks and we seemed so close. And . . . and . . . I don't swim very well."

They both make half-hearted attempts at levity the rest of the way back to the marina, but the closeness and warmth of the afternoon was gone. Simon seemed detached, his mind was elsewhere. And Barbara had a layer of hostility barely covered by skin that was ready to erupt with any provocation. The reactions seemed strange to me. Sure, we had taken a risk. It wasn't the smartest thing to do. But the effect it had on both of them was dramatic, much more dramatic than the situation merited, I thought.

We tied up at the berth and after they collected their belongings, I walked them to their car. Barbara made an attempt at congeniality now, thanking me profusely for the wonderful day. And as I closed Barbara's door for her, I saw something else in her eyes. It was fear. I know that look. I've seen it before. And it didn't fit here, not back on dry land. Not now. I apologized for the scare, and suggested a repeat performance, without the rocks. They both smiled and nodded, but I was sure Barbara would not come sailing again.

"Simon, I'll have the prints for you Tuesday or Wednesday. What is this all about? I'm speaking as a reporter now. If there's a story here, I think I should have it."

He paused, as if considering what to tell me. "Dave, I don't know what, or if, there is anything to this. But if there's a story there, it's all yours."

Back at the boat I hosed the salt from the deck, and quickly converted the boat back to a live-aboard. Lange came over and we settled down with a couple of beers. Lange is just Lange, and to my knowledge goes by no other name. He is a good head taller than me and lanky, gaunt even, if he didn't have such a healthy out-of-doors look. His face is ageless, allowing one to pick a number between the forties to the early sixties. "So tell me about the reception. Who was there? I nearly went, but I hadn't quite finished my business for the day. I already know that you drank too much."

"Oh, that was after the reception. All of the consulates were represented. The ambassador from Taiwan was here on his way to Washington. That was why Elliston chose this time for the reception. All of the City's department heads were there, Ralph Hunt of Public Works; Enoch Worth, City Engineer. Of course all of the Supervisors were there, including isolationist William Cochrane. Even the Mayor put in an appearance, and was quite complimentary to Elliston. With as much as they hate each other I didn't know they were capable of cordiality in the other's presence. But since both are pushing Pacific Rim trade, they had to make nice." Lange is a venture capitalist who, like me, lives on his boat, an immaculately maintained 54-foot cruiser. I told him some of the bits of information I picked up and whatever gossip I could remember. He likes gossip, and is quite adept at pulling secrets from people.

"And how was your cruise?"

"It was good for the most part. But toward the end it got strange." I shared with Lange my perception of Simon and Barbara and then the abrupt change after the Lands' End. His questions were virtually the same as mine. Why would there be water coming from an outflow, when there had not been any rain all summer? Why was Simon so intensely interested that he wanted photo documentation? And why was Barbara so affected by this? Sure it was risky. But her reaction was more than the fear of crashing on the rocks. There was real fear deep inside.

It was nearly dark when Angie showed up at the boat. Lange and I had just opened another beer and were debating whether to make a cooperative dinner, or to eat out. We had pretty well decided to eat out, neither one of us feeling any culinary creativity. Nor did we see her coming until she was right at the boat. The first I knew she was here was a tentative, "Hi."

"I left a few things on the boat I thought I should retrieve before you threw them out. Hi Lange." She acknowledged him.

"Sure, come on aboard. Want a beer?"

"No. I won't be staying. I just wanted to pick up my things." There was a long pause as she stepped onto the deck. "About last night, David, I wanted to say I'm sorry for how I acted." Although sincere, her voice had a quality I recognized, but had never thought about before. The experience was over and she had already written it out of her life. There was no sense of loss. It was time to move on, and she did. Some people go from experience to experience, capturing them as they go along. But I wonder if they really feel any sense of attachment during the experience, or have any sensation about the experience after it is over. I found myself questioning if our relationship was only an experience of the moment to her. There were odd little things that I thought nothing of at the time. But looking back at them the made me wonder if she was really emotionally involved in our relationship at all.

"I accept that. You were just expressing frustration at . . ."

"No! It wasn't the right way, and I'm sorry."

Lange stood and moved toward the rail. "I'm going next door. Let me know what you decide on dinner."

"Lange, don't go. I won't be but a minute. I've said all I have to say." Angie disappeared into the hatch. Moments later she returned with a scarf, sweatshirt and tennis shoes in her hands. At the rail she turned, "David, please don't be terribly angry with me. I'll talk with you later. Lange, good to see you." And she was gone.

Lange watched her all the way off the pier, and then resumed his seat. We sat silently for minutes, lost in our own thoughts. I didn't know how I felt at this point. Or more accurately, I was feeling different emotions, all at the same time. Part of me felt a sense of loss. I was fond of Angie, and I knew I was going to miss her. But part of me was relieved. She had been growing increasingly pushy about our relationship. I thought it was that she was trying to get me to make a commitment. But now I'm not sure she wasn't just trying to goad me into making the first move. Whether or not I would ever remarry, I didn't want to feel pushed into it. There was even a third part of me that was ambivalent, almost a fatalistic outlook--whatever is, is. It was a like I was standing outside of myself, passively watching the events of my life go on around me.

"Look, if you're not up to socializing, we'll do it later." Lange broke the silence.

"No, no, it's okay. To tell you the truth, I'm not sure how I feel about this. I liked Angie well enough, but other than my wounded pride, I'm not sure I'm all that hurt." Lange nodded his head in understanding. We talked for a few minutes about how couples build strange, complex relationships for themselves. Lange opined that he liked women well enough on occasion, but found they encumbered his life on a sustained basis. The thought occurred to me that just maybe I was pretty much the same way. Completing our discussion on the turmoil instigated by the fairer sex, we locked our respective ships and, just as the stars began to appear, we strolled the two blocks to a tiny, hole-in-the-wall Italian restaurant. It was across the street from the Marina supermarket. Pirelli's restaurant fronted a door and one window on the street, easily overlooked by casual passersby. But it served the best pasta in all of San Francisco. With a good meal and a bottle of Chianti under our belts we retired to our respective boats to sleep the sleep of the innocents we liked to pretend we were.

SUNDAY

I awoke early Sunday and lay in my bunk drinking in the sounds around me. I couldn't imagine anything so pleasant in an apartment. By the time the sun sliced the eastern hills across the bay, I had gotten my Sunday newspapers and had a pot of coffee brewing. Besides the Clarion, I usually read the competition and at least one out-of-town paper. There is a lot of information in a newspaper--more than some people want to digest. But by reading newspapers a person at least stands a chance to understand what is going on behind the event. Most people think that it is a natural trait for me, being a reporter. But I think it's the other way around. I respect the written word and its closer representation to facts than is available from the show biz of television news. Television news is a show, as staged as any entertainment.

I don't mean that it is wrong, just that in the few minutes TV gives for a news story it is impossible to present the full perspective of a situation. A station must get the most impact it can so, understandably, most stations play the emotional angle. They go for the gut not the head. There are a few stations that have hour-long news programs, and spend a little more time on a story. The result is the difference between a sound-bite and an understanding. I have a little television tucked away in one of the lockers that I get out every once in a while for a national news event, the World Series, or just to see if it still plays.

However, I didn't get a chance to read all my newspapers. There was a light rap on the deck and I poked my head up to find Simon staring at me from the dock.

"Can I come on board?" He spoke softly, barely above a whisper; as if he were afraid he would be overheard.

"Sure, hop on. I've got a pot of coffee going."

He had no more than landed on the deck than he started talking in an excited whisper. "I've got to ask you for a big favor. I've got to go back out to the outfall. Something strange is going on. I don't know what it is."

I hadn't really looked at him closely at first. But as he climbed into the cabin, I noticed that he looked rumpled, with beard stubble and dark circles around his eyes, as if he hadn't slept. "Here, Simon. Have a cup of coffee. What can I do for you?"

"You've got to take me back out to the outfall, David. I've got to take samples. Something is very wrong. Please help me."

"Sure, Simon. What is it that is so wrong?

"I'm not sure, things just don't add up. I was checking the project all night. There are things that don't hang together, and the closure of that line was not scheduled for another two months. I've had suspicions, but this just doesn't make sense."

I had plenty of time to motor out to the area and back before my dates for the picnic were due to show. The timing was perfect. It was slack tide, which meant that there was no current into or out of the Bay. This made it much easier to maneuver near the rocks. Water was still flowing from the outfall and Simon collected a dozen samples of the water as close as we could get to the bottom of the cliff. I also collected a few samples of my own, unseen by Simon. Back at the marina Simon bounded off the boat before we were even tied up.

"Don't tell anyone I was here. I'll call you!" He shouted, heading up the dock. If he was worried about someone overhearing him before, he certainly wasn't now.

I had cleaned up and was just back into my newspapers, when Margaret Elliston, my date for the newspaper picnic arrived. She was early by a full three quarters of an hour and was breathless, as if she had run all the way, or was hyperventilating from excitement.

"I know I'm early, but I didn't want to be late so I set my alarm an hour early and got tired of waiting at home." The words tumbled out, bumping into each other. Dressed casually, Margaret had much more of a figure than the evening dress had allowed showing. Her mid-calf white pants and pink knit top accentuated her slightness and height, and displayed that she had some shape. Standing beside me on the deck she was about my height. Her blonde hair was pulled back and tied with a silk scarf in shades of pink.

"It's okay. I wasn't going to leave without you. We'll have a few more coming with us, a couple of reporters and associated spouse or friend. Most of the staff is taking the ferryboat to Angel Island." We had a cup of coffee as I showed her through the boat.

"This is really nice, but your whole boat is smaller than my bedroom. What's it like, living on a boat this size?"

"Well, you have to be an outdoors person. This isn't just a floating room. I sail it, so I have the whole out-of-doors. If I were restricted to just the cabin, I'd go stir crazy pretty quickly." I described waking up to the morning sounds, and watching the sun set over the Golden Gate Bridge or drifting off to sleep to a chorus of fog horns and the gentle rocking of the water motion. "The first month I was here, it rained every-other day and the sun didn't shine once, and I loved it."

Just as I finished making a fresh pot of coffee, Ernie Stahl arrived with his wife, Susan, and their four-year-old son, Jacob. They were in their twenties. I think sometimes he envied my life style of being single and living on a boat. Ernie still had a lot to learn, but he was a talented and creative writer just beginning to hit his stride. We had no more than finished introductions than Lorraine West, the City Hall reporter, came striding down the wharf dragging her latest beau behind. There was nothing dainty about Lorraine. She was a large woman, not fat, just large, easily pushing the six foot mark. A San Francisco native, Lorraine had been news papering for over thirty years. She knew everyone who was anyone and where most, if not all, of the bodies were buried. One of her best attributes was her wonderful, cynical humor. After the introductions and coffee all around, we were ready to shove off.

"All right, yea land lubbers, listen up. These here are the rules of the ship." I proceeded to give the safety information and pass out life jackets. We put a life jacket on Jacob and hooked a line to him because children can move so fast at that age they can be overboard before you know it. We sailed to Sausalito, then turned downwind toward Tiburon and entered Raccoon Strait, the half-mile-wide channel that separates the Tiburon peninsula from Angel Island. Angel Island anchorage is adjacent to Raccoon Strait and we tied up at the anchorage guest wharf.

The picnic is just one of the many events sponsored by the newspaper. The Clarion management believes in providing a variety of events for its employees, but it is unable to pick up all the costs. It covers the basics and the employees are expected to chip in with a few dollars. All the planning is done by the employees. This picnic was a good old fashioned picnic with three-legged races, bag races, egg races, a water balloon toss, volleyball and horseshoes. There were nearly two hundred people, what with family or dates. We played and had a great time. I had been a afraid I'd have to introduce Margaret around and that she'd be a wall flower. But she joined right in as one of the gang.

At an opportune moment I got Ernie aside and told him of the sailing episode with Simon and Barbara. Since the sewer project came under his public works beat Ernie had first claim to any story that may develop. Simon and Barbara's behavior piqued his interest, but drew a blank on any unusual circumstances. He suggested I pursue it, if I was interested, because he was loaded with work.

It was a little after four o'clock when I suggested to my crew that we might want to leave soon. Fog normally creeps under the Golden Gate Bridge in the late afternoon and early evening. As we rounded Angel Island to the open bay, I saw indeed that the fog was creeping under the bridge. With it came the cooler air. "If anyone needs a jacket or sweater, I have some one-size-variety in the cabin." I like to stay out of the fog unless it is really open water, so I set a course for the Ferry Building, well down the bay from Gas House Cove Marina. This was a longer route, cutting across the Bay than following the shoreline, but we would avoid a risk of collision in the fog. Thirty minutes later we were approaching the Ferry Building, and the fog was no longer creeping. It was bounding through the Gate on a wind that was whistling straight through the Gate into the bay. Sailing against the wind is slow work and it forced us to tack several times. But forty-five minutes later we were at the marina.

Margaret lingered after the other guests had gone. I wasn't sure if she was expecting dinner or just wanted to talk. Requiring little direction, she helped me make the boat into a live-aboard again. When we were done, I asked, "Want something to drink, a coke, a beer or a glass of wine?"

"Wine sounds good. A white, if you have it." As I was uncorking the bottle and poured us each a glass, she told me what a great time she had today. "I don't get a chance to be with real people very much." I lifted an eyebrow. "No, it's true. You know my father has money. He came from money, and my mother uses it to orbit us in the highest social circle she can reach. It's always this tea, or that reception, or tennis with the Blakeley's and dinner at the club. These people are unreal. They're above the everyday struggles. They have no concept of what it would be like to work because you *had to* work for survival. Neither do I, for that matter, but I know I don't live in the real world. Today was wonderful because I found I could be accepted by everyone else."

"I don't know what to say. I guess I didn't think of your environment as being so stifling. Now that you mention it, I suppose that if the elite didn't mix with the elite, they'd either be lonely or have to mix with the common folk. Kind of like social incest, isn't it?"

She laughed and nodded in agreement. "The sad part is that I don't know what to do."

"Get a job, of course."

"Doing what? I'm not equipped for anything. Here I am a college grad with a useless degree in anthropology. But look, I don't want to bore you with my complaints. I just wanted you to know why I found today so special. Thank you for a wonderful time." She stood and turned to go, then turned back to me. She planted a kiss on my beard before she hopped over the side to the dock. "Thank you," she called. I watched her to the gate, where she turned and waved before heading across the parking lot. I felt a little strange, like I had done a good deed, and not learned of it until later. During the day we had played in the games and I didn't think of her as a date, rather like a kid sister. I understood why she might not find many young men of her social set interesting.

The fog brought a real chill, and most of the Marina Green players had left, though it was not late. I stayed on deck for a time watching the fog darken the sky. Lange was not about. I suspected he was off on a weekend jaunt that he would tell me about in due time. He was a natural explorer and an avid historian, but unlike most amateur historians, I think of Lange as a prospector. His jaunts explore business prospects and their environments. He studies the history of similar endeavors and the factors that influenced their success or failure. Beginning to feel the chill myself, I went below. There was so much food at the picnic that I decided on a light dinner of scrambled eggs. Dishes washed and everything cleaned up, I had just settled down with one of Tolstoy's classics when the phone rang.

It was Barbara Blare. Her voice sounded as if she were near hysterics. "Do you know where Simon is? He didn't come home last night, and I've been calling everywhere today, but no one has seen him. I don't know where he is. I don't know what happened to him . . ."

"No, Barbara, I don't know where he is. He came by this morning for a little bit, then left."

"Did he say where he was going? Or tell you what he was up to?"

"He didn't tell me anything. But let's start at the beginning. Tell me what you did after you left the boat." I don't know why I didn't tell Barbara that we had spent two hours together, and had gone back out to Lands' End.

"Nothing. I mean we went home. He seemed to be brooding on something. Then about seven he left. He said he was going to the office. Later, around nine he called and said not to wait up, he had some things to check on and would be home late." She said she had gone to bed about eleven and the first she knew Simon had not returned was when she awakened about seven this morning.

"When he called, did he say where he was calling from?"

"No. I assumed it was his office. I think it has something to do with the water coming out of the cliff."

"Why do you say that?"

"He seemed agitated after he saw it."

"Has he ever been away over night before?"

"Never, not like this. He's gone to conferences, but I knew where he was, and we talked by phone every day. I'm so worried."

She had checked all the hospitals and even had called the police. "But they said I can't file a missing persons report for three days. They act like it's a domestic matter."

I was a little surprised at what sounded like the edge of panic in her voice. Yesterday, on the boat, I didn't feel that Barbara was as enamored of Simon as he was of her. But, I suppose each person has his or her own way of showing affection. And, after all, I didn't know her. "Hang in there, Barbara. Let me see what I can find out. I'll let you know.

As I hung up the phone I remembered the pictures Simon had taken. I had forgotten all about the film still in the camera. I emptied the camera, stuck the film in my pocket, and reloaded. That way it was always ready. I didn't know if the water coming from the outfall had anything to do with Simon's disappearance, but I didn't want to take any chances.

But what to do with it? If I used the newspaper's darkroom I'd have to sign into the building. Then I'd get questions from Max, the editor. And I didn't have any answers, or even know where to start. If it took it to a fast-service commercial processor it would be twenty-four hours before I could see what we had. I could take the film to Tim Feldman, a staff photographer, to process in his home darkroom. But he talks a lot, and I didn't want to have premature exposure, if there was a connection between the outfall and Simon's disappearance. Then I remembered Lorraine. Her hobby is photography and she has her own darkroom. And more importantly, she is as tight-mouthed as they come, when she wants to be.

I locked the boat, jumped into my 1967 VW bug and fifteen minutes later was looking for a parking spot near Lorraine's apartment on Telegraph Hill. I prayed she was home and wasn't entertaining the silent dude she brought to the picnic. I parked illegally with a half-a-dozen other cars a block from her building. At the door I scrutinized the names next to the bell buttons. The bell for Lorraine's apartment was simply marked LW. I rang. No answer. I rang again. Still no answer. I rang four or five more times, not wanting to give up. Just as I was turning to leave, her voice came over the intercom.

"Who is it?"

"Hi, Lorraine. It's me, David. Can I talk with you for a moment, or are you busy?"

Without an answer the door buzzed and I opened it. Lorraine lived on the top floor of an old, but nicely kept three-story building. She was waiting at her door when I puffed my way to the top of the stairs.

"Well if it isn't our seagoing reporter. Now that the weekend's over are you looking for an old crow's nest to roost in?"

"Matter of fact someone said you were an old crow, but I didn't believe it." With that she took a playful swing at me. "What I really wanted to know is if I could borrow your darkroom. I have this roll of nearly pornographic film that I need to process. I'll pay for the chemicals and paper, of course."

"Of course you will, but there are strings attached. I'm cooking lasagna. If you'll help me eat it and split a bottle of Chianti, I'll let you use the darkroom. I'll even throw in the chemicals and paper, if you like the lasagna. Now if that isn't bribery I don't know what is."

"Aw, shucks, I've already eaten supper, but I'll share some wine with you."

"Okay, but you'll have to at least taste the lasagna. Now, I'm in the middle of doing laundry. The darkroom is in there, help yourself." She pointed to a door as she picked up a basket of clothes and headed for the stairway.

Lorraine's darkroom was a tiny closet next to the bathroom. Though compact, it was well equipped to process both black and white, and color film. I developed the film and, while I was waiting for it to dry enough to be printed, I sat in Lorraine's living room and sipped wine. The artwork was exclusively photographs, many of them hers. Most of her prints were of San Francisco buildings in an artsy style. "You should sell some of these. They are much better than the ones I see by the street artists."

"I haven't got the patience. These are strictly for my pleasure and for gifts to my friends--the one thing they can count on, another picture from Auntie Lorraine."

When the film was dry enough, I went back into the darkroom. Using the enlarger to expand the images, I looked at the shots Simon had taken. There were six which adequately showed the water flowing from the pipe, and one that put it all in perspective, a wide enough angle to capture background and identify the area. I printed one of the total perspective, two of the pipe, well up on the cliff, and then enlarged these to focus on the volume of water spewing from the pipe. For the record I printed four from the beginning of the roll. In these I had captured Angie, nearly nude, in some very suggestive poses. These I showed to Lorraine as the reason for my need to use her darkroom.

"As a cheesecake photographer you're not great, but I understand why you didn't want these going through a commercial shop." Then looking closer she said, "Say, I know her. That's Angela Dinucchi."

"I . . . Ye. . . Yes. You . . . You know her?" I hadn't expected that, even though Lorraine knows nearly everybody. Then a greater fear hit me. What if they were friends?

"I know who she is. She works for Hibber, Quaid and Shockley, only the City's largest law firm. I've seen her in court. Her firm does a lot of the City's trial work. How'd you get her to pose like that? I thought she was so stiff she'd break if she smiled." She looked at me and winked. "On second thought, don't tell me. I'd rather not know."

Lorraine and I visited until nearly midnight, talking about San Francisco, the people and the all the issues. It was better than any San Francisco history or sociology class. I even tasted the lasagna. Since she told me it was a new recipe, I suggested she might want to find another recipe, and she threw a piece of French bread at me.

Before I left, I clipped the negatives of Angie from the rest of the roll and stuck them in the envelope with the photographs. The negatives of the pipe I put in another envelope and, without telling Lorraine or even thinking why I did it, I taped them to the underside of her darkroom counter. Over the years I guess I've learned to take precautions, even when there is no apparent reason.

Chapter 3

Monday

———————◆◆◆◆———————

I had awakened to the mournful moan of fog horns. It was typical San Francisco summer weather. Tourists at Fisherman's Wharf would be shivering in their shorts and T-shirts, disbelieving that the City could be so cold in the summer. After all, wasn't this the California of the sunny beaches, tanned surfers and warm waters touted in the travel brochures? For sure San Diego is. And Los Angeles usually. But here in San Francisco, rarely in the summer. Saturday's beautiful sail with the Blares was the exception, not the rule. Nice weather comes in the spring and fall...when, the air is swept crystal clear by fresh sea breezes. The days are warm but not hot, and the nights are balmy, with just enough chill for good sleeping.

Thinking of the sail with the Blares brought me to full consciousness. I showered and dressed in my work-day clothes -- slacks, turtleneck sweater and a jacket. I didn't stop for breakfast, the most important meal of the day for me, planning to get some later. On the way out I shoved a reporter's notebook in my jacket pocket and grabbed the sewer pipe photographs and the three little jars of water I collected at Lands' End. I wanted to get to a friend at the Federal Building before reporting to work at eight-thirty.

One of the more difficult adjustments I had to make on this job was satisfying the requirement to be at the office at eight-thirty every day. During my ten years with the U.P. there were no set office hours. Completing the assignment by deadline was the crucial requirement. While occasionally I goofed off, more likely it was a sixty- to eighty-hour work week that included weekends. On top of that, I was often on an airplane at odd hours of the night to some inhospitable place. One of the reasons I left U.P. was for a more normal life. And I got it, including the 8:30 a.m. to 5:30 p.m. routine, Monday through Friday. But somehow the job still accrued more than 40 hours a week.

I pulled into the last parking spot across the street from the Federal Building a little before seven-thirty. As I stepped off the elevator on the fourth floor my friend was at the door to his office, juggling a coffee cup, newspaper and attaché case while trying to unlock the door. "Hey, Danny, it looks like you need a third hand. Can I help you?"

"David. Thank you. How are you?"

Dr. Daniel Marshall and I went way back. He was the medic with my unit in Vietnam. After his tour he returned to school and became a doctor. Disenchanted with private practice, Danny joined the federal Public Health Service and was eventually assigned to San Francisco. We had kept in touch and he was a strong advocate for San Francisco when I was deciding where to settle.

"I'm fine, Danny. How're Mindy and the kids? By the way, did Mindy ever get over my sabotage of her matchmaking effort? More to the point, will she ever invite me back for one of her wonderful dinners?" The last time I had been at his house for dinner, Mindy played matchmaker, inviting a very nice young lady to join us. To Mindy's dismay, I spent the evening telling old war stories and dirty jokes, which thoroughly disinterested the young lady.

"I think she was angrier at me," said Danny. I had told her it wouldn't work, which it didn't and she hates it when I'm right. Fortunately you read the scene correctly and played it perfectly. But you didn't come here for a social call. What's up?"

"How can you tell if there has been raw sewage dumped into the bay?"

"That's easy. We have tests for that. Usually it's done by the state people, but we often get called in to check out a particular contaminate. Who's been dumping?"

"Do you ever make these tests, yourself?" I ignored his question.

"Oh, sure. All the time. That's a part of my job, seeing that the tests are run and checking the results."

So I told Danny a little of what Simon and I had seen. But I left Simon out as the one who identified the water as coming from a sewer outfall. "Here are three samples I picked up from the area. After you check it out, we could go for a little sail? I could pick you up a little after lunch and we could go check it out."

Danny checked his schedule and agreed on two o'clock.

"Oh, by the way, here are two passes for the Labor Day races at Sears Point. All you have to do is act like a press photographer. The passes will get even you into the pits." Danny liked sports car racing, and had done a little himself. So when I could, I'd get the press passes for him. The Clarion never covered the races, but the paper usually got the passes anyway. Once in a while we'd even run one of his pictures, photo credit and all.

"Oh, great! Thanks a lot."

On the way out I grabbed a bagel from the building coffee shop, and then headed for the Clarion. I instinctively cringed as I signed in at the reception desk at eight-twenty-eight, another job requirement. After the usual "good morning" to the lady at the switchboard and the classified girls I took a cup of coffee to my desk in the editorial newsroom. Lorraine and I had adjacent desks. She was already at her desk checking our competition, the Evening Exchange and the morning News-Sentinel. We often feel the big daily papers had an edge over us, publishing on the weekends, so we were quick to check what they cover on the weekends. More often than not it's a rehash of the week's news and a lot of wire copy, very little that we aren't already working on. Some of their weekend analysis articles were really expansions on what we had published earlier. But we had to check, anyway.

"Hey, Lorraine, here is the real reason I wanted to use your darkroom last night. These are photos Simon took of an outfall near Lands' End Saturday. You can see some sort of water coming out of it. Simon thought it was sewage." While she was looking through the photos, I told her I had a contact in the federal health service that would run tests of the water for us this afternoon. Then I dropped the bomb, "By the way, I got a call last night from Barbara Blare. It seems Simon is missing."

"No! You're kidding?"

"Nope. He left home Saturday evening. She thought I might have seen him. She reported his disappearance to the police, but according to Barbara they are treating it like a domestic situation for at least 72 hours."

"This is serious. We'd better bring it up at Staff."

Max Delacroix, our editor, held a newsroom staff meeting every workday morning. It lasted fifteen to thirty minutes and provided an opportunity to coordinate news coverage, making sure the important issues were covered. Being strictly a San Francisco newspaper, without wire stories and with only a few syndicated columns, pushed us to dig deeper into a news story. Under Max's tutelage the Clarion had developed a reputation for accurate, factual and insightful news reporting, capturing the essence of San Francisco. The Clarion had won several state and national awards for its City news coverage.

"All right, you turkeys. The weekend's over and now I gotta retrain all of you," Max bellowed from his office door. Max had an office at one corner of the news room for privacy, but spent most of the day at a desk in the center of the newsroom. He now perched on one corner of that desk, his stomach creeping over the top of his belt. "Good grief, it's almost nine o'clock on a Monday morning and there isn't a scrap of copy in the copy box. What do you expect me to put in all of that white space for Tuesday's paper?" For all of his gruffness, he was like a favorite grandfather. The Clarion's fourteen reporters and two photographers gathered around Max.

"Well, who's got any news?"

"I can give you a background piece on the dispute between the Superintendent Rowley and the Board of Education President Jack Everly," Lorraine offered. "It's not front page, though. It's over the special education budget that Everly wants to add into the general Ed fund rather than leaving it as Special Ed. It's on the Tuesday night's school board agenda."

Max nodded, made a note on his yellow tablet and looked at the next reporter. In a few words she outlined a business feature she would have completed by today's deadline. We continued around the circle of reporters until it was my turn.

"There's something smelly with the sewer project." This brought a chorus of groans and "Ughs" "See, it is bad. Either it rained a lot over the weekend, or there's one hell of a back-up in one of the main sewer lines. Simon Blare, the project engineer, was sailing and saw what he though was waste water flowing from an outfall near Lands' End. Lorraine and I need to speak with you after the meeting." Although we were all schooled to keep this kind of information private, it didn't seem worth the risk of disclosure to mention Simon's disappearance yet.

"Also, I heard that County Supervisor Robert Davis is going to negotiate a settlement to the Carpenters Union suit, although it is against City law for supervisors to directly negotiate." All labor negotiation was responsibility of the mayor or the Chief Administrator's office. According to the City charter, the Board of Supervisors could neither participate directly in the operation of a department nor could it participate directly in labor mediation or negotiation. The Board of Supervisors was a law and policy setting body, only. This covert negotiation represented a major political move by Davis. My source was a member of the union's executive board, so I was pretty sure of the facts. When the staff meeting was over Max motioned Lorraine and me to his office.

"So, what's so private it can't be discussed in the newsroom?"

"Simon Blare is missing. We went sailing Saturday, that's how I got the outfall information. Then last evening I got a frantic call from Barbara, his wife, asking if I had seen him." I related that Barbara said he had gone out Saturday evening and, other than one phone call, she had not heard from him again. "However, he came to my boat early Sunday morning, practically pleading with me to take him back out. He collected some water samples, and when we got back to the marina he ran off into the parking lot. I don't know why, but I didn't tell Barbara this last part."

Max nodded. "It's just as well to not have this around the newsroom yet. Stay close to it. We wouldn't want to get beaten on this, especially since we knew it first." We mapped out a little strategy for coverage. Max agreed with the idea of collecting and testing water samples from near the outfall.

Before heading to City Hall, I called Danny to tell him that our trip was on, and that I'd pick him up at two o'clock. At City Hall I hunted down the young deputy City Attorney handling the suit for the City. I caught up with him just as he was headed for his office, and trapped him inside.

"Hi. I'm David Montgomery of the Clarion. I understand you're handling the Carpenters Union suit for the City. I wanted to ask a couple of questions."

"Yeah, I know who you are. I don't know what I can tell you. It's really one of these things that is likely to drag on for a while. And I really am busy."

"This won't take long." After a few questions to pin down the available options and relax him, I fired my heavy shot. "You say you're ready to go to trial. Why then are you going to ask for a continuance at today's hearing?"

He had been looking at some papers on his desk, and with that question his head shot up. He had the guilty look of having been caught with his hand in the cookie jar. His reaction told me I was right on target. A few more questions and he had trapped himself into a position that forced him to acknowledge there would be private negotiations between Supervisor Davis and the union president. Based on what the union was telling him, he said it was even possible to reach a tentative agreement today. Once opened, he spilled information like a ruptured pipe. I made notes the whole time.

"You aren't going to put all of this in a story, are you?" He fidgeted nervously while I finished writing.

"Of course I am." I gave him a big reassuring smile. "Now, how do you spell your name?"

"Oh, my god! You won't use my name, will you?

"Don't you want to be quoted?" I gave him an innocent smile.

"Oh, shit. You use it and I'll lose my job."

"Don't get upset. I don't have to identify that the information came from you…only that if came from the City Attorney's office. By the way, what time and where are they meeting?"

He told me everything I wanted to know, that Davis would enter the third-floor law library through a little used door at 12:00 noon. The union attorney and president would use the main entrance of the City Attorney's office on the second floor and climb an inside stairway to the law library.

I reassured the young deputy attorney his identity would be protected, and headed for the pay telephones. The City provides a room for the press in City Hall. Each of the credentialed media organizations has a desk and a telephone there. I could have used that phone, but you never know who is listening. Max answered on the fifth ring. I told him what was happening and I thought we might be able to get a photograph of Davis entering the law library. "You mean it's really going to happen. Davis is exceeding his authority and you're going to catch him on film. I love it. I'll send Tim Feldman to meet you at the press room at eleven."

"Better make it the snack shop. The other press might think something is up."

"Right!"

The hearing was scheduled for eleven-thirty. If I could catch the union attorney before the hearing Tim and I would have more time to set up for the shot. The court room for the hearing was across the building and on the second floor. The best place to intercept him was at the elevator, but there would be other union people with him. The trick would be to get him by himself long enough to ask him a couple of questions. I hurried down stairs to the first floor and positioned myself near the elevators, and pretended to be deeply absorbed in my notes. I didn't have long to wait before rotund, red-faced William Cochrane came puffing across the rotunda trailing a retinue of union officials. Still apparently involved in my notes I followed him into the elevator. I made it obvious that I looked at him, pulled out one of my cards, scribbled a few words on the back and handed it to him. He took it, looked at it, looked at me, looked at the card again and by then we were at the second floor. He excused himself from the retinue and headed for the men's room. I trailed behind.

Inside, I found him trying to peer at the back of his pants. "Oh, don't worry, there's no gum on your pants seat. I needed to speak to you privately." I flashed my press identification.

"You have a lot of gall."

"I've been told that. But I've also been told you're about to strike a deal with the City to get this case out of court."

"Who told you that? I can assure you . . ."

I held up my hand to stop him. "I already have most of the information. I just wanted to give you an opportunity to tell your side." As I told him what I had learned his bluster changed to incredulity. "Is this substantially correct?" He nodded. "Now, I understand you were the one who engineered this breakthrough. I won't use your name, unless you give me permission." He was now on the horns of a dilemma between taking credit for engineering a solution and his complicity in back room negotiations.

He thought for a moment before answering. "Well, I don't know where you got your information, but I won't deny it. You may even quote me that we are very near an equitable settlement, and I mean very near--like in the immediate future.

"And on the minority thing, we welcome into the membership all qualified workers. Why just this week the Board of Trustees voted to establish a training program for those less skilled so that they can enter the apprenticeship program once the training is completed."

"This week? This is only Monday."

"Well, yes. They voted unanimously on it this very morning."

"Is that part of the settlement?"

"Being as the City has a concern over the integration of minorities, women and gays into the unions that work for the City, I would say this will definitely ease their concerns."

"And in turn the City will proceed with its contract negotiations with the union. Correct?"

"I don't see anything to stand in the way."

"Thank you Mr. Cochrane. You've been most helpful." As he left the men's room I smiled at him and he winked back. The whole interchange had taken less than five minutes.

There was still some time before I had to meet Tim down stairs so, since Simon's office was on this floor I went to see if he had shown up. He worked in City Engineering, under the Chief Engineer and Public Works Director Ralph Hunt, and his office was directly across the hall from the Public Works Department offices.

The Blare's secretary's name was Elaine, and I guessed her age at somewhere between bubble gum and high heels. She told me she was new, a recent secretary school graduate who passed the latest city examination and has been on the job about a whole month. "No, I haven't seen Mr. Blare today, but I think Mr. Hunt spoke to him. No, I didn't talk to Mr. Blare directly. Mr. Hunt said Mr. Blare wanted this report typed. No, you just missed Mr. Hunt, but check with his office across the hall."

The one worthwhile nugget of information she did impart was that Ralph Hunt was frequently in here to talk with Mr. Blare about the waste water projects.

Across the hall in the Department of Public Works I started the process all over again. I showed the secretary my press identification and asked if I could see Mr. Hunt.

"He's not in right now, but if you care to wait, I'm sure he'll see you when he returns." Her voice had a melodic ring. And when she smiled her eyes twinkled. She was, I guessed, thirty-three or thirty-four with a trim figure, from what I could see of it from across the desk. Rich auburn curls framed her face, which displayed just a hint of makeup.

"Bet you get freckles." I smiled back at her.

"Oh, because of my red hair. All the time. I've gotten use to them, and it's wonderful what makeup can do. But I still don't like to be called 'Red'. And you didn't speculate that I had a temper, which is what most people say." Her laugh had the same melodious ring. I could have easily spent the afternoon waiting for Mr. Hunt, but it was time to meet Tim.

"I'm sorry I can't wait. But I'll be back, probably tomorrow. Could you, by chance, tell me when would be the best time to catch him?"

"Certainly, let me get his appointment book from my desk." She walked across the room to a desk outside his office door, and picked up an appointment book. I realized she was Hunt's secretary, and that she was filling in for the receptionist.

"I'm sorry I didn't introduce myself. I'm David Montgomery and I with the Clarion." I offered my hand to shake. Her hand was smooth and her grip was firm, like she was comfortable shaking hands with men, which I guessed she would be, working for Public Works and meeting all the contractors and site engineers.

"Hi, I'm Sally Dunstan, Mr. Hunt's secretary." She looked in the book. "He'll be available after three tomorrow afternoon. Can I make an appointment for you?"

"Better not just yet. I don't have my schedule with me. I'll call if that works for me. Do I reach you through the main number?"

She shook her head and gave me her direct number. "Call me here and I'll set it up for you." She smiled again as we said good-bye.

I was right on time to meet Tim in the basement snack shop. I briefed him on how the action was supposed to go, and we headed for the third floor. The door to the law library was unmarked, except for the room number, 331. We casually walked past the door and I tried the handle. It was locked. There were no room doors across the hall, but there was a men's room about fifteen feet back the way we had come. Upon retracing our steps I heard a click, as if a latch were being turned on the door to room 331. At the men's room, Tim pulled an official looking "Out of Order" sign from his jacket pocket and hung it on the door. "You'd be surprised how often this comes in handy," he quipped. Once inside he opened the door a crack and looked through the camera. "It will do fine, if he shows enough face to identify. I would have preferred to shoot over a transom, but this will do."

We took up our vigil, Tim poised with his camera at the door and me standing on tip toes to see over his head. If anyone had pulled the door open we would have been very embarrassed for there was no mistaking that we were trying to take pictures surreptitiously.

We didn't have long to wait. There were footsteps on the stairs next to the men's room. Tim signaled me to run water in the sinks and flush the toilets to validate the out of order sign and to cover the sound of his camera and its automatic winder. I hit the handles on the five toilets and turned the sink faucets on full force. Tim was firing as fast as his winder went. All I saw when I got back to the door was Davis' back as he closed the door to Room 331.

"I got him good," was all Tim would say. Later at the paper he showed me a beautiful sequence of shots showing Davis from the time his foot hit the top step of the stairway until he closed the Room 331 door. There were a number of positive ID photos, including one of him glancing over his shoulder to see if anyone saw him enter the law library.

Back at the paper I started punching out the story on my terminal.

"S.F. CITY HALL -- City Supervisor Robert Davis met secretly with Carpenters Union President Angelo Marichetti Monday to negotiate a settlement to the union's suit against the City for its refusal to bargain on a new contract.

The involvement by Davis in this dispute is an unprecedented move. City Law requires that all negotiated settlements are to be handled by the Mayor's office or the Office of the Chief Administrator. The secret meeting took place at 12 noon in the City Attorney's Law Library -- Marichetti entering through the City Attorney's main entrance on the second floor, while Davis slipped into the third-floor law library back door.

Union attorney William Cochrane, who is rumored to have engineered the agreement, said he expected an equitable settlement "in the immediate future."

The two key issues in dispute were the safety provisions for workmen on City projects and the number of minorities, women and gays to be hired into union positions on the City payroll. These two controversial issues had been buried in point seven of the Union's suit.

Just that morning the Union Trustees had approved a pre-apprenticeship training program to bring more minorities into the Union.

Earlier in the day, attorneys for both sides met in a pre-trial hearing at which the City asked for a continuance, ostensibly to gather additional data...."

*   *   *

I included background on the issues of the suit, the legal maneuvering that already had occurred, and the City Charter sections which forbid the direct involvement by members of the Board of Supervisors.

About the time I finished the article, Tim had printed the photographs. Max loved it. You could see his joy at nailing a politician sneaking around trying to undercut other politicians -- all part of the political world, but it is fun to be able to point to such a blatant example of shenanigans. It also gave us a scoop over the larger dailies. Max had instructed one of the City Hall reporters to get reactions from the Mayor's office and other City Supervisors. The reaction sidebar, sent later from City Hall, had elected officials expressing outrage at Davis' actions.

I rushed to make it on time, but it was still five minutes after two o'clock before I pulled up in front of the Federal Building. I felt relief when I saw Danny just coming out the door. I hate it when people aren't on time, so I try not to be late. I'm not always on time because of my crazy schedule, but I do try to call if I'm going to be more than a minute or ·

two late. Danny swung a black doctor's bag into the back seat and folded into the front seat beside me. "When are you going to buy a real car? I hate having to peddle."

"Ohhh? You don't like my bug. I'm hurt."

"As a bug, I suppose it's all right. I just don't like riding insects."

We traded barbs for the twenty-minute ride to the marina. When we arrived there were two police cars next to the gate for my dock. Looking out the dock I saw one policeman standing by my boat talking with Lange. I swung into the first available parking spot, and bolted from the car, shouting at Danny to lock the car, that something was up.

"What's going on?"

"Are you the owner of this boat?" The officer asked, pointing to my boat.

I nodded.

"This gentleman called that two men were breaking into your boat. It's good you are here and can tell if anything was taken. I think we arrived before they could make off with much of anything. Thanks to Mr. Lange here, we have the license number and make of car." The other officer emerged from my cabin as Danny came puffing up, lugging his case.

"If anything was taken, I can't tell. It was pretty well tossed though. Looks like they were looking for something specific," the other police officer said.

After checking my identification and taking a statement from Lange and from me they left. Lange told me he returned from his jaunt to find the hatch on my boat open, heard noises and caught a glimpse of one of the men. He pretended to pay no attention, but as soon as he was below decks on his boat he called 911, the emergency number.

The officer had been right. The interior of the cabin indeed had been tossed. In the mess I couldn't tell if anything had been taken. It did appear that someone was looking for something specific. I introduced Danny to Lange and left them to chat while I checked out the workings of the boat. Nothing had been damaged, the engine ran well and none of the running gear had been stolen or sabotaged. I told Lange that I had to take Danny out to Lands' End. Lange said we could talk when Danny and I got back.

I checked the fuel level and decided to motor out rather than to sail. It would take less time and I would have better control near the rocks. The tide was just reaching the high point, so it was smooth running and less current than I had with the Blares Saturday afternoon. When we got close to the outfall I pointed it out to Danny. I took the boat as close to the shore as I could. It looked like there was still a trickle of water falling from the pipe, but not near the quantity there had been Saturday. As we worked our way along the shore, Danny rapidly dipped water samples. After three passes he had collected all the samples he wanted.

"If there's anything there, I'll find it. We have a broad enough sampling to allow for the current. It would be a lot better if I could collect the samples from the land side. But I don't see any kind of trail down that cliff, and there's precious little to stand on at the bottom."

As Danny packed up his gear, I headed back for the marina. When the boat was snugly tied into the berth, Danny offered to help me straighten up the cabin. "Thanks for the offer, but I needed to reorganize my stuff anyway. Let me get you back to your office. I've got all evening to clean up." Danny refused to let me drive him back to the Federal Building. He insisted on catching a cab. "Besides, I'm tired of peddling." I finally gave in.

I sat at the top of the cabin steps and surveyed the damage. Every drawer had been emptied onto the cabin floor. All of the lockers had been opened and the contents strewn across the cabin. Even the sheets had been pulled off my bunk. It appeared that nothing of value was missing. If they had been regular burglars, there were plenty of items to take; all the sailing instruments, binoculars, the lenses to my film camera, and personal items that easily could be hocked or sold at a flea-market. I felt the boat shift, and looked up as Lange swung on board. He handed me a beer and peered over my shoulder into the cabin for a moment, then seated himself at the top of the steps to the cabin.

"They sure weren't very tidy, were they? It does look like they were searching for something specific." Lange told me that the two guys didn't look like burglars. For one, they were dressed in suits, rather conspicuous in a marina. He described them as being solidly built, muscular even. "These two looked like they might be enforcers. You did pay your bookie, didn't you?" He knew that the only gambling I do is an occasional dollar on a Lottery "Quick Pick", and nickel-dime poker with friends.

It was time to straighten up, so I waded into the cabin. I started organizing things into piles, kitchen items, clothing, out-of-doors items, sailing paraphernalia, bedding and the other categories. All of a sudden I knew what they were looking for, and what they had taken. I found my photo albums, and two of my three negative books. But I couldn't find the newest negative book. "Negatives!" I hollered to Lange. They could look at the photos and know what it was they were looking at, but it is much harder to tell what you are looking at in a negative. "They took the negatives!"

It's bad enough having someone break into your home, but to take your photo negatives.--.that's getting personal. Now I really felt violated. I can tell a lot about people from the negatives they shoot. Photos can be altered, highlighted, or cropped to tell the story the photographer wants to tell. But a collection of a person's negatives tell what's inside the person. They can show the level of self-confidence, how the photographer relates to people, and even a level of integrity. The negatives in the book were personal, not business. And I suppose I was fortunate they took only the latest book for it only contained shots of San Francisco and Northern California. These were replaceable after a fashion. It would be hard to explain the photos I shot, but the best explanation was that I shot for mood. So while I could replace the shot of the subject, I might not find the same mood or setting. Or I might not feel in the same mood when looking at the subject I had taken before. The negatives in either of the other two books were not replaceable. They contained shots from all over the world, taken during my travels. Any negatives I had shot for work were locked up in the Clarion. The only negatives I could think of that someone might want were the shots Simon took of the outfall. But how would anyone know Simon took photos and that I would have the film. Only Barbara and Simon Blare knew I had the film. No, not quite true, I had talked with Lange and showed Lorraine and Max the prints.

"What are you thinking?" Lange had come to the companion way and seated himself on the top step, watching me in the cabin.

"The only people who know of the photographs are you, Max, Lorraine, Simon and Barbara Blare. Ruling out you, Max and Lorraine, it had to be Simon or Barbara. But Simon only had to ask me for the negatives, if he were around, so Barbara..."

"What do you mean, if he were around?"

"Oh, that's right. I hadn't told you. Simon apparently is missing. Sunday night Barbara Blare called, nearly hysterical. She wanted to know if I had seen Simon. He hadn't been home since Saturday evening. She said the police were treating it like a domestic thing and wouldn't take a missing person report for seventy-two hours."

"Well, she certainly is a candidate. After telling you Simon is missing she can't very well say 'By the way, now that Simon's missing can I have the photos and negatives Simon shot of the pipe with the water running out?'"

"True, but for the sake of argument, Simon could have told someone else."

The duffel was stowed and everything ship-shape by early evening. We migrated to Lange's cruiser for dinner and continued to explore even the most remote possibility, but we always came back to the probability that the break-in was the result of information from either Simon or Barbara. But what was the motive? What would be so incriminating in the photographs?

Chapter 4

Tuesday

———➤◆◀———

T uesday morning again brought the sound of fog horns, and the sound of soft spats as water dropped from the rigging to the deck. It was a very wet fog to condense on the rigging. My little luxury is to lay in bed after awakening, enjoying the morning sounds and mentally organizing the day. It felt good to have scooped the competition on the secret union negotiations, but it was a real quandary about Simon Blare's disappearance. Where was he? Did the sewage coming from the outfall have anything to do with his disappearance? Did he have enemies? Although he did not seem the type, was he off on a bender? And the burglary; were they really after photos and negatives? Why? All they showed was water coming from a large pipe. If they were after the photos, who told them, Barbara or Simon? Who were the thugs working for? What was the motive? The questions kept going on and on. There were so many they finally nagged me out of bed. With all that going on in my head, how could I lay there and enjoy the morning sounds?

Open questions are unfinished business, and I don't like to have things unfinished. Like having my boat organized so I can sail at a moment's notice, I like to keep the rest of my life neat and orderly--at least in an intellectual sense. And now I had two pieces of unfinished business, the second being my relationship with Angie. With everything going on, she hadn't been in the forefront of my thoughts. Never-the-less, she was a presence in my mind. I made a mental note to call her today. By 6:30 I was on my second cup of coffee, having showered, dressed, eaten breakfast, washed the dishes and written a to-do list. There was nothing left to do but go to the paper and start some research.

It was real windshield-wiper fog, almost a drizzle. Only the die-hards were out pounding their feet on Marina Greens. My VW started, but it took more than the usual coaxing. The bug doesn't like damp air. I also found it had a leak on the left side of the windshield. But if I held my left leg to the right, it only dripped onto my trousers when I reached for the clutch. I would have to get some sealant for where ever the leak was. Fortunately, it was early and traffic was light enough I made it to the office with a minimum of gear-shifting.

Early morning in the newsroom is a stark contrast to the roar that constantly builds through the day to a deafening crescendo at deadline. Phones ringing, reporters hollering across the room, the radio scanner squawking, printers humming, keyboards clicking, people moving and talking are all absent at this time of day. Newspapers run on what I call crisis cycles. Everything builds during the day to the time when all the press plates have to be made. This is a one-day crisis cycle, a very short crisis cycle. For our newspaper, each crisis is only one day long. Every day the paper starts with a clean slate. To be sure, there are stories, columns, features, comics and other material that can be put onto pages in advance. But the news hole always starts empty. All day long writers, photographers, and editors frantically work to fill these voids around the advertising. Once the reporters have gathered the news and the stories are written, and after the photographers have taken the pictures, developed the film and printed the photographs, and after the editors have polished, buffed and molded the articles, the makeup editors fitted them on pages, and after the pages are made into plates that go on the presses, then the presses start to roll. For the Clarion, 11:00 p.m. is that moment when the rumble in the bowels of the building starts. Today, much of the process is done by computer, but it still takes hours to make the pages of the paper into a visually attractive product.

I started my research in our morgue, the files of past articles, dead editions of the paper, clips organized by subject and name. To my surprise, the morgue files yielded more on Simon than I would have thought. Much of the activity started after he and Barbara married. Nearly every major social event in the past year listed the Blares in attendance. There was a biography of Simon written when he was appointed to head up the sewer design team. It listed him as a fourth generation San Francisco native, a graduate of Lowell High School and of the University of San Francisco. He had a degree in civil engineering and was active in the local professional engineering society. The City appeared to have been his only employer for the past fifteen years. Simon's father had been a prominent physician, but both of his parents died in a car accident leaving him a substantial inheritance. He had no brothers or sisters, but did have relatives in the Bay Area. Earlier articles listed him as an eligible bachelor, but he was never engaged until he met Barbara. The news clips substantiated some of what I already knew that he was a quiet, unassuming person. But now, with a little more knowledge, there was a starting point from which to ask more questions.

Barbara was more of a mystery. There was very little beyond what I already knew from our sailing excursion.

She was active in the historical society and raised money for a battered women's' shelter. Beyond that, her principal activities seemed to be attending social functions. It struck me as odd that there was no mention of her parents in the society clip of their wedding, and it listed her home town as Las Vegas, not some small town in Iowa. I made a note to call the Las Vegas newspapers. Perhaps they had more information on Barbara.

After culling all the information I could from the Blare clips, I started on the mammoth files reporting on the City's sewer project. San Francisco is one of the only two cities in the United States which has a single combined sewer system containing both sanitary sewage and rain water runoff. The system might have been adequate until the 1940s, but the population growth after World War II saturated the capacity. Sewage processing capacity never caught up. Catch-up projects strung together piece-meal, trying to get the outdated sewage treatment plants to carry the load. But when the volume was too great for the sewer lines, or for the processing plants to handle, such as in the rainy season, the system simply overflowed. It dumped waste into the Bay and ocean through outfalls, such as the one we had seen running Saturday.

The City had been expanding the capacity of its sewage treatment plants, but nothing had been done to increase the size of sewer lines. The number of times the system overflowed had increased from once or twice a year to more than thirty times last year. The beaches were no longer safe to use half the year and the state had issued cease-and-desist orders. It had been threatening to freeze all construction in the City until the City corrected the problem. This was the situation that gave birth to the massive sewer building project, now expected to cost about $1 billion. And Simon headed up the design team.

The sewer project is so vast that it was broken into different major projects. There were sub-projects by neighborhood, financing, construction bids, project management, a total of eight major projects. I was deeply immersed in the first file when Max came sauntering by toward his office.

"Good god, Montgomery! You're an hour early. Did that scoop go to your head?"

"Well, boss, I did want to grab a few hundred copies for relatives and closest friends, and I didn't want you to catch me scrounging." Then I explained I needed to do some research. Since we were the only ones in the newsroom, told him about the break-in of my boat.

"And you think it's connected to Simon's disappearance?"

"Since they only took the newest negatives, and nothing else of value, I have to think there's some connection."

"What about the photos and negatives?"

"They're secure."

Max nodded and thought for a few moments. "Tell you what. I'll give you as much support as I can on this. Lorraine and Ernie know the players and can help evaluate what you are told. I want the story on Blare as early as we can substantiate it. It won't hurt the police investigation, and breaking it early may help solve it. Sometimes a good story generates leads. After staff we need to plan strategy.

I had gotten through the second file by the time the news staff began drifting in. Lorraine observed the stack of sewer project files on my desk. "Excuse me, but are you trying to become an instant sewer expert?"

"Yeah, I want to become a real shit disturber." We chuckled. "Actually, I was looking for background on Blare. There's a lot of stuff in his file, but I thought I should also take a look at his project. By the way, Max wants to see us after the staff meeting." I didn't tell Lorraine of the break-in yet, but I was glad I hid the negatives at her place.

Before the staff meeting I called Simon's house. Barbara answered, and sounded as if she had been crying. I identified myself and asked her she had heard anything about Simon. She said no, that she was just on her way to the police station to file a missing person report. I asked if she had spoken with anyone from his office. She said she had spoken with Ralph Hunt, Simon's boss, but he had not heard from Simon either.

The staff meeting was routine, and I caught some complimentary jabs for the Davis story. "You three," Max roared at the end of the meeting point to Lorraine, Ernie and me, "I want to see you in my office." Once inside he pointed to chairs and perched on the corner of his desk. "I think we have something going on with the sewer project, and I think we need to organize to go after it." He paused, pulling a cigar from a box on his desk. After peeling the wrapper from it he stuffed it, unlighted, in the corner of his mouth. Occasionally, I like a cigar myself, but we were all thankful he didn't light it. His cigars were the foulest smelling things I've ever encountered. "Now, Ernie, have you noticed anything peculiar, anything that doesn't quite fit the pattern over at Public Works?"

Ernie shook his head. "I've not seen anything unusual, but then I've not been watching it closely. With the other public works activities and airport construction assignments I haven't been following it closely."

"Lorraine, you've got your nose everywhere. You hear of anything funny going on over in Public Works, or on the sewer project?"

Lorraine shook her head. "The only thing I hear is that the sewer project is so large it seems like total confusion. No one I know has a total picture of it."

"Okay. The only evidence we have to go on is that Blare freaked when he saw water coming from an old sewer pipe.

He takes pictures. No one would want photos of sewage discharge, unless he's weird or the situation is weird. Then Blare disappears. Someone breaks into Montgomery's boat to steal the negatives." Max's summarization's are renowned. "So, either of you got any ideas?"

"Broke into your boat?" Ernie's surprise echoed in his voice. I nodded. "And they only took negatives?" I nodded again. Lorraine gave me a knowing look. Now she knew why I wanted to use her darkroom.

No one spoke for several moments, so I laid out what I've been thinking since last night. "I think there are only three options for Simon's disappearance. They're the obvious ones. He's being held, he ran off, or he's dead."

I explained my reasoning. Simon has a lot of personal money, enough that I doubted he would be tempted to steal from the City. It's also unlikely he would run off and leave Barbara, being deeply in love with her. So I ruled out a voluntary disappearance. If he had been kidnapped, there should have been a ransom note, or at least some communication by now. He has been gone for three nights, two for which he is unaccounted.

If he were dead, it could have been accidental, like a holdup or mugging that went awry, or it was intentional. No body has been found, so if he were dead I doubted that it was accidental. If he was killed intentionally, most likely it was for greed or to keep him from talking about something. If it was for greed, Barbara stood the most to gain financially. But if he was silenced, the best guess is that it had to do with his work. It fits with the theft of my negatives and I haven't found any other reasons to kill him.

"You're making a pretty strong case for him being dead," Lorraine observed.

"I guess I am. But I can't think of anything else that fits with the circumstances? Can you?"

"Okay," said Max. "I want to get a copy of the missing person report as soon as possible. Then we need to get the reaction from the City Engineer and Public Works people on how this will affect the project. We need to weave in Barbara Blare's reaction and a bio of the guy. David, I want this one for tomorrow. Touch base with the head of engineering at San Francisco University for a professional view. I understand Blare was close to him."

"Next, let's look at the project. Is it on schedule and within budget? Have there been any problems that haven't been made public? Cost over-runs? Personnel or union problems? Anything that affects the outcome of the project. Ernie, that's yours because you're closest. It may take a day or two."

"Lorraine, I want you to pull the political implications. Will this hurt the future bond election? Tap all your sources for any funny feelings--on the project, that is. This will give us a start. We'll huddle again tomorrow morning. Let me know as you turn up anything."

"What about the companies involved in the project? What are their histories?" I asked.

"Good point. We'll catch that next."

As we stood to leave Max's telephone rang, and he cupped it in his paw and mumbled into the mouthpiece. "Montgomery, wait." He turned back to the phone. "We'll be right there."

"Mrs. R. wants to see us in her office -- now."

Mrs. P. Richmond is the publisher of the Clarion. She had inherited the newspaper and a couple of small businesses when her husband died five years ago. Deciding against a caretaker publisher, she made the Clarion her primary interest and runs it herself. The other businesses are handled by a management firm. Through her devotion to the Clarion it had thrived, nearly doubling in size, and had grown a strong financial base. There were even rumors that the Clarion would soon move from its present decrepit building into new, yet-to-be built, quarters.

She rose as we were ushered into her office by her dour secretary. Her tailored clothes and stylish hair-do made it difficult to believe that she was over sixty-years-old.

"Good morning, Mr. Delacroix, Mr. Montgomery."

"Good morning, Mrs. Richmond," we chorused.

Mrs. R., as everyone affectionately calls her behind her back, is slender, and stands taller than I. Behind her desk she appeared even stately. She reminds me a little of Margaret Thacher, a former English prime minister. No one knows what her first initial, "P", stands for, Priscilla for all I know, but it is immaterial. I can't imagine anyone calling her by a first name. She motioned us to two chairs directly in front of her desk, and seated herself.

"That was a particularly striking story you wrote for the front page of today's paper, Mr. Montgomery.

"Thank you."

"I don't believe Mr. Daily is complimenting you. Actually, he tried to say it never happened, and is ready to sue us, which of course he won't. It would be thrown out if he did because he is a public figure. But it was good foresight to have photographs."

"Thank you."

"Good judgment you have. But I'm not sure the politicians are ready to stand up to the visibility you put them under."

"Are you displeased with my reporting?"

"Quite the contrary, I am delighted with your work. I have no difficulty with the fact that we are building a more controversial newspaper, or of telling Mr. Davis to go to hell. I don't mind telling you we'd had a pretty staid operation until Mr. Delacroix joined us, and now you. I want people to sit up and take notice of us. I asked you here because I hadn't really talked with you much since you joined us. And I invited Mr. Delacroix because I think it's only fair that employees' managers hear what I say to them.

"What I want to say is that your articles appear to be most accurate and demonstrate fairness. These are qualities I value highly, and I appreciate your good work."

"Thank you very much." Her sincere compliment caught me by surprise, and I felt embarrassed. A journalist rarely gets pats on the back without people wanting something in return. "I can only say I like it here and I'll give the best I've got."

"I know you will. Mr. Delacroix tells me you may have stumbled onto something else that may turn into a substantial story." Seeing my apprehension over the disclosure of information, she hurriedly interjected, "Oh, don't worry. I know nothing about it, only that it could be a good story. I want you to know that probing and digging is what I expect and I'll support your efforts."

We talked for a few more minutes. Rather, she talked, mostly of her dreams for the paper and the role it could play in the community. She envisioned it championing just causes and exposing evil conspiracies -- a rather idealistic view, I thought. However, this is the direction she is steering the paper and it is growing. And more uniquely, it is making money as more advertisers join the paper. She even eluded to employee participation in profits sometime in the future -- a relatively unheard of practice in newspapers, because they operate on such very slim margins.

As Max and I rose to leave she tossed out an additional surprise.

"Oh, I almost forgot. Saturday night is the Mayor's Gala. I'd like the two of you and your dates to be the guests of the paper. We have two tables, and I'd hate to be stuck with stuffy bureaucrats or politicians as the only ones around me. Could you please join me?"

Max and I looked at each other and mumbled our acceptances. Outside her office Max grumbled. "I've been here two years and she does this to me all the time. I'm going to have to start taking my weekends out of town." I gathered that Max didn't care for these large social events, either.

Back at my desk I found a telephone message from Danny. It was market "Urgent! Call me!" I dialed his number. "Boy, that's some kind of poison. I hope all your shots are up to date."

"Why? What did you find?"

"Besides enough coliform bacteria to make everyone in the City sick, there was Salmonella typhus. Have you had typhoid shots recently?" Danny described a number of other bugs he found, but none as serious as the typhoid. "I'm going to have to have the sewer line that leads to that outfall checked out. Something's really wrong. There has to be standing sewage for this to occur."

"I'm current on the shots. But can you hold off a couple of days?"

"What? And have half the City come down with typhoid, or cholera? You gotta be out of your skull to even think that way. As it is, the earliest we're likely to get any action from the yo-yos at City Hall is tomorrow or Thursday. Why do you want me to wait?"

"There may be some funny stuff going on with the sewer project. There are some things we want to check out before this gets public."

"I'd guess there really is some funny stuff. Look, I won't start beating on the Mayor's door until the City has done nothing for twenty-four hours. But I gotta turn in this report, now. And I'll have to elevate it pretty quickly or I wouldn't be doing my job."

I told him I understood, and that I'd just have to work faster. Then I called the missing persons department at police headquarters, but was told they don't give that kind of information over the telephone.

Before going to police headquarters, I checked on the newspapers in Las Vegas. There were three, a daily and two weeklies. I called the daily and spoke with the City Editor. He said he'd be glad to help, but his librarian was on vacation through the end of the week. "None of the casino people go by their real names here, anyway. But if you could fax me a photo, it would help speed up the process." I told him I would, adding it to my check list of things to do later.

Police headquarters shouldn't have to appear depressing. But even in broad daylight, a person just looking at this drab, gray stone building has to feel a sense of foreboding. The halls are poorly lit, further accentuating the drabness.

The missing persons department is on the third floor, so I waited for an elevator. I was standing to one side of the elevator doors when one opened and out stepped Barbara Blare. She didn't see me, and I was about to speak to her when she put her hand on the arm of a man next to her. It was the kind of touch you give a close friend, so I held back to watch. She talked to him as the two of them walked toward the front of the building, and I had the feeling they had known each other for some time. The man was Ralph Hunt, the City's public works director. I was tempted to follow, but I had a lot of ground to cover before I could write the story on Simon's disappearance.

My reception at Missing Persons was somewhere between negative and hostile. There must have been twenty people in the waiting area huddling in small groups of two or three filling out forms. A sergeant was sitting at one of the desks behind the counter reading a newspaper. He didn't bother to look up when I rang the little bell on the counter.

"Yeah, whadya want?"

I told him who I was and that I wanted to see a missing persons report.

"Oh, yeah. You're the one I just spoke to. Didn't waste any time getting here." He looked at me for the first time. "So whadda ya wanta know?"

"I understand that one Simon Blare, age 36, six feet tall, brown hair, and brown eyes, has been reported missing. I'd like to see the report."

"Ya do, huh?" We stared at each other for a moment, and then he pushed his belly off the desk and extracted himself from the chair. Without another word he lumbered through a door into another office. It was a good five minutes before he returned.

"I don't have anything on him."

"Nothing? Nothing at all?" I let my voice sound incredulous.

"Like I said, I don't have anything on him . . . at all." He registered finality with his voice. I didn't respond, but let the silence hang pregnantly between us. Finally he broke it.

"He works for the City, right? In Engineering, right?" He also gave me Simon's home address and telephone number.

"I thought you didn't have anything on him?"

"I don't. But you seemed so all-fired interested in this guy I thought I'd see if there was any other information on him. He's got a parking ticket from two weeks ago.

"I don't understand why you can't find a report on him. I saw Mrs. Blare downstairs, and she was just here to file the report."

"I don't know what you're talking about. I haven't seen a Mrs. Blare, and there is no missing persons report on a Simon Blare." The sergeant's tone was testy and it was evident was not going to be cooperative. He returned to the desk, perched his belly on the edge and eased himself back into his chair. "First of all, if she had just filed a report, I'd have it right here on top of my desk, which I don't."

"But I just saw her with Ralph Hunt downstairs, Sergeant..." I waited for him to supply a name.

"It doesn't matter. If you saw her, get a copy from her. Everyone who files . . ."

"Excuse me, Sergeant. What is your name?"

"Look, Mr. Wise Guy Reporter. If you think you're going to get me in trouble for not giving you a report which I don't have, forget it. I'll explain it once more, as nicely as I can. I don't have a missing persons report on a Simon Blare. I haven't seen Mrs. Blare or that other dude, whatever his name is. And my name is Stan Skowski, Sergeant Stanley Skowski."

"Forget it." I could feel my anger building and I knew I wasn't going to get anywhere if I let my temper get the best of me. So I turned and walked out of the office. The frustration was neck high as I stood in the hall by the elevators. It was possible that particular officer did not have the report, but he certainly had to have seen Barbara.

"Hey, Montgomery. Why the long face?"

"Hi, Lieutenant. I'm just frustrated. The sergeant in Missing Persons is stonewalling me and I'm trying to figure out where to go next."

It was Lieutenant Andrew Sullivan of homicide. I hadn't seen him since I wrote a series of articles about several Chinatown killings he had investigated when I first joined the Clarion. I didn't get under foot or pester him with a bunch of questions, but I confirmed all my facts with him. This made him comfortable with my style. In the articles I had noted the difficulty of getting witnesses to talk to police in Chinatown, which had helped generate interest. This and good police work enabled him to solve the killings.

"Tell me about it." So I did. "Go get a cup of coffee and I'll meet you in the cafeteria in fifteen minutes. I know another way to get it, if it really is there."

Ten minutes later the lieutenant handed me a copy of the report. "They tell me this is very hush-hush because someone in City Hall is afraid the exposure will really have bad repercussions on the project bonds. I think that's a line of bull and the hold is being done as a favor. But that's my opinion. Anyway, a missing person report should be public knowledge. You don't fill out a report and then ask us to sit on it. The person will never be found that way. Just don't tell anyone where you got it."

"I owe you one, Lieutenant."

"No you don't. And my name is Andy."

"Thanks, Andy."

My next stop was San Francisco University. It was close to lunch time, but I hoped to catch Dr. Lawrence, the head of engineering, before he left for lunch. The university is nestled on the side of a low hill gently sloping toward the Pacific. Some of the campus and several university buildings had views of the Bay. The vista must have been spectacular before the surrounding housing was built, apartments and some mini-mansions as a show of opulence to show that the inhabitants have arrived. The houses of area are not my style, not because I'm not wealthy and probably never will be, certainly not as a journalist. I just prefer a simpler life.

Parking is a problem everywhere in San Francisco, and the campus was no exception. But after my third tour of the student lots I found a spot a half-a-block from the engineering building. I half ran to the building, but I might as well have saved the energy. Once the department assistant leaned what I wanted, she told me Dr. Lawrence rarely eats lunch out and that his last class ends in five minutes. "Have a seat. He'll be in momentarily. You can almost set your watch by him."

Seven minutes later a tall, slender man strode through the doorway. His gray English tweed sports jacket sported a maroon handkerchief in the breast pocket that picked up the same color in his tie, a fashion rarely seen any more in California. His white hair and clipped military mustache gave him a distinguished appearance.

"Dr. Lawrence, this reporter -- I'm sorry I misplaced your card -- wants to speak with you."

"Dr. Lawrence, I'm David Montgomery. I want to speak with you about Simon Blare."

"Oh, yes. How is Simon?"

"That's what I wanted to speak with you about. May we use your office?"

Inside I told him of Simon's disappearance and that Barbara had filed a missing persons report. "I understand that he was a student of yours, and that you may have kept in contact."

"Oh, my! Oh dear. Yes, of course. We have stayed in contact and are, I would say, friendly. We are both active in the local engineering society, in which we've both held office -- though not presently." He paused. I saw him swallow. "I saw him just last week. We had dinner . . . we often do that . . . about every week or so . . . have dinner together." He paused again, and swallowed. "I am quite distressed by this, I must say."

"Look, if you would rather I come back later..."

"Oh, not by you. Just the idea of him disappearing, vanishing into the ether. This is so strange . . . so uncharacteristic of . . ." He took a few deep breaths and seemed to recover his composure. "Well, how can I help you? I'll do anything I can for Simon."

"Tell me about him. What was he like? I knew him only a little bit, but I like what I saw of him."

"Yes. He is a very likable person. He's almost like a son to me, you know. But of course, you don't." Dr. Lawrence paused several moments before continuing. He gazed out the office window without really looking at anything. "His parents died in an automobile accident when he was a freshman here at SFU. I was a recent widower. Out of our respective losses, I suppose, we were drawn together. It was very hard for him, so I took him under my wing. It helped me move outside my own grief, also." Dr. Lawrence told me of Simon's development into an outstanding scholar. "He wasn't a book worm. Simon was too slight to play football, and he lacked the agility for basketball, but my, that boy could run. He held the conference record for the eight-eighty and the mile for years."

Dr. Lawrence told me Simon could have been employed anywhere, that he had the skills. "But I think he is just too closely tied to San Francisco. Maybe it's because of his parents' death, or because the only family he has is in the Bay area. But he never seemed to want to advance or become more prominent in his profession."

"Can you tell me about the family he has in the Bay Area? And if you could give me their names and where they live, that would be helpful."

"Certainly." He opened an address book on his desk and scribbled some names and telephone numbers on a piece of note paper.

In our conversation he had little to say about Barbara, but his very lack of comment left me with the feeling that he disliked her. "I'm not sure she appreciates what she has in Simon," was the only critical comment he made of her. It was clear that she was never a part of his dinners with Simon.

We had pretty well exhausted Simon's personal life. There were no skeletons or known problems there. "Did Simon ever indicate any problems or uneasiness about the sewer project?"

"No. Not to speak of. We talked about the project, of course -- a great deal." He paused, his eye brows lifted as he remembered something. "However, now that you call it to mind, his discussion of the project had been diminishing in recent months. Nothing I can put my finger on, but he seemed guarded in our discussions. I hadn't thought of it until now, and it simply may have been that he felt overloaded. Do you suspect anything with the project?"

"No. Not directly." I told him of the outfall and how Simon had become agitated, followed by Simon's disappearance, and that there was evidence someone was looking for the photographs. "It's all pretty circumstantial."

"As I said earlier, I'll do anything I can to help Simon. This project represents a tremendous amount of money -- probably more than two billion dollars with all the side work, before it's done. It wouldn't surprise me if someone were scheming to illegally reap some of that money. I suspect the easiest way would be to phony the work. Perhaps I could help validate some of the work. I have sufficient time, for I only teach two classes now."

I told him that he had a good idea and that I appreciated his offer. Certainly his knowledge of the subject would be most helpful. "Before you start anything, I need to talk with my editor and publisher to determine our direction and what resources may be available to us. But as of now, you are a member of the team." I caught a fleeting smile at my pronouncement.

"What are the police doing?"

"Not much yet. They've just gotten the report. I'm sure they'll have it on the street quickly." I dispensed more confidence than I felt from what Andy had told me. There was no reason to upset this kindly old gentleman with the fact the police were sitting on it. Besides, I suspected it would be sprung it loose shortly.

Before I took my leave from Dr. Lawrence, I asked to use his telephone. "Hello, Miss Dunston, Sally? . . . This is David Montgomery. We met yesterday and you offered to make an appointment for me with Mr. Hunt? . . . I'll take you up on your offer, if it's still good?. . . . Three-thirty is good. I'll look forward to seeing you. . . . Thank you very much. . . . Good-by." I just love that voice, and was reflecting on it until I was jolted back to reality.

"One of the most reprehensible human beings I've ever met. I suppose he fits with the politicians, but he's no engineer, nor manager, nor project leader, nor anything else productive."

"Who? Ralph Hunt?" His pronouncement on the character of the man piqued my curiosity.

"Himself."

"Tell me about him."

"Oh, not much to tell. I just don't like the man. He is weaselly or slimy. I think he bends the figures on things. Nothing specific, though."

"Did you ever have a run-in with him?" Dr. Lawrence shook his head and I was unable to get anything more out of him on Hunt.

I took my leave from Dr. Lawrence and got my car. I had enough time to grab a sandwich and stop by Barbara and Simon Blare's house. The sandwich I picked up from a fast food drive-through a few blocks from the campus, and ate it on the way to the Blare's house.

I knocked, then rang the bell several times before I heard any movement inside. When Barbara answered the door she was a little disheveled, as if I had awakened her from a nap. "Did I wake you? I'm sorry."

"Oh, no. I haven't gotten much sleep so I was lying down. But I wasn't asleep." She didn't invite me inside.

I explained that I needed to make a copy of the missing person report. The copier in missing persons was broken and the officer couldn't let me take it out of the department to make a copy on another floor. Although I had the copy Andy had given me, this was the only excuse I could think of for stopping by her house. When she went to get it, I stepped inside the doorway. From the entry, I could see most of the living room. It was neat and orderly, modern furniture in black, white and glass. There were two glasses on the coffee table, and it looked like they still had ice cubes in them. She quickly returned and handed me an envelope. Maybe it was a whisper of movement or inaudible breathing, but it felt like someone else was still in the house. Well, if there were anyone there, I'd give him or her something to think about.

"You don't know who ask the police to sit on the report, do you?"

"What? Sit on the report? Of course not. Why?"

"Well, someone asked them to sit on it. And until the report is released, it won't be out on the street -- which means they won't be looking for Simon until it is."

"Oh, my god! What do we do?"

"You might talk with Mr. Hunt and suggest he could put some pressure to have the report released. Meanwhile, I have a couple of tactics I'll try. I'll get this report back to you tomorrow." Not having any other reason to hang around, I left. I had plenty of time, so I drove around the corner, made a U-turn and parked at the corner where I could see the house. I had a hunch that if someone else were in the house, they'd soon leave. I didn't have long to wait. A tall, slender man came out of the house and walked briskly up the block away from me. I couldn't see his face because he was wearing hat with a brim. A few houses away, he got into a black Porsche. His car was facing my direction, and I expected him to come towards me. But he made a U-turn from the parking space and sped around the corner before I could get the license number. I wasn't prepared for that, so I didn't even have my engine running. By the time I got to that corner, he was gone. There was a main street was a few blocks away, and I figured he headed that direction. But there was no black Porsche in sight when I got to California Street either. So I drove on over to Geary Street and turned toward City Hall.

Since I had extra time, I stopped at the Engineering Services office to see if I could get a map of the City's sewer lines. He brought out a book of maps which showed every sewer connection, block by block and building by building. "Don't you have something a little more general, one that just shows the main sewer lines, like that map on the wall?" He went back among some cabinets stacked six feet tall. I heard him opening drawers and finally he produced one. It was about six years old.

"That's great. I'll take it. How much is it?"

"You don't want this one. It's out of date. I'm out of the new ones with the project areas market. They're on order and I'll have one delivered as soon as they come in."

"That's fine. I can still use this one for general reference now. How soon will the other ones be in?"

"About a week. It will cost you $50, and I can let you have this one for $10. You can pay me for both when I send the new one over, C.O.D. Now which firm are you with?"

"Richman Construction," I lied, and gave him the newspaper's address. I stowed the old map at our desk in the press room, and went to the Public Works offices.

Sally was busily writing on the computer when I came into the offices.

"Can I help you?" The receptionist asked.

"No, I'm here to see the little red-headed girl with freckles." Hearing that, Sally turned toward me.

"Oh, hello, Mr. Montgomery..."

"David."

"David. Mr. Hunt isn't back from his two o'clock meeting yet. He'll be here shortly." She was, I guessed, about thirty-three or thirty-four. A tailored skirt and blouse nicely fit her trim figure. She used light makeup and her auburn hair framed her face. She invited me to have a seat near her desk while I waited. With a minimum of query, she told me that she had lived in the East Bay all of her life, except for the five years she was married. During that time she lived in San Francisco and had gotten a job with the City. But now that she is divorced, she shares an apartment with two other unmarried women.

"I really like the City, but it's too expensive on my salary, especially in the areas with the nicer weather." We were having a delightful conversation, and I had just invited her for dinner Friday evening, when Hunt walked in.

Hunt's figure fit the typical bureaucratic image, slightly overweight, slightly balding, slightly rumpled. But his demeanor was much more that of a politician than of a bureaucrat, anticipating questions before they were asked and answering in a measured voice.

"Of course I'll see Mr. Montgomery. I always make myself available to the press. Come on in Mr. Montgomery," indicating the open door to his office. "Would you care for a cup of coffee or tea?"

I thanked him but declined. He closed the door and motioned me to a sofa placed against one wall, seating himself in a chair facing the sofa. I didn't like the setting. The sofa was lower than the chair, which would give him a slight psychological advantage by having his guest look up to him. Instead of sitting where he indicated, I grabbed a straight-backed chair from a table and swung it around to face him. This made him shift his chair. As he did, I whipped out my notebook and pen, and sat poised to take down every word he said. The maneuver was meant to startle him. It succeeded.

"Yes . . . ah . . . well, now . . . ah, Mr. Montgomery. What can I do for you? What is it you would like to speak about?"

"Simon Blare, Mr. Hunt. Where is he?" The frontal attack was also calculated to keep him off balance. People often display more in body language when they can't concentrate on control. His movements were jerky and he didn't seem to know what to do with his hands. He was certainly unsure of how much I knew, and didn't know what to tell me.

"Ah . . . well, now. Mr. Montgomery, I was under the impression that Mr. Blare was taking a few days off due to some . . . ah . . . that is . . . for . . . ah . . . personal reasons."

"Did Mr. Blare tell you that himself?"

"Well, not in so many words, so to speak."

"Who did tell you that, if anyone?"

"Well . . . I . . . actually, his wife. She called and . . . ah . . . when he wasn't going to be at work."

"What did she actually say?"

"Well, it was something about taking some time off, I believe."

"Mr. Hunt, I don't think that was what she said at all. Now what did she say?"

"I don't exactly . . . I don't think I should be telling you what goes on between one of our employees and his wife." He was recovering and desperately trying to lead me off track.

"Come on, Mr. Hunt. You know that's not true. Barbara Blare called you to ask where Simon was, that he had disappeared." Then to change stride and keep him off balance, "What's wrong with the sewer project?"

"Why . . . wrong with the sewer project? . . . Why, nothing."

"Then why did Simon disappear when he started investigating a suspicious discharge from an outfall at Land's End?"

"How . . . I don't know what you're talking about."

"Simon Blare is missing, and has been since Sunday. You knew about it because Mrs. Blare called you Monday morning at the latest, because Simon worked for you. Today she filed a missing person report, the earliest the police would accept one, and you know about it." I paused. He took a breath as if to say something, but clamped his jaws together. "So just now, when I asked you if you knew where Simon was, you first implied that he was having personal problems and then suggested that his wife called to say that he was taking time off. You're lying to me. Now, where is Simon Blare? Why are you lying to me?"

I sat and waited for his reaction. I could figuratively see the gears turning in his head. He was between a rock and a hard spot. Almost anything he said could be damaging now. He twitched a few times as we sat in silence. Then I could see him gathering his inner resources. He pulled up his chest to reflect his full officialdom.

"Look, Mr. Montgomery, I'm a very busy man, but I always want to make sure that the press has all the accurate information necessary. I'm willing to take this time with you, particularly since you seem to think I might be hiding something."

"I want to be very clear that I never lie to the press. But you must understand that we have the City's largest project going. There is a lot riding on a successful bond issue coming up in a few months. The disappearance of a city official who is a key member of the project team could make a very bad impression and seriously jeopardize the funding of the project."

"You are right. I do know about Mr. Blare's disappearance. But we don't know anything about the circumstances of it. There are innumerable possibilities, including domestic reasons. I felt that until we know more about the circumstances of his disappearance, it was best to let people believe he was just absent from his desk." Hunt appeared pleased with the logic of his explanation.

In fishing terms, it was now time to set the hook. "I appreciate the explanation. It provides some logical reasoning." I smiled my disarming smile, then pulled the line tight. "But how long were you going to just let Simon Blare be absent from his desk? Until after the bond election next spring?" The pleasure was starting to drain from Hunt's face. "Is that why you asked the police to sit on the missing person report?"

He inhaled sharply. The color drained from his face. I waited silently for his response, a tactic that didn't help his composure. It must have been nearly two minutes before he began stammering.

"I . . . I . . . well . . . but . . . I . . . it isn't what it . . . it seemed best to keep it . . . confidential . . . for the moment, that is . . . until . . . well, until the . . . until the police have more information." His eyes wandered the room as if seeking answers or assurances. His face was now turning red as he groped for the right words to say. "And it's not unrealistic that . . . that it is . . . ah, domestic. He could very easily have taken time off . . . to think things through . . . I mean, really . . . you don't know his wife. I mean . . . well . . ."

"Oh, come, Mr. Hunt. If you expect me to believe you, you have to be specific. You're making insinuations, but it could just as easily be a smoke screen to cover your own culpability. How can you tell me that a responsible, dedicated man, like Simon Blare, wouldn't have called you personally if he were going to take time off, for any reason?"

"And so far as the police turning up any more information, they won't. And the reason they won't is because they are sitting on the report, at your request. I am becoming suspicious that you don't even want him found. Now why would that be?"

"You have no proof that I asked them to sit on it." His anger was building. He was going to bully his way through.

"Oh yes I do, Mr. Hunt. You were in the police headquarters this morning. You requested missing persons to delay action on the report for at least a few days."

"You can't . . ."

"Oh, yes I can. I was there. I saw you." His face again drained of color. Perspiration made beads of moisture on his face. His mouth worked but no sounds came from it. "Do you have something you wish to tell me?" He stared at me, shook his head and swallowed, almost convulsively. I stood in preparation to leave. There was little more I would get from him. He couldn't provide any more information without further involving himself. "In that case, you won't have any objection if I browse through Simon's office, or speak to the other members of your staff."

"No, damn it! Now get the hell out!" He was screaming.

I walked out leaving the door open and he immediately slammed it behind me, rattling the pictures on the wall.

"Oh, it sounded like you might have had a stormy session." Sally observed.

"I think he was a little upset. Does he often get angry?" I noticed that one of the lights on Sally's telephone lit. I wondered who Hunt was calling.

"He does have a temper, but he usually keeps it under wraps.

"Mr. Hunt said I could browse through Mr. Blare's office. Do I need a key or anything?"

"Really? Is anything wrong with Mr. Blare?"

"We don't know. He's absent and I'm trying to track him down."

"I'll tell Elaine Wilson, Mr. Blare's secretary, to let you in."

As I left I told Sally I was looking forward to having dinner with her Friday night, and would pick her up here at City Hall. Across the hall, Elaine opened the door to Simon's office. I wondered if she was still chewing the same wad of gum she had in her mouth yesterday. She stood awkwardly in the doorway watching me walk around the office looking at the framed credentials on the walls. Besides his engineering certification and diploma, there were several citations for design accomplishments. A framed picture of Barbara was all that was on his desk. Similar to Hunt's office, there was a sofa, a couple of side chairs, a small conference table and four straight-backed chairs. There was a map of the major sewer lines on a drafting table. Under it was a cross section of what looked like a tunnel with all the engineering notations. A random collection of pens and pencils were in one desk drawer. A few folders with project papers were in the other drawers. It was so orderly that it was obvious to me that someone else had gone through all the papers here, and tidied up.

"Was Mr. Blare always this neat?"

"Gosh, no. He must have cleaned it up Friday evening after I left.

"Was that the last time you saw him, Friday evening?"

"Yeah. I asked him if he wanted anything before I left. He had stacks of papers and folders all over his desk. He had me make some copies of things before I left. When I came in Monday I found notes he had left, things for me to do."

"Where did he normally keep papers?" There were no filing cabinets in his office.

"I don't know what was there Friday. He kept some papers in his desk and I guess the rest are from the files out here." She indicated the large outer office.

"Would you know if any of the files were missing from the filing cabinets?"

"Maybe, some of them. I don't know much about what they do, just that they plan the City's projects -- everything from streets and sewers to the convention center remodeling. Why are you asking all these questions? Has anything happened to Mr. Blare?"

"I hope not. But no one has seen him for a few days. Did he act strangely on Friday?" She shook her head no. "Those notes he left for you, do you still have them?"

"I might have one or two, let me check." I followed her out to her desk and closed the door to Simon's office after me. I wasn't going to find anything there. Anything incriminating was gone. She rummaged around in the waste basket and came up with two that she handed to me. "I have one more, but I'm not done with the work yet." I put the two hand-written notes in an envelope she gave to me, and asked her if she could copy the other one, so I could have the original. She ran it through the copy machine near her desk and handed the original to me. I gave her my card and asked her to, "Call me if you think of anything else."

I picked up the map from the press room and headed for the Clarion to write a story.

Chapter 5

Tuesday Afternoon
and Evening

———⟫◆⟪———

B ack at the office, in front of my terminal, I pounded out the story. Although the Editor has the final say on headlines, the paste-up editor writes the headlines to fit the space, the reporters are encouraged to suggest headlines that fit the intent of the story. This makes it less likely to have an unrelated headline, which occasionally happens in some of the larger newspapers.

CITY OFFICIAL DISAPPEARS

Key San Francisco Sewer Team Leader Vanishes

By David Montgomery

SF CITY HALL -- A key member of the City's $2 billion, massive waste water construction project has disappeared without a trace. Simon Blare, 36, left his home Saturday evening, supposedly to go to the office, and has not been seen or heard from since early Sunday morning.

Blare, a Deputy City Engineer, was in charge of engineering design for the new sewer project, currently under construction.

His disappearance was hidden from the public by City officials for two days, ostensibly until they could learn more about the circumstances of his disappearance. Public Works Director Ralph Hunt had requested the police department to delay the investigation until they could develop additional information, he told the Clarion. Barbara Blare, Blare's wife, had earlier filed a missing person's report, which was not available to the press because of Hunt's request.

Hunt suggested that Blare's disappearance was possibly due to domestic matters, which he was unable to substantiate. To the contrary, associates of Blare dispute Hunt's allegation, depicting the domestic relationship as warm and loving.

Although there is no established connection, Blare had been investigating an unusual sewage discharge at Lands End. The photographs shown here were taken Saturday by Blare. Water samples taken at the location by the US. Health Department indicate that the discharge was untreated sewage, and may have contained the Salmonella typhi bacteria--typhoid fever bacteria. The report was hand delivered to the City's Health and Public Works

Departments Monday, but no action was taken as of Tuesday evening.

Blare's wife of just over one year said Tuesday, the last she heard from Simon was ..."

* * *

Although a missing person story does not usually merit front page placement, Max felt there was enough behind this story to start it on page one. He set it up to run with a large mug shot of Simon and one of the sewer discharge photos on page one. The rest of the story and an additional photo would run inside. He even gave Blare photo credit for the discharge photo.

I finished writing about six o'clock, and was catching my breath when Ernie came running in. He told me that Hunt had called a press conference for five o'clock, and that he had attended.

"But Hunt sure wasn't prepared. He had little to say, and couldn't seem to answer any of the reporters' questions."

Ernie said that only four reporters had attended and there was no one was from the electronic media. I figured the rest of the media would be deep into it tomorrow, after our story. With that kind of pressure, the police would have to start investigating and hopefully the trail wasn't too cold.

Once Max was finished with the story, we went to Mrs. Richman's office. We wanted to advise her of the turmoil we were likely to create.

"Aren't you leading the reader to believe something malevolent has happened to Mr. Blare, and that it has to do with the sewer project--possibly even Mr. Hunt?"

"I don't think so," Max responded. He filled her in on what we knew that was not in the story, including the break-in of my boat, that we think was for the very photographs we were running. "From everything we know, Simon is not the type of person to walk away from anything."

"Thank you for appraising me of the circumstances. Controversy is so exhilarating. Is there anything you need from the paper to continue your investigation?"

"I think we could use some expertise." I told Mrs. Richman and Max of Dr. Lawrence's offer to help evaluate the sewer project. "But I'm not sure he has the necessary resources available to him. I think we need a civil engineering firm that would work with us and Dr. Lawrence to evaluate all the project pieces; someone who is not involved with the project."

Mrs. Richman was thoughtful for a moment, then suggested, "I might know of someone. I'll call him in the morning and sound him out. We can't afford consulting fees, but maybe for public recognition he would volunteer his firm."

I thanked her for her assistance and Max and I went back to editorial. I remembered I had to fax a photo of Barbara to the Las Vegas newspaper. I sent two, one of the wedding announcement, which is what she would have looked like when she left Las Vegas, and a current society shot. Closing up my desk, I remembered that I wanted to call Angie. I felt things had stagnated long enough between us, so I dialed her office number. But all I got was the answering service. The voice said she had just left for the day, was it urgent, or did I want to leave a message. "Just tell her David called." I didn't call her apartment, even though she lived near the office in one of the high-rise buildings near the Bay. I had to wonder why I didn't call. She could easily have been home by now. Was I really so upset in talking with her? Should I or should I not call. If I did, would it look like I was chasing after her? And would she get the wrong impression: the impression that I was willing to make concessions? Her pronouncements were so matter of fact...almost cold. It was a side of her I had not paid attention to earlier. But looking back I could see it was always there.

I wasn't quite ready to go back to the boat, so I told Lorraine and a couple of the other Clarion writers I'd join them for a quick beer at Ole's Tavern, the Clarion staff hangout down the block. Ernie was just finishing at his terminal. "Hey, Ernie, want to stop for a beer? We're going to Ole's for a quick one."

"Yeah, go ahead. I'll be along as soon as I turn this in."

Ole's is in an old brick building, a block from the Embarcadero. It's always been a labor bar, and its history goes back to the reconstruction after the 1906 earthquake. When San Francisco was still a port city, the longshoremen drank there. During the war years, it offered good jazz, catering to the servicemen. This lasted into the 1970s, but it was on the wrong side of Market Street to attract the evening tourist trade. It had good lunch trade from all the offices, but evenings were pretty quiet. This made it a good place for us to unwind. The current owner, Tim O'Conner, knew us all by name. He had a private back room for parties and it had a pool table in it. He was not licensed for pool, so this was strictly for his privileged regular clients. He would let us play for free if we wanted. But it seemed that no one was in the mood for pool tonight and the lights were off in the back room. O'Conner, himself, was tending bar when we came in.

"Yo! Montgomery! Some big dude was just here looking for you."

"Oh? Did he have a name?" O'Conner shook his head as he drew a beer for a customer at the bar.

"You know I never ask names. I told him to check the paper. So if you didn't see him there, he must not have stopped. Anyone have a beef against you?"

"No, why?"

"That's what he looked like, trouble."

"Thanks, Tim." It was a curious incident. The thought that immediately leaped to mind was that it might be one of the two men who had ransacked my boat. I didn't know anyone who would look for me here because I don't stop here very often. It had to be someone checking me out for some reason. I hadn't seen anyone on the walk from the paper, but then we were talking and I didn't pay any attention. I filed it as information to keep on tap and put it out of my mind.

Ernie arrived and we grabbed a table with the other writers. There is not a lot of socialization among the staff, but the occasional after-work beer helps keep the information exchange going. It makes for good cross reference on people and situations. After a few minutes the conversation got around to the respective news beats. Each reporter is assigned an area to cover, often correlating to some expertise or knowledge. Lorraine had covered City Hall political scene for years. She knew all the City players; the department heads, members of Board of Supervisors, their staffs, most of the neighborhood group leaders and all the interest groups. Now she was on her second tour of the school district. Other reporters' beats cover police and crime, transportation issues, science, public and private health issues, City planning, business, and of course local sports. Several of the beats, like City Hall, were so complex it needed more than one reporter assigned.

I mentioned that Simon was missing and that it might have something to do with the sewer project. "Funny. The last missing city official was Ralph Hunt's predecessor," commented the police reporter. "He was never found. It looked like he stole city money, but I always thought he could be part of the civic center foundation."

"How come?"

"Oh, nothing specific. Just that things didn't quite add up for him to have absconded with City funds.

"How long ago was this?"

"What was it, Lorraine, six or eight years ago?"

"I thought it was five, but it could have been six."

"Where's Hunt from?"

"Some place back east. I don't remember, but I'm sure we have a full biography on him. He worked for a year as the Manager of project planning in Public Works before the director disappeared and he was promoted to Director of the department."

This gave me another avenue to check out. One thing about this business, there are always different leads and each one takes you in a different direction. We talked for a while longer, then my beer finished, it was time for me to leave. "Anyone want a ride toward the marina?"

"Thanks, but I might be better off on the buses. The worst that can happen there is to get mugged. Remember the last time you gave me a ride, your door just popped open and I thought you were going to fall out just as we started down the Hyde Street hill. But what the heck, why not live dangerously?"

"Thanks, Lorraine. Just for that I'll leave it to you in my will."

Lorraine and I walked to the employee parking lot, and got into the bug. Pulling out of the parking lot, I noticed a car pull out of a space in front of the paper. I turned the corner, and the other car followed. I remembered Tim's information about a big dude looking for me, and I wondered if this was trouble or coincidence. I felt the hair on the back of my neck stand up. There was no way I could outrun anything but a peddle-car in a 1967 VW. But if I made it obvious I thought I was being followed, maybe they'd back off -- and if I wasn't being followed, there was no problem. At the next corner I turned right. So did the car behind me.

"Montgomery, are you lost, or did you forget your navigating equipment?" Lorraine glanced at me and saw me looking in the rear view mirror. "Maybe the next time I won't live quite do dangerously," she muttered.

I turned right again, back to the street on which the Clarion is located. My tail followed. But when I turned right toward the Clarion, the trailing car went straight. To be safe, I made an illegal U-turn in front of the Clarion and pulled to the curb, cutting my lights.

"Now what was that all about?"

"I thought that car might be following us, but I guess not." Maybe this whole thing with the break-in just has me overly nervous, for the dark sedan did not re-appear. All the way to Signal Hill to drop Lorraine at her apartment I kept checking my rear-view mirror. But I was not followed.

On her departure from the bug, she leaned back in for a parting observation. "I'll tell you, Montgomery, there's no getting around it. You are a magnet for unusual happenstances. The first time I ride with you, your door flies open, now being followed. Being around you is certainly more exciting than a TV murder mystery."

The rest of the trip to the marina was uneventful. I stopped at a market near the marina to picked up a few groceries for dinner and when I came out of the grocery there was nothing unusual. While dinner cooked, I read more about the sewer project. I wanted to finish as much of the background as I could so it would be more difficult for anyone to snow me on the real information.

Tuesday night is laundry night for me, so when dinner was over I grabbed the duffel bag of dirty clothes, a bottle of laundry soap and a sewer book. The Laundromat was a couple of blocks away. It being a pleasant evening, I walked. The street was quiet. After dark there are no people and hardly any cars on the neighborhood streets. Only the main streets seem to carry any traffic. People in California don't walk much. That doesn't mean they don't go hiking in the woods, back-packing in the Sierra Mountains, a stroll in the park, or jogging on Marina Greens. But in the cities they don't walk, and pedestrians are particularly out of vogue when you get away from the Greens. I enjoy walking, even when the weather isn't good. The fog was already in, and I could hear my footsteps echo hollowly off the houses.

The Laundromat was all but deserted. There was a couple making a big production of doing one load of laundry at a time, and a black woman who kept watching the door, as if she were waiting for someone. My laundry style is very unceremonious. I divided the clothing evenly and indiscriminately between two or three washers, punched in some coins, dump in some laundry detergent, set the dials and settled back to read. When all three machines had stopped spinning, I dumped the clothes into a rolling cart, divided them evenly between two dryers, inserted the coins and returned to my reading. When everything was dry, I stuffed it all back into the duffel bag, put the soap and book on top, and closed and latched the bag.

I headed for the boat, duffel bag slung over my shoulder. The fog was much thicker now. Visibility was down to half a block. I crossed the street and headed down the first of the two blocks toward the marina. Half way down the first block, the echoes of my footsteps got echoes of their own. I altered my pace. There were definitely footsteps coming from behind. I quickened my pace and the footsteps behind speeded up. Ahead, I sensed a shadow moving in my direction.

Whenever it appears there is a possibility of physical conflict, my philosophy is to force the other side to make a premature move. So I slipped between parked cars and crossed the street. The footsteps behind me also changed sides and were drawing closer. The shadow ahead also changed sides of the street. They both started closing rapidly. I knew the one in back would wait for a move from the one in front -- supposedly to hold my attention. I slowed my pace to throw off their timing. My face felt flushed as the adrenaline started to pump through me. It gave me a high that felt good. All my senses were alive.

The one in front, trying to compensate for my change of speed, broke into a run for me. At the same time I heard the shuffle of steps gaining from behind. At the last possible moment, before the attackers were upon me, I swung in a circle, launching the duffel bag hard into the midriff of the man behind. As I came out of the spin I brought my foot up high and hard, catching the front one just under the chin. He took a long slow dive into the bushes along the sidewalk. In a continuation of the move I turned to face the rear attacker, dropping into a crouch. My move took me to the left of where I had been standing. The impact of the duffel bag had the desired effect of momentarily slowing him. He was already diving for the spot where I had been standing. I brought my knee up into his side and my double-handed fist down hard on the back of his neck, destroying his planned landing. As he hit the sidewalk I was already in the air and planted my heels on either side of his back bone. Had I been dead center I would have broken his back. He writhed in agony then lay still, the wind knocked out of him.

The scuffle had been virtually silent. Now there were the sounds of heavy breathing and moaning.

The man in the bushes was starting to move. I pulled him out and slammed him against a parked car. But he didn't have any fight left. His jaw was broken. I relieved him of a knife, a .38 revolver and his wallet. Keeping an eye on him, I went to the one on the sidewalk. He was out cold. I rolled him over, and took a .45 automatic and his wallet. from him He was regaining consciousness and debating if he wanted to move, so I cocked the .45 and stuck it in his ear. He stopped breathing, his eyes glued to mine. "Nasty little boys with nasty little toys. You're lucky to be alive. Tell your boss, when he bails you out, that he's dealing with a pro. I don't scare easily and you'll never get a second chance, because . . . bang, you'll be dead." Through the hatred flowing from his eyes there was also wariness. He had been easily beaten, not something he would quickly forget.

Then I screamed as loudly as I could. Both toughs cringed. In seconds front lights up and down the block came on. No one would come out; they were all waiting to see if they heard what they thought they heard. I screamed again and knew that a dozen fingers were dialing 911. Broken jaw collapsed against the car and slid to the ground when I screamed. He must of thought the end was near. The one on the sidewalk just groaned. He had at least two broken ribs, and possibly a dislocated shoulder. In the dim light I checked their wallets and made a mental note of their names. I tossed the wallets beside them. In less than three minutes I heard a police siren. I cleared the weapons, making them safe, wiped my prints from them and tossed the .38 to broken jaw and the .45 to the one on the sidewalk. Then, after collecting my duffel bag, I stepped into the street and waved down the police car.

"Over here, officer. There must have been some kind of accident because those two guys seem hurt."

"What happened?" One officer approached me while the other one went to the two on the ground.

"I wouldn't know. I was returning from doing my laundry down there at the Laundromat, and found them here."

"Hey, Mac, these guys are armed. Get the Sage." The first called for his commander and then for an ambulance. They took my name, address and noted my press identification. As soon as I could, I took my duffel bag and walked off. As I left a third squad car was pulling up. Two of the officers were trying to question the thugs, but all they got were groans. I walked to the marina and felt the post-high euphoria that an adrenaline rush gives me. It had been a while since I needed to use my martial arts training. Thinking about it, I wasn't at all sure my timing would still be good. But it all came back like it was only yesterday. I probably could have gotten information from them, but out in the open someone might have come along any moment. I didn't want to be directly tied to this incident. There would have been too many questions to answer.

Something rang a bell in the back of my head. What if I hadn't gone to do laundry? Would they have come onto the boat to work me over, or kill me? In the open I had a better chance to fight back. In the confines of the boat it would have been harder to fight back. They could have been on me before I could even set up a defense. I made a mental note to make the boat more defensible. It didn't make sense that they would want to kill me, but I believe they did want to discourage me. However, I didn't know anything damaging . . . but I was working on it. Did these guys work for Hunt? If his looks could have killed, I would have been dead this afternoon.

Activity like that brought back lots of memories, most of which were unpleasant. As a result I spent a restless night alternating between surrealistic dreams and staring at the faintly lit overhead. Even when I was staring at the overhead I was in limbo, not knowing if I was awake or asleep and dreaming that I was awake.

Chapter 6

Wednesday A.M.

———⟫◆⟪———

When I decided I would roll out I found it was only an hour before my normal wake up time. I must have slept more than I thought. The fog was gone and I could see a few stars when I opened the hatch. After a shower and breakfast I felt pretty good.

I read some more sewer stuff before leaving for the paper. What was a mystery now was that I felt like I was beginning to understand the project. I made notes of questions and items that were not clear to me. The intent of the project was to make some of the main sewer lines large enough in places they could act as temporary retention basins. These basins would contain peak flows that could then be processed at the capacity rate of the process plants. Two new process plants were planned and the combination sewer retention basins and more processing capacity was calculated to reduce the number of overflows to once or twice a year. In a sustained rainy period there might be an overflow, but it would be diluted by the volume of rain water and be much less damaging to the environment than it was today.

The total project was broken into eleven major parts, each part a full project in itself. The City had estimated a total cost of $800 million, but under pressure admitted this was a very preliminary number. The State and Federal governments were expected to cough up a substantial portion of the cost. But there was still no figure for the City's share of the cost to be generated by a future bond election. The way it was organized it appeared that the only person who had total visibility of the project's performance was Ralph Hunt, Public Works Director, and Simon, if he were around.

I finished reading the last folder just when it was time to leave for work. Ernie was already at his desk when I arrived. He was examining project progress reports looking for inconsistencies, and putting all the data into a spreadsheet for analysis. I asked him if he had a list of all the companies working on any of the projects.

"Of course, Monty. I just updated it. Here's an extra copy." Being called Monty after the W.W.II British General Montgomery, grates on me. To most of the people who call me that, I jab back with a quick retort. But Ernie means well and I do work with him, so I let it die. Anyway, it doesn't happen often.

"Thanks, Ernie." The two-page list contained over seventy companies, and I knew just who I could get to wring them out. If there was anything the least bit peculiar, we'd know it. Lange was a master at deciphering company entanglements, and I knew he would be delighted with this kind of project. Unraveling company connections are for him like working a crossword puzzle is for puzzle devotes.

Staff meeting brought a lot of chit-chat. The dailies had not picked up on Simon's disappearance at all, apparently giving it little of the significance we had given it. Hunt's disorganized press conference also led them to discount the significance. It was our second scoop in as many days. We could bet that the dailies and the electronic media would be all over the story today with twice as many reporters as we had. The morning staff meeting was nearly finished when Mrs. Richman stepped into the newsroom. All conversation stopped, even Max paused and looked at Mrs. R. Although she was not a stranger to the newsroom, she did not commonly come to the morning staff meetings.

"Oh, please carry on. I'm sorry to interrupt. I thought you might be finished." She parked herself by the door as the remaining reporters hurriedly identified their stories, the aside comments and off-color comments held. As the meeting broke up, reporters and photographers heading for their desks or to meetings, Mrs. R. handed me a piece of her note paper. On it, in school-book handwriting, was a man's name, company name, address and telephone number. "Here is the person who has offered his help in analyzing the sewer project. His company has not been involved in any of the projects. He seemed almost eager to participate with us. You'll need to arrange an appointment." I thanked her for her assistance and said I would make an appointment right away.

Before calling the number she had given me, I collared the police reporter, Sid, and asked him to check on the two thugs picked up near the marina. Basically, I told him the same story I gave the police, but added that there was a personal interest in finding out what happened to them. Sid agreed.

I dialed the number Mrs. R. had given me. "This is Mr. Bates' office." It was a direct line to the man's secretary. I explained who I was and that I had been referred to Mr. Bates by my publisher, Mrs. Richman. "Oh, yes. Will you hold for a moment. He's on another line and will be right with you." I waited a good five minutes, during which the secretary came back on the line twice to reassure me that I was not forgotten.

"Mr. Montgomery, I'm so sorry to have kept you waiting. How can I help you. Mrs. Richman explained a little of your needs, and that is exactly the kind of project in which we would be delighted to participate." He had a rich cultured voice, like the voice of a person who has been voice-trained for radio. From his voice I imagined him as lean sophisticated, and a sharp dresser. The project is to take existing project information and plot it on a computer. The results should indicate the level of efficiency in running the projects, holes, inconsistencies and perhaps financial discrepancies. The need was for the use of an experienced project person, some data entry time and the use of the computer.

"Mr. Montgomery, I have just the person, Alexis Treller. She is an engineer, manages projects for me and is, at this moment, between projects. She knows our computer analysis software, and can put together a staff that can run through this in no time."

We set a time later in the morning for me to come to Bates Engineering and meet with Ms. Treller.

"Oh, one more thing, Mr. Bates. I forgot to ask at the beginning if you were presently, or had been involved in any of the City's waste water projects? I wouldn't want there to be the appearance of any improprieties on either side."

"I'm glad you asked. We have not participated in any of the City's projects for the past four or five years now."

"Why is that?"

"We've not won any bids recently. Perhaps we are overpriced for what the City wants." His answer was sufficiently vague that it raised more questions than it answered. Perhaps that was his intention, or it could be his normal manner of speaking about his business to someone he doesn't know. Either way I let it drop, to be pursued when I met with him later.

In the mean time I had a lot of preparation work for this meeting with Bates Engineering and Ms. Alexis

Treller. City reports are public documents, unless they involve personnel matters. As a matter of course most newspapers collect these various City reports. They provide part of the factual background from which reporters write their articles. The Clarion collected City reports on every aspect of the City operation. A well-organized newspaper library provides a wealth of information on the City, its operations and its proficiency. We put a college intern to work making copies of all the sewer project reports and records the Clarion had collected over the past two years. This would provide the actual design criteria as well as the basis for the comparison to the hypothetical project performance.

While the intern was busily copying the files, I started checking the Clarion files on some of the company names from the list of contractors Ernie had given me. There were files on only a few of the companies, and none of these seemed to have much of a history in the City. It was not surprising for there are thousands of companies in the City. Unless they are a City institution or have achieved some level of notoriety, separate company files were rarely maintained. The business reference books were also devoid of entries for many of the companies, although several did belong to the Chamber of Commerce.

I made copious notes on everything I found and put them in a folder with the list so that I could show Lange that I had at least done something with the list before handing it over to him. Eight of the contractors on the list had offices in the same building as Bates Engineering, one of the high-rise buildings along the Embarcadero. Another ten had offices in nearby locations. An interesting coincidence, I thought, but probably not significant. There are lot of high-rise business buildings near the foot of Market Street, where it meets the Embarcadero.

The Embarcadero rims a third of the City at the Bay along the north and north-east sides of the City. Originally it was the haulage road linking the shipping piers. At the peak of San Francisco's sailing ship days, the Embarcadero was paved in brick and cobblestones that had been collected for ship ballast for ships with lighter loads or partially empty on their way back to the East Coast. Most of the return trips found the ships loaded with cargoes of lumber or hides. During the gold rush, thousands of people a day arrived, and they needed provisions, equipment and sustenance, more food than could be provided by the small gardening plots around the City. This gave rise to the increasing farms down the peninsula and across the bay.

As shipping went to steam, the Embarcadero was widened, cemented over and a rail line was added to collect freight for shipment to the burgeoning farming and lumbering communities up and down the state. Today, it provides only the wide street separation between the City proper and the waterfront, some of which was being revitalized into urban walkways and parks as the old piers collapsed or burn to the waterline. The Ferry Building, opposite the end of Market Street, provided a central point along the Embarcadero for trendy business activities. Modern ferries now run between San Francisco and Marin County or Oakland bringing a newer form of commuter, the middle-aged yuppie and young executive.

By 10:30 a.m. the copying was finished, neatly stapled and filled a box to overflowing. I added a few more background files and lugged the box to my bug. The box was too large to fit in the front storage compartment, so I had to place it on the front passenger seat. Settling into the driver's seat, I found that the driver's door refused to latch. I slammed it and banged it but still it refused to latch. In desperation over the prospects of being late to an appointment arranged by the publisher, I drove the mile to the high-rise office building holding the door closed with my left hand, while shifting and steering with the right. If this was a TV sitcom, it might have been funny, but right then I couldn't find any humor in it. Just as I pulled in front of the building, I hit a pot hole and the door latched. Miserable old car. Maybe Danny was right. Maybe I should get a better vehicle. But one look at this and no one would want to steal it. And no one could tell the new parking dents from the old ones. Besides I've gotten use to the temperament of my piece of junk. I know how it is going to behave in a range of conditions. Or, maybe it is just that our personalities fit together.

Street parking in the San Francisco business district is virtually impossible and high-rise building parking costs a fortune. Not that I wouldn't get reimbursed for the expense, its just that I don't like to pay extortion fees to anyone, and especially for this car. I was about to give up and park in the building when I saw two-thirds of a space worth of unmarked curb, just enough for the bug. I swung in just ahead of a black Porsche angling for the same spot. The driver gave me a dirty look as he wheeled around the corner. I was still gloating as I lugged the box of paper into the building lobby.

"Hey, bud. You can't bring that box through here, deliveries are around the corner." The security guard at the information counter shattered my sense of wellbeing.

"It's not a delivery."

"Yeah? What is it, some new kind of Gucci attaché case for carrying your business papers?"

"As a matter of fact, yes. And I'm kind of in a hurry for a meeting with Mr. Bates at Bates Engineering. I'd appreciate it if you'd let it go this time." Bates must have some clout with the building management for I saw the guard's expression change when I mentioned his name.

"I'll let it go this time. But in the future all deliveries larger than a attaché case have to go through building receiving. The rules..."

"Thanks, I'll be careful in the future." I wondered what kind of rules there were with a rush mail delivery person, as I rode up to the 16th floor. The Bates receptionist wasn't much friendlier than the security guard until I mentioned that Mr. Bates was expecting me. She spoke softly into the phone and nodded me toward some modern chairs against one wall. I set my box down, but stood near the desk. After a few minutes I wandered across the room to examine the wall decorations. They could hardly be called art, more like geometric representations of hills and valleys in pale mauves and faint gray-blues. A braided rug of the same shades hung on the wall behind the receptionist.

It wasn't until 11:15 that a young man came from the inner sanctum to collect me and my material. As I picked it up he offered to help me with it and I wondered if he was proposing to take one end of the box, or the whole thing. He just stood and watched with a perplexed expression as I lifted it to chest height. "That's all right. I have it. If you can just help me with the door and lead the way, that would be fine."

He led me around a couple of turns to a main hallway where a side hall intersected at a conference room. The room had two glass walls. One looked out on the hallway from which we had just entered and the other looked into another room with half a dozen people working at computers. "Ms. Treller will be with you momentarily." With that my guide nodded his way out of the room. I set my box on the glass-top conference table. It was certainly not a room in which people would play toes-ies under the table. It was another five minutes before Ms. Treller did indeed appear.

I knew it was her when I saw her coming down the side hall. She walked purposefully and her bearing was all business - the professional woman. She was medium height, but looked taller in her smartly tailored business suit. No matter how severely cut her suit, it couldn't hide the fact that she was a woman. She wore her dusty-blond hair short to take away the narrowness of her face. She wasn't pretty, but the way she wore makeup made her striking, accentuating her gray-green eyes.

"Mr. Montgomery, I terribly sorry to keep you waiting. Mr. Bates cannot join us right now, but he will join us for lunch, that is if your schedule allows."

I knew I didn't have anything scheduled, but produced my pocket date book to let her know I kept to schedules. "I think that will work. I don't have a meeting until one-thirty, Miss Treller."

"Good. Call me Alexis. Now what is this project we are going to help you with?"

I explained that we weren't sure the City was appropriately managing the sewer projects, and were even less sure of how the expenditures were handled. We already knew the City's cost estimates were well below the actual cost. Several of the projects were beginning to show cost overruns. We weren't making any allegations, but it was possible that with the amount of money that these projects represent, some people might be tempted to develop sticky fingers. "We'd like to take the existing designs and calculate what these projects should cost at today's prices for design, labor and material. Then we can compare them to what they are actually costing and evaluate the differences."

I pointed to the box. "Here are all the project design criteria as published by the City. There are also some of the status reports. We'll have more later."

She pulled a stack of papers out of the box and flipped through them, reading the type of information they contained quickly. "This will work very well…" We spent the next half hour discussing the approach to the project, the type of reports that we could use and how we wanted it presented. She was bright, articulate and easy to talk with. It must have come from her exposure to the male-dominated construction industry. Bates had been correct in telling me she would be perfect for the job. She asked me how I happened to be interested in this project.

"Well, with the disappearance of Simon Blare, we thought we ought to take a look at the projects."

"That's right; you were the one who wrote the article on his disappearance." But something in the way she said that, made me feel she knew I had written that article before she ever entered the room. "So what do you think happened to him?"

"My honest appraisal?" She nodded to my question. "I haven't the foggiest idea."

"Maybe he absconded with some of this money?" She phrased it as a question, almost as a suggestion. "But he didn't really seem the type."

"Oh, you'd met him?"

"Yes, a couple of times, but I didn't know him. I got that feeling from your article...pillar of society, and all that. But those are often the ones who do. Are you investigating his disappearance? I mean you, personally. It must be exciting to investigate such things for your paper." It didn't dawn on me at the time that she knew more about my job than I would have suspected. Of course it was possible that Mrs. R. had told Mr. Bates what my role was, and he in turn passed it on to Alexis.

"Actually, most of my work is sifting through old records looking for discrepancies – like trying to make sense out of this waste water project. It's not at all like being a private investigator. And as for Simon Blare, I assume the police are looking for him and will turn up something." She asked several more questions that I also evaded in a similar manner. It was difficult to break her train of questions about Simon and what we knew about him and the waste water projects. She was a skillful interrogator, coming back to items I had responded to earlier.

"You have an insatiable curiosity about our approach to this."

"I guess it's just my background and that I am always curious how the press looks at public projects.

"What is your background?"

She gave a cursory explanation that she grew up in the oil fields, her father being a wildcatter. Raised as a tomboy, she had a natural affinity for science and became a civil engineer. "I worked a few other areas before coming to San Francisco and going to work for Mr. Bates.

A tall, slender man passed in front of the windows and entered the conference room. I guessed his age in the mid-50s. He wore the tan of an outdoors man, but was immaculately dressed in a brown, hounds-tooth jacket, beige slacks, white shirt and brown tie with a hint of geometric-modern background in it - silk, of course. He almost perfectly matched my mental image.

Mr. Montgomery, I'm sorry I couldn't join you earlier, but there were just too many things demanding my attention. I trust Alexis has been picking your brains and is ready to start working." We shook hands and made some small talk for a couple of minutes. "Shall we go to lunch. We have reservations at the International Club in the Ferry Building across the Embarcadero. Does that sound all right?"

We didn't speak much on the elevator down as it stopped at other floors to pick up the lunch-time crowd. At the bottom, the lobby between the elevator banks was crowded. The doors were just closing on the elevator across from ours on its way up and I saw a face I recognized. I recognized it, but at the moment did not put a name to it. I wasn't until we were crossing the Embarcadero that I could name the face. It was Ralph Hunt. There must be a million legitimate reasons why he was in that building at lunch time, but right then I couldn't think of any. I almost excused myself to go back and see if I could find out what company he was visiting. But that would have been ridiculous. There were easily fifty companies in that building, besides eight of which were contractors on the City's sewer project. And even if he were visiting one of them, it could be perfectly legitimate.

Both Alexis and Mr. Bates saw my momentary lapse. "Is everything okay?" Alexis was the first to speak.

"Oh, yes." I had, by then, recovered. "I thought I had forgotten something, but then I remembered that it had been taken care of. Thank you." The International Club was not really a club. You could pay a membership fee and receive preferential treatment, but anyone with the financial resources could drink and dine there. We were immediately ushered to a table by the window with a view of the bay. The fog had burned off and there were now sailboats dotting the bay. I would have much preferred to be out there among them than having lunch here. Bates noticed my longing gaze at the Bay.

"Do you like the water?"

"Well, yes, Mr. Bates. I love to sail."

"Oh, that's interesting. I have a cruiser. It's berthed at the San Francisco Yacht Club."

"We're practically neighbors. My boat is just a quarter of a mile away. Do you have any trouble with theft there?" My question popped out, without any thought.

"Of course not. We have very good security and the harbormaster knows each of us, so he can spot people who do not belong." The answer was more abrupt that I expected. And he didn't follow up with the normal question of 'why'.

"We have reasonable security, but someone broke into my boat the other day. What they took surprised me. It wasn't any of the electronic gear, just a book of photograph negatives." His reaction surprised me. He totally ignored my comment and shifted subjects to the project we were working on.

"So tell me about what it is you are looking at."

Before I could open my mouth, Alexis outlined the project.

"Isn't that about right, David?"

I agreed. She had a good handle on it. She then told him about our following discussion on investigating Simon's disappearance. She must have used some code words, for when Bates started questioning me about what we knew, he probed behind some of Alexis' earlier questions. He was a master interrogator. By the end of lunch I felt like my head had been squeezed in a vice, and I couldn't even remember what I had eaten for lunch, or if I had eaten lunch. I don't think I told him much, but neither did I get much from him. When I asked him why he had such an avid interest in the sewer projects, his answer appeared to be direct. But thinking back on it, he never said very much.

"Look, I've bid on a lot of the contracts for design work, engineering and project management with the City. Nothing has ever materialized. I won't say something strange is going on, but I'm curious why I don't get any contracts. That's why I volunteered our resources to examine the projects. If I had done it on my own, the results would have been suspect, no matter what the results." He spun off the answer like he had rehearsed it, calculated to sound altruistic. He excused himself before coffee arrived. I suspected he felt he had learned all he was going to learn in this sitting. Alexis hardly said a word after he started his inquisition.

"Is he always like that?"

"Like what?"

"Oh, come on. He was pretty intense. Did you just tune out?

"Yes, that's Randolph. I sometimes think he is a manic-depressive. When he is on, he is like that. Other times, he's a pussy cat. I guess if you're not use to him, it can be pretty... uncomfortable. He doesn't mean anything by it, really."

Back at the paper I wrote the second-day follow-up on Simon's disappearance from phone calls to the Police and to people in City Hall. According to the mouth piece at the Chief Administrator's Office, they didn't even know he was gone, and had no idea what kind of implication that could have on the future bond election. They certainly didn't know if any funds were missing, and no, they weren't about to launch an audit. The Mayor's office had even less interest in the goings-on over in the Public Works Department.

It was about five when I turned the story in to Max. "How'd Mrs. R. find that Bates character." I asked Max after telling him I felt like I had spent a day in an interrogation room as the subject.

"I don't know, but I'll ask?" I knew he would. Max is funny about using or protecting sources. It is a place where his idealism shows through. He would protect a source to the death, I am convinced. But the source had better be absolutely straight or Max will throw him to the wolves. This is one of the ways he jealously protects the integrity of information going into the paper.

I was stuffing copies of few files into a bag to take to the boat with me for the evening's study session when I got a call from the receptionist. A Miss Margaret Elliston was in the lobby and wanted to speak with me. I came down to the lobby, my arms loaded with books and the bag of files. "Hi, Margaret. I was just on my way out. What can I do for you?"

It seemed that she wanted to talk, but not here. Maybe over dinner?

"Tell you what. Let me put these in the car, and I'll buy you a drink at Ole's, the company hang out." She trailed along as I put the books and files in the car and locked it. At Ole's, I ordered drinks and we settled into a corner booth, away from the normal action area.

"Oh, I've never been in a place like this, before. A real news person's bar."

"Actually they do a better trade as a lunch-time sandwich shop than they do as an evening bar. So what do you want to talk about?"

She started with how much last Sunday had meant to her, and thanked me again for the good time. I thought at first she was trying to make a play for me, but I could see that there was something else chewing at her, inside. I had been quiet throughout her conversation, but I finally said that she should just spit it out and we could make sense out of it later.

"Okay. I think my father is in trouble. He is being threatened. I overheard him being threatened, but he doesn't know I heard. He would be upset if he knew I heard. These things are not supposed to come into the family." Once unlocked, the words just flowed. "I don't know why he is being threatened, but I think it has to do with something in the sewer projects. I heard the man say that my father could also find himself over his head in sewage, if he didn't do what he was supposed to do."

"What did the man look like?"

"I didn't see him, other than afterward from the window. He was tall and slender. That's all I could tell."

"What was your father supposed to do?

"I don't know. He didn't say what it was, just that my father had to do what he was supposed to do, or he would pay the penalty."

I asked a lot of other questions, for which Margaret had no answers. "I don't know what I can do without more information."

"I know. I just needed someone to talk to about it."

"I really can't go to dinner tonight. I have work to do. Are you going to be all right? Do you have any girlfriends you can go visit."

"No. It's okay. I feel better already, just talking with you." With that, she got up and left. Her drink was hardly touched. It was almost as if she was to deliver a message. And when it was done, she left. Strange. There are a lot of strange people in San Francisco, but two regular people who act strange in one day are more than a little unusual.

As I was leaving Ole's, Sid, the police reporter came in.

"Hey, Montgomery, you'll never guess who bailed out those two hoods. Your girlfriend."

"Girlfriend?"

"Yeah! The attorney, Angela Denuchi. They were being held on weapons charges. One of 'em was a convicted felon." He added more, but the shock of who bailed them had given me hearing paralysis. Although she was not at the bottom of the totem pole in the large law firm and subject to a range of assignments, criminal law was not in her field. And, whoever wanted them out had to put up a lot of money for her firm to handle it.

My head was puzzling on Angela's action for the two hoods all the way home. When I got to the boat, I reached over and tapped a quick rhythm on Lange's hull, our signal to get together. I had this project for him. And, besides, at this point Margaret was not the only one who needed to talk.

Lange was home, and popped his head out of the cabin within moments of my knock.

"So, home is the hunter, and all that. Was hunting good today?"

"I'm not sure. I don't have any trophies. As a matter of fact, I'm rather confused. I also have some minor exercise for your organization probing talents."

"I was just putting the finishing touches on a loin roast. If you could find a decent bottle of red in your barge, something in the late Napa 70s or early 80s is preferable, you would be welcome to join me. We can discuss our mutual interests over a savory meal." Lange was a gourmet chef, among his other accomplishments. How was it that he could eat all the excellent food he prepared and remain toothpick-thin was a mystery to me. It had to be his metabolism, for I've never seen him exercise. Me, I gain ten pounds just looking at what Lange polishes off in one sitting.

It had to be a special occasion for either of us to prepare beef. Neither Lange nor I ate much beef, although we both enjoyed it. Besides the health aspects of a high-beef diet, it is not so easy to carry beef on a cruise, as it is for some other foods. Beef consumes a disproportionately large amount of refrigerator space for the number of meals it serves. Also, it requires heavier refrigeration to keep it fresh. The last thing one wants on a cruise is to have one's mouth watering for a delicious steak and find the meat has aged beyond a consumable level.

"I think I can scrounge something up. At the worst, I can bring over a bottle of '93 Alex's Cabernet." It was my prize purchase. The winery was new on the market, and I had lucked into a distributor who didn't know the quality of what he had. I had purchased a case at $17 a bottle. Most places today were now selling a bottle at $50 and everyone expected the prices to skyrocket. It was a superb cabernet sauvignon. "So what's the occasion?"

"My weekend junket paid good dividends. I'll tell you all about it over dinner."

Onboard my boat I washed up, changed into a pair of jeans, sneakers and a pullover, and grabbed a prize bottle of cabernet from the storage locker under one of the bench seats. It was the one area that had not been seriously trashed in the break-in. Maybe they had more respect for good wine than they did for the rest of my personal property. I also called Angie's office and apartment. There was no answer other than her mechanical voice on the answering machine, but I left messages at both locations.

I boarded Lange's boat. It was a strange sensation to look back at my boat from his deck. Lange's deck was a good three to four feet above the top of my cabin, even higher than the boom that holds the foot of my mainsail. My boat isn't large, but it isn't tiny, either. However, when seen from this vantage point, it does look small. The smells coming from Lange's cabin started my mouth watering. There is a step up from the deck to the floor of the deckhouse on Lange's boat. I almost always nearly trip on it going in. But this time, carrying my prized wine, I easily negotiated the step. The deckhouse functions as the living area and dining room, and doubles as a wheel-house when cruising during bad weather. There is a flying bridge above.

The galley is down about three steps forward of the deckhouse, where Lange was busily creating his gastronomic masterpiece. Forward of the galley was a storage area, a head, and the crew bunk room. From the aft end of the deckhouse another set of steps lead to the owner's stateroom and another stateroom, somewhat smaller than the owner's, but each with their own heads. It could sleep nine comfortably, including crew and, if the two settees in the deckhouse were used, eleven. Built for cruising long distances comfortably, with a deep V-hull, it boasted large fuel and water tanks. Lange had added good refrigeration and the latest in navigation equipment. His log book showed he had been all the way to the Far East, and several times to Hawaii, Alaska and the Aleutian Islands. But at present, he was content to make shorter soirees through the California waterways and along the coast.

"Here." Lange tossed me a wine opener. "Even jug wine is better if it is allowed to breathe for a bit before consumption. In the meantime you know where the bar is. Pour yourself a scotch and me bourbon. I'll have the usual." Lange's bar was small, but stocked with such items as single malt scotch whiskey and Wild Turkey bourbon - all good sipping whiskey.

"So what are you confused about?"

"I'll get to that in a moment. First let me tell you about being interrogated at Bates Engineering." I related the episode, trying to remember the questions and intonation exactly as Bates had asked them. "Do you know anything about Randolph Bates?"

Lange came up into the deckhouse and perched on the chair mounted before the steering wheel. "Let's see. He must have started seven or eight years ago. It was about the time when I was winding up my employment with San Francisco General Bank and Trust Company. I thought I could do much better on my own, and of course I have . . . even with some ups and downs. As I recall he was looking for capital. I think he wanted to buy out a partner, or an investor, I'm not sure which. It seemed like an expensive way to go, borrowing to buy out an investor, but then maybe not in his case. It seems like he had been doing work for the City for a while, but I've not followed his business.

Lange continued, "He does seem a bit eccentric, but then I've only met him a few times. Seems like I recall him having some association or relationship back East, but then these engineering firms can wander quite far for business. Look at Bechtel, they are all over the world in dozens of different projects."

I described how Bates would be helping us, and described how we had the projects set up.

"The only thing you need to do is make sure that all the assumptions are indicated, like what weight steel reinforcing is used in the cement and the cement thickness. Then you can spot check the arithmetic." He made some other suggestions about validating the project. "It might be a good practice to check the purchase orders against the specifications, just to be sure they are buying the right grade steel, etc."

Lange tended to look at everything from a project management point of view. "There has to be a task list, resources must be assigned, a time-line drawn, and performance evaluation to track the progress."

These were elements missing from our documentation.

"Do you have anyone who is willing to do the study validation?"

"Yes, Dr. Lawrence of San Francisco University. He has a deep attachment to Simon and has already volunteered to help any way he can." I explained a little of their relationship. Lange knew of Dr. Lawrence, but had never met him. I was a little surprised that he knew about Dr. Lawrence, but then I am beginning get over being surprised at who Lange knows or knows about. He once explained that when you are a venture capitalist, you have to know people, and everything there is to know about them. Companies are only as good as the people in them.

As we were talking, Lange released a polished teak table that folded into a cupboard against one of the deckhouse walls. Fully opened, with leaves, the table would comfortably seat nine, so he only opened it part way. Returning to the galley, Lange handed up plates and silverware. "Here, you can set the table. We'll use the place mats from the cupboard beside the table." I had no more than finished setting the table than he began bringing up dishes of food.

"Excuse my neglect of starters…appetizers if you prefer. I simply forgot them when we started talking." Besides the roast loin of beef topped with mushrooms, he had made his own version of potato puffs, braised asparagus with a lemon cream sauce, and a sautéed vegetable medley. I felt ravenous. We finished our whiskeys and I put the bottle of cabernet between us on the table.

"Before we immerse ourselves in the sewer stuff, no reflection on the meal, tell me about your weekend triumph," I suggested.

Lange related that he had met with the owners of a small computer software company in Mendocino, north of San Francisco a couple of hundred miles up the California coast. "It is a delightful location, Mendocino. You should spend a weekend there. You can't sail there, though. There is no harbor or good anchorage. These guys have a fully functional product and all they lack is the marketing." Lange had been able to put together a marketing program, and bring in a software marketing company for less money than they had expected to pay. For this he receive shares in the company and royalties on the sales. They retain majority ownership, something many young entrepreneurs are unable to do. "Pretty good for a few day's work, if I do say so myself. Now tell me where we're at with the Blare disappearance."

"Where to begin… I suppose the first is that I was attacked on my way back from the Laundromat last night."

"No!"

"It could have been the same thugs that tossed the boat. They were both carrying, but I think they just wanted to rough me up. I was ready for them and they were rudely surprised. One may do a little hospital time. I think I broke his jaw." I explained the scenario and there was no doubt in either of our minds that they were specifically after me.

"What is confusing is, I heard that the attorney who bailed them out was Angie. Although they were being held at the prison wing of the county hospital, she had them bailed within three hours of their arrival. It's strange that she is the attorney on this. She's not been practicing criminal law, not that she couldn't if she chose. Whoever paid them to rough me up had to pay big bucks for that law firm. I have a call in to her at the office and a message on her machine at home, but so far she's not returned any of my calls.

"Here is a list of about 30 companies which are working on one or more of the eleven sewer projects. I'll go through the City records and library to dig up what I can about them. Your sources may be able to shed some additional light on them." I told him that the marks by eighteen of the names were companies located in the same building as Bates Engineering or one of the adjacent buildings. "I only marked them because I saw Hunt in that building at lunch time."

Lange scanned the list. "I recognize the names of a few of these companies, but nothing pops right out. Most of them are unknowns. I'll check them out." He paused for several seconds. "It seems a little strange that Bates Engineering isn't on your list. The firm is eminently qualified for design and for project management."

"I asked Bates if the firm was involved in any City projects. He said not, that his bids always seemed to come out too high, but made it sound like there might be something going on in City Hall."

On that note it was time to go home. Lange said he would start researching the companies in the morning.

I had just gotten settled into my cabin, with another wastewater file open on the table, when the phone rang. It was Margaret. She thanked me for meeting with her earlier, then shifted to her father's behavior.

"He just isn't himself," she said. "He used to be funny and good company to be with. But now it is like he is in this funk all the time. Is it alright if I come over?"

I turned her down. I felt like a heel, because I knew she needed to talk and she considered me a good listener. And I am. But right now there were too many things going through my head. And she being the daughter of one of my suspects just didn't seem right. For all I know she could be a setup to distract me. But on the other hand she could be totally innocent and very concerned about her father.

"Margaret, listen to me very carefully. Here is what I want you to do." I laid out a set of instructions; what she should say to her father and how she should say them. I told her they had to be delivered with absolute confidence, like she has command of the earth. "He won't want to hear this, especially from you. But stand firm. This will be how your dad can get everything square."

She sounded relieved that there was something she could do, when she hung up.

I went back to the wastewater files. By eleven o'clock the words were dancing on the page and I had lost all ability to concentrate. So I crawled into my bunk and was immediately asleep.

Chapter 7

Thursday – After Finding Simon

———— ❖ ————

The fresh air was finally starting to take effect. The sour sewer smell was fading from my nose and I didn't feel quite so slimy.

"Any way, Lieutenant, it was a perfectly normal sail, really nice until we got to the Cliff House and Mile Light. Both of them were acting perfectly normal . . . your typical loving newly-weds, only they weren't; not really newly-weds. Simon said they had been married a little over a year."

The personal stuff I left out including the Sunday picnic, or where I developed the film. But I couldn't help thinking that if I had checked out the sewer discharge instead of playing, the result might have been different. I had settled into an easy life and was getting lazy. Had I used my instincts the way I use to, the way they'd kept me alive in the past, I would have picked up on Simon's focus and anticipated what he might have done. I know thinking this way is not productive. Lange says that self recriminations, feeling guilty about something you can't control, is a wasted emotion and energy. He's right. But if I had done something different maybe, just maybe I wouldn't have been looking at Simon's body in a sewer.

"So, Lieutenant, that's how I know there was water coming from that outfall."

"Is there any chance it could have been a different outfall, maybe a little farther along the cliff?"

"Aw, Lieutenant...."

"Okay, okay. I had to ask. Your story brings another perspective into play. And we know that someone at City Hall wanted the Police to sit on the missing persons report." A coroner's wagon pulled to the curb behind one of the squad cars. "The lab guys should be about done. When they are, we'll take the body down town. You're welcome to tag along." I nodded acceptance.

The two coroner's deputies pulled a basket from the wagon and disappeared down the manhole. Several minutes later one of them reappeared, hanging on to one end of a rope. Once out of the manhole he turned and began pulling on the line. The basket was gradually drawn from the hole, the other deputy pushing from the bottom. Simon's body was encased in a black body bag, strapped to the basket. My eyes burned and tears formed at the corners from anger, frustration, and sadness. I had seen lots of body bags over the years from the war, terrorist attacks, disasters. But body bags are so depersonalizing. With the body safely hidden inside, it's easy to forget that it had been a real living, breathing person a short while before, a person with a name, hopes and dreams, loves and hates. And this was just that. It was such a waste. A talented young man, deeply in love, just reaching his prime, now lifeless. His body stuffed in a body bag. Now, that life is gone, it's just another body in a body bag.

The deputies slid the basket unceremoniously into the back of the wagon, casually got in the front and pulled away. A couple of the lab guys climbed out of the manhole followed by a uniformed officer. The one that had been vomiting already stood by a squad car. "They'll have the whole thing wrapped up by five AM.," called one of the lab men to the lieutenant.

"Lieutenant..."

"Call me Andy."

"Andy, what time did the sewer guys find the body?"

"It had to be just after midnight. We had an officer here by one a.m."

"Why were they there at that time of the morning?"

"I wondered that, too. It seems that they do this kind of checking after midnight because the flow is less than any other time of the day. I'm going to head downtown. Do you want a ride?"

"Thanks, Andy, but I have my car. By the way, everyone who was down there this morning should make sure they have current shots for typhoid fever. The public health doctor I took to the outfall found typhoid bacteria in the water. He said this indicates there was standing sewage."

Having been up for more than two hours now, and with the sewer smell dissipating, I was hungry. So I stopped at an all-night beanery on Geary Boulevard. It was in the Tenderloin, a seedy neighborhood at the edge of downtown. But a lot of cops eat there so I knew it had good food, and cheap. Andy beat me to the door by a couple of seconds.

One of the other homicide cops and a uniformed cop, who had been in the sewer, joined us in a booth. My presence initially stifled conversation until Andy told them I had been trying to track the guy and probably knew more about the incident than any of them.

"So tell me again about taking the guy sailing." Then as explanation to the other officers, "Montgomery here lives on a sailboat." So I reviewed the day again, and told the officers of the change in both Simon and Barbara once Simon started taking pictures of the outfall. Then I told them of the return trip Simon and I made to the outfall and the call I received from Barbara Sunday evening.

"So, what do you make of it?" Andy probed the officers, but they shrugged their shoulders and shook their heads. Unless you're on the inside, cops don't offer speculations. After eating, we all headed to the Hall of Justice where the homicide and coroner's offices are located.

A police headquarters should not have to look depressing. But just the appearance of this drab, gray stone, seven-story building covering half a city block next to the freeway, can't help but overpower one with a sense of foreboding. Built in the 1930s with federal funds as an edifice to justice, it was devoid of any of ornamentation that gives other buildings of that era character, or a hint of grandeur. Most mausoleums are more attractive, but it obviously was not built to be attractive. The building houses the police chief's administrative offices and staff, specialty departments such as homicide or missing persons, the downtown precinct station, six municipal courts for misdemeanors, four superior criminal courts and a temporary jail. It was into its yawning portal and through its electronic sensors that I headed for Lt. Sullivan's office.

Passing between a pair of metal detectors, I entered the large lobby. Empty now, its gray marble floors and marble half-walls echoed my steps back to me. At one side was a chest-high window, behind which sat one of the City's finest at a thankless task. The sergeant's face, behind the bullet-proof glass window was sallow, reflecting the grayness of the room and the green fluorescence of the lights. When I told him through the metal voice grill that Lt. Andrew Sullivan was expecting me, he scrutinized me for several moments before requesting identification. He gave me a blank look as I flashed my press card. Slowly, he reached under the counter for the door buzzer to let me in.

Once inside he pointed down the hall. "Second door on the left," he barked.

Andy had already started tapping out the first lines of his report with two fingers on an upright Underwood typewriter as I dropped into the metal chair by his desk in the corner of the room. The City certainly hadn't overspent its budget on the furniture in the homicide squad room. Scarred wooden desks of the 1930s and 40s were intermixed with dented metal desks from the 1950s strewn around the room. A random arrangement of different sized filing cabinets lined two of the walls. It looked as if at one time someone might have tried to line up the desks. But it would have been impossible. The desks were all different sizes and shapes.

"My, god! I haven't seen a typewriter like that since typing class in high school. And then they were already throwing them out."

"Yeah, I know. You threw 'em, we got 'em." He didn't look up but kept plunking at the keyboard. "That was Saturday or Sunday you took them sailing?"

"Saturday."

"And what was it you saw?"

"You already have this."

"Yeah, I know, but it's easier if you tell me than for me to try to read my notes."

I went back over the events of the trip after we passed the Cliff House.

"And what did you say was his reaction?"

"I hadn't said. But he was rather agitated after seeing the water coming out of the outfall. By the way, do you have any speculations on how he died?"

"Not really. There was no blood on his clothes, so rule out gunshot or stab wound. It didn't look like he was strangled, although it's hard to tell with the condition of the body. So it doesn't appear to have been a violent death. This means we'll have to find something else to say it was murder."

"You mean it could have been accidental?"

"Too early to tell. The circumstances don't exactly point that way, so I am inclined to treat it like a homicide. We'll know a whole lot more once we have the autopsy report. Anyway, I thought I'd get a little of this paperwork out of the way while we wait for his wife to make a positive ID."

"She's coming down here?"

"Yeah. One of the guys has gone to get her. I called her from the car."

"How'd she take it?"

"Not happy at being awakened."

"No, I meant. . ."

"I know. It was hard to tell. She wasn't hysterical, if that's what you mean." I nodded. "She was actually pretty calm."

"Like she was expecting it?"

"Couldn't tell." Andy and I were nearly the only ones in the squad room. One other officer across the room was deeply engrossed in a back issue of Playboy magazine. I left Andy squinting at his notes and wandered over to a table in the corner that sported a coffee pot. I lifted the pot to my nose. The scorched smell told me it was made sometime yesterday, or before. Even sugar, which I almost never use, couldn't have helped this mud.

"Hey, Montgomery. What was that you said about funny stuff on the project?"

"I didn't say that. I said that Simon said there were things going on that he didn't understand. But he didn't say what they were, other than water coming out of the outfall. He had spent the night checking out stuff, he said, but he didn't say what he was checking. But he must have had some pretty strong suspicions of something to spend all Saturday night working on it, rather than waiting for Monday morning."

"Have there been any problems over there, that you know of?"

"No, it's not my regular beat, but I haven't heard or read anything."

We spent about 40 minutes exercising my memory, but there was only a trickle of additional information. By then Andy thought it was about time to go over to the morgue, a two-story building attached to the back of the Hall of Justice. "They'll have him cleaned up by now so Mrs. Blare won't see him in quite the shape we did."

The hallways, empty now, would soon be bustling as the establishment prepared to deal with the night's collection of drunks, muggers, robbers, thieves and whores. We left the building by a back door into the police parking lot. It was already daylight, and the sun was breaking the horizon somewhere on the other side of the building. We walked silently across the parking lot to the morgue entrance. Inside the lobby, there was another window, but this time without a face behind it. Andy pushed the bell button. It was a couple of minutes before an attendant appeared behind the glass. Andy asked for Dr. Naguchi, the pathologist in charge. "He ain't here," was the curt reply. "He don't come in 'till eight."

Andy flashed his badge. "Look, I just talked to him. So don't give me any shit."

"Sorry, sir. He don't want no one to know he's here this early. I'll let you right in." He buzzed the door and Andy pushed through with me in his wake. Usually they don't let the press in. Besides being disruptive for the morgue staff, information inadvertently leaked by pathologists and lab assistants, or unofficially released copies of autopsy reports, could damage a police investigation. The attendant didn't know I was press and Andy didn't say anything to stop me. So I walked along like I was supposed to be there. It was only the second time I had been in this morgue. But Andy acted as if I wasn't there or more specifically as if I were supposed to be there. Which was fine by me? I'd get first-hand knowledge of all that happened.

We located Dr. Kenneth Chong inside one of the operating theaters. He was just washing up after his preliminary examination of Simon. Naguchi was a small Japanese-American, whose brilliant forensic work and abrupt, outspoken personality had drawn national attention. Andy introduced me only as David Montgomery, without reference to my profession. Chong barely grunted acknowledgment of my presence, probably assuming I was a police officer, while he and Andy settled into a patter borne of familiarity.

"Your stiff?"

"Guess so. Any thoughts?"

"Some. But we've got to test."

"What do you have so far?"

"He was gagged, you know. He probably strangled on his own vomit."

"That makes it harder."

"Well, he didn't do it willingly. He was bound and probably not conscious."

"Drugged?"

"Likely. That's what the tests will show. No evidence of struggle against the bonds as he strangled."

"The wife will be here soon to ID him."

"I hate these show-and-shrieks."

"You don't have to be here. She's coming with someone, her attorney I think."

"Good. I'll have Steve do the presentation. His sympathy smile is good. I suppose you want the report yesterday."

"Before that." Andy gave a mock smile to which Chong scowled. Chong called in his assistant and gave instructions. Andy and I found an alcove with a coffee machine. Coffee in a paper cup, especially from a machine, is one of taste's greatest insults, but at this time of the morning it seemed better than nothing. Fortunately we didn't get a chance to drink much of it, for a few moments later Steve, Dr. Chong's assistant, told us Barbara had arrived. We met Barbara as she, a police officer and another man entered from the lobby. She introduced the man as Marvin Bagley, her attorney. The name tickled a couple of gray cells in the back of my mind, like I should have known the name, but nothing leaped to the foreground. He was probably some attorney I had seen in court, or City Hall. It occurred to me later that it would have helped put things together much faster if I had been able to place him then.

Barbara seemed surprised to see me, but acted like I was a friend she could lean on in her hour of need. "Oh, David, I'm so glad you are here. I know how Simon felt about you."

Andy introduced himself and Steve. "I'm sorry we have to do it this way, but we need a positive identification by a family member or very close friend. I trust Mr. Bagley has explained all this to you." Barbara nodded.

"I realize this is necessary, but I really don't understand why we had to do it so early in the morning." Bagley said.

"I know that it is inconvenient, but the condition of the body makes it imperative that the autopsy be performed as soon as possible."

"I'm not sure Barbara wants an autopsy. It would seem..."

"The state has the rights in this case," Andy interrupted. "With the possibility of homicide an autopsy is mandatory."

Bagley said nothing, so Andy nodded to Steve.

"This way folks. I do need to caution you that although the body has been cleaned up, the facial features are swollen and distorted. Would you prefer to use the video viewer? It might make it a little easier." The County had purchased a closed circuit video system that was piped into a couple of conference rooms. The theory is that people have gotten use to seeing bodies on television, and therefore are less emotional than when viewing the actual body.

"I . . . I don't think so." Although Barbara's voice sounded hesitant, but the strong movements of her body language said she was ready to get on with it.

Steve led us into a white room with what appeared as square white locker doors in two walls. The room smelled faintly of disinfectant with a hint of something like formaldehyde. Steve paused before one of the lockers.

"I'm sorry to have to say this, but you must realize that this person has been dead for several days. The features are not as pronounced as they were in life, and the skin is discolored. There are no obvious marks, and we don't yet know how he died." With that Steve opened the locker door and rolled out a sheet-draped cart. He moved around, placing himself between Barbara and the body as he drew the sheet down from the head. Simon had obviously been cleaned up from when I had seen him earlier. Steve continued to partially shield Barbara from the body as he turned toward her. "Just take a quick glance and turn away for a moment. It will make it a little easier." Naguchi was right. Steve did have a good sympathy smile.

Bagley gripped her arm as she looked across Steve's arm at the exposed head, then turned her head for a second, but did not shrink back. I saw a tear form at the corner of one eye as slowly she turned back. "Oh, God. Why?"

Bagley turned her toward the door. Over his shoulder he snarled at Andy, "Satisfied?"

"I need to speak with her. How soon can that be?"

"I wouldn't count on today. Was this all necessary?" By the time they reached the door Barbara was sobbing. Having nothing else to do, since it wasn't time to go to the office and all the City offices were still closed, I trailed behind and tried not be obvious.

I was still trailing when I pulled into a parking place down the block from Barbara and Simon's house in the Avenues. However, Barbara and Bagley had left me well behind when they left the morgue. To retrieve my car I had to walk to the other side of the Hall of Justice.

The Blare house was one of the grand old homes built in the late 1800s, unpretentious by neighborhood standards, but still showing enough gingerbread to fit in. Most of the homes on this block had garages under the house, and there was a Lincoln parked across the sidewalk at Blare's garage entrance. I assumed it was Bagley's. It was light enough to get a shot, so out of idleness I dragged out my camera. As I was focusing, I realized there was a man standing in the shadows near the house. There was another one on the other side of the house by the corner, both were wearing suits. I got shots of them both. I didn't know if they had seen me or not, but for about 30 minutes they never moved.

Sitting in the car watching the house, my mind and attention wandered. It was hard to imagine how the police could work a stake-out. It was only Thursday but it seemed like forever since I started tracking Simon. Was it really just Monday that I started tracking him?

A black Porsche swung into view in my mirror. I slid down in my seat to avoid detection. He parked about two cars away, on the other side of the street. I got a photo of him locking his car door through my passenger window. I leaned farther over the passenger seat, and shot a sequence of him walking to the house, climbing the steps to the front door, and entering the house. There was something familiar about him, but I couldn't place it right then.

"Okay, now give me the memory chip," I heard from a heavy voice right outside my window. At the same time, I felt something hard pressed against my head. I assumed it was a gun.

"Don't turn around. Just carefully empty the camera, and hand over the chip," the voice continued. "And no tricks, like the other night."

I thought of a lot of clever retorts, but none of them made it to my lips. Instead, I made a big show of opening the camera. At the same time, I slowly shifted my left foot, till it was against the driver's door. The latch on the driver-side door had not been holding very well. Occasionally the door just popped open while I was driving. I had been meaning to get it fixed.

At the same moment I opened the camera, I straightened my leg with all my might. I prayed that the door latch would not pick this time to hold.

WANG!

The door edge caught the goon across the face and in the groin. The gun went off and sounded like the loudest explosion I've ever heard. I was not hit, but did catch some of the muzzle flash on my neck and my ears were ringing like I was in a bell tower at noon.

The goon was rolling on the ground in agony, trying desperately to recover the .45 he had dropped as it went off. From the corner of my eye, I saw another one, probably 'broken jaw, running toward us – a gun in his hand.

I hit the key, popped the bug into gear and, without looking peeled into the street. I heard a gut-wrenching squeal of brakes, but did not feel any impact. I tore down the street and ran the stop sign at the corner. As I turned, I saw a blue sedan pull out behind the car, which almost hit me. I zigzagged down some alleys and around a few blocks before I slowed to a more normal speed. Now that it was over, I was almost shaking like a leaf from the excitement.

The fact that a shot was fired told me that those goons would be playing a lot tougher game the next time I saw them. The best protection, I figured, was to avoid being the exclusive owner of information. The quicker I could pass it on, and the more people who knew about it, the safer I was.

With my cell phone I called police headquarters. When I reached Andy, I explained what had just happened. I told him I had someone on the camera going into Barbara's house. He expressed interest, and I suggested we meet at Lorraine's apartment, where there was a computer and good printer. He agreed, so I gave him Lorraine's address and telephone number.

Wanting to be sure I was not followed, I took a circuitous route to Lorraine's place. I expected them to watch the Clarion, where there were computers and photo printing equipment. If they were still thinking of film processing, they knew there was no darkroom on the boat, but I did have a computer and printer.

I felt like I was living right, for I caught Lorraine just as she was arriving for lunch. I explained a little of what was happening, and asked for the use of her computer and printer.

"Good lord, Montgomery. You're like a little boy, still playing cops and robbers," she observed. She was reluctant to let me use it, until I explained the alternative. It probably was not safe for me to use the Clarion because they might be watching for me, or my computer and printer on the boat, so I could let the police extract the images from the memory chip, and take whatever prints they wanted. And there was stuff I didn't think I wanted them to see.

"Oh, Hell No!" she exclaimed. "Don't give those bastards a damn thing." With that, she opened her apartment for me. "I'll make some sandwiches" she said, and unlatched the door.

"You probably should make an extra one, Lt. Sullivan will be joining us."

Using Lorraine's computer, I had already downloaded the memory chip and copied it to a CD by the time Andy arrived. Using photographic paper, I had also printed a couple of Simon's shots of Lands' End, similar to the one we had run in the paper. He watched me print a set of photos taken in the sewer tunnel earlier in the day. Then I printed two sets of the man arriving at Barbara's house. When I was printing the pictures, I knew who the man was. It was Dan Kirkman, TV reporter.

"Do you think he's involved, that it is one of those love triangle things?" Andy asked.

"There may be some involvement, but not with the murder." I answered. "It just doesn't make sense with the other stuff, and the goons. I don't see him just walking in like that, if he were involved with a murder."

As we were talking, Andy had been dialing a number on his phone. With no apparent answer he redialed. Finally after the seventh try, he got an answer.

The conversation was brief. Then just before he hung up, he asked me if I would like to go for a short sail this afternoon.

"Sure, just bring the sandwiches and beer," I quipped.

He relayed my agreement. Listened for a second, and hung up.

"The guy I was talking with works for the State Attorney General's office. He is in the organized crime task group. He works undercover, so I can't give you his identity. But I thought, at this point, we all might be able to help each other...unofficially, of course."

I gave Andy a set of the photographs, and when he was not looking, I taped a copy of the CD under Lorraine's desk.

Andy thanked Lorraine for the sandwich as we left her apartment. Andy headed for police headquarters and I drove to the newspaper. I checked the streets for uninvited guests, but all seemed normal. The page editors were in, making up the pages in preparation to make the plates for the printers, so I felt safe entering.

Max was not at his desk, so I put the photos on Max's desk, with a note of explanation. I wrote a short article about Simon's death, and persuaded one of the plate-makers to put the bulletin about Simon's body being found, on the front page. Then I headed for home.

The normal Marina activity seemed completely out of place, contrasted to what I had experienced so far today. It was hard to realize that other lives were engaged in normal activity and recreation.

I showered and dressed in clean clothes, but the memory of the odor lingered on . . . even after burying the soiled clothing in the bottom of the dirty clothes locker.

I had just finished when Andy and his contact arrived.

Once they were on board, I disconnected the water, power, and telephone; started the engine, cast off, then backed out of the berth.

"I understand I can't have your real name, but for convenience sake, what do I call you?" I asked the contact.

"Just call me Cliff," he answered. There was something about him that made me wary of him. I felt like he could smile at you while he was stealing your wallet or stabbing you in the back. He was, I guessed, in his late-forties – clean shaven, and had an olive complexion that showed some exposure to the sun. At about five-foot, nine, he was trim, but with a small paunch starting to show. His facial features were clearly Mediterranean, with a knife scar under his left eye. His steel gray hair was slightly wavy, and combed straight back. There was a hardness about him, which could only have been earned from a rough environment. His hands were heavy, like a workman's, but they sported a recent manicure.

Once out of the marina, we set sail and headed toward Angel Island.

"I understand you are interested in the McKee Corporation," he said, flatly. His voice was coarse and gravely. He gave me a sickly smile.

I told him it was the largest contractor on the sewer project.

"Well, you're probably just chasing your tail. We've looked at these companies, and so far there is no evidence they are operating illegally…although, there are some organized crime contact with the parent company," he said, again with the sick smile.

"You mean like McKelig Corporation and McKraskie?" I asked.

He smiled and nodded.

"What about Lawrence Languitini?" I asked. "He is listed as the representative for both of them."

"Oh, I guess you might call him an organizer, but there is nothing you could pin on him." Cliff answered, vaguely.

"Is McKee active in other areas?" I asked.

"Well, the firm is involved in perhaps a dozen construction projects around the state. But, like I say, there is nothing we see that they are doing wrong."

"Since they're keeping such a low profile," Andy spoke for the first time, "are they likely to use rough stuff?" He was referring to the strong-armed stuff used against me this morning.

"That wasn't the first time, either," I added. I told them about the incident Tuesday night. "Since the area is not an area for muggings, I thought they were trying to discourage my inquisitiveness."

"Well, if they are involved in something, we haven't seen it. I suppose they could be trying to discourage you," Cliff responded sourly. "But I really think it is more likely a coincidence."

We discussed Barbara and her contact with Dan Kirkman. We speculated on what that relationship might mean.

"My first reaction was that she was just screwing around," I said. "But that was before those goons wanted the memory chip."

"You know, Kirkman is a top investigative TV journalist," Andy noted. "That is why they made him news director. He's the one who broke the story on the legislator pay-offs a few years ago. He's had four or five good scandal stories over the past few years...I mean ones which have sent people to prison.

"Since he became news director, his news team has been digging into more of the behind-the-scene kinds of stories," Andy continued. "You can bet they'll be riding herd of this thing over Simon Blare...that is, unless Kirkman pulls them off."

"Kirkman married?" I asked.

"Yes," both Andy and Cliff answered together. The fact that Cliff answered surprised me.

"Do you know Kirkman?" I asked Cliff.

"Well, I've met him...on the legislative pay-offs," he answered. "Okay, so what possible situations do we have with this liaison?" he changed the subject.

"If we assume the goons are working for the McKee people, then we have to assume their interest is to protect, or hide the liaison," I said. "Is that a fair assumption?"

Andy nodded agreement.

"If you assume that they work for McKee," Cliff answered.

"Then the question is, what purpose does this liaison serve?" I continued.

"You're suggesting a conspiracy," Cliff said.

"Perhaps'" I answered. "But if the liaison doesn't serve a purpose for McKee, why would they have attempted to protect it?"

"You don't think Blair was simply killed because his wife was screwing around with another man?" Cliff queried. "I mean, doesn't it make more sense that Kirkman hired the goons to do away with Blair?"

"We don't know that it was murder, yet," Andy said, vaguely. We'll have the preliminary autopsy report tonight. But what you suggest about Kirkman just doesn't fit."

"Kirkman is married to this society gal," he continued. "If he even suggested a divorce for any reason, she'd serve him his head on a platter...make a real stink. It would be the scandal of the century. He'd probably lose his job at the station."

"Dave, what do you know about her?" Andy asked.

"Well, she came from Iowa with a dream of becoming a dancer in Hollywood, and get into the movies. After a few years she went to Las Vegas for more steady work. That's where she met Simon," I related.

"Vegas, huh?" Andy grunted.

"Yeah. They've been married about a year and a half," I said.

"What did she do there?" Andy asked.

Cliff sat silently, listening with a sick smile on his face.

"She said she was a chorus girl, and that she had worked around at different spots." I answered.

"Okay!" Andy exclaimed.

"Are you suggesting she has mafia connections?" I asked.

"It is quite possible," he answered. "Especially true if she was there any amount of time…a pretty girl, eager to meet the right people…very susceptible for recruitment."

"Oh, come on." Cliff said. "I think you both are trying to conjure a case out of thin air."

We admitted that there certainly wasn't enough evidence to take it to court.

"But," said Andy, "when you put it all together, it looks something like this…particularly when you have companies working on a tremendously large project, like the sewer project…Simon's project…which we now know have hidden relationships and some mafia connections.

"I'm just a dumb City cop, but even I know of organized crime's interest in construction," Andy said. "So what I see here, circumstantially, is the beginnings of a case.

"What we are missing, is the knowledge of how they operate," he said. "Now how do we pin down the information, Cliff? Don't your people know how they operate?"

Andy and Cliff were staring at each other, almost nose to nose.

"Maybe I can help," I said.

In unison their heads snapped toward me. I immediately regretted saying anything, but now that it was out, I had to continue.

"The sewer construction represents a multi-billion dollar project." I said. "There is not only the possibility of gross mismanagement; there is an overwhelming opportunity for all kinds of graft."

"Simon's disappearance, and now death, has only reinforced our strong suspicion about the project," I continued. "To monitor this project we have made arrangements with an independent engineering firm to provide a full construction analysis. We also have gained the assistance of a top university professor to work with the engineering firm on how to design the analysis.

"When will they have a report?" Cliff asked intently.

"I'm not sure," I answered cautiously.

"Will their work be available to … us?" he questioned. There was something in his tone, which made me uncomfortable.

"Of course, after we've written all the articles on their findings," I answered.

"That's not good enough," Cliff said. Which firm?"

"Sorry," I said, indicating I would not go any farther.

"Look, man! They'll all be gone, and their records destroyed. The moment your story hits the street," he said, angrily.

"Hey, this is news scoop. I hear what you're saying, but I'm not going to let this out so some other news agency can beat us to it," I retorted. It was possible Cliff could get a subpoena, and just take everything they wanted. That would leave us with a lot of hard work, and nothing to show.

There was also a warning in the back of my head. The avid interest he showed now was certainly a turn-around from a few minutes ago.

"How about a deal?" Cliff asked.

"What's the deal?"

"Give us the report and some lead time to round up all that we'll need for a case," Cliff said.

"Twenty-four hours," I said. "And you don't give anything to anyone else. We have the exclusive all the way."

"Oh, come on! That will barely give us the time to get subpoenas and search warrants. Speaking of subpoenas, you know we could get one to confiscate your records. We could even jail you for withholding evidence," he said smugly.

"I don't think so," I said, bluffing. "You, yourself, said no crime has been committed. You'd have to prove that a crime has taken place. And, if you did jail me, you know the story would be out long before you could have the information you want. You know how the press is about jailing one of their own."

All you could hear was the lap of the water and a little flutter of the sail, as we sat silently, staring at each other.

"You strike a hard bargain," Cliff said finally. "I only wish we had more time. The exclusive is no problem."

"I'll give you the best that I can," I said. "You've probably a couple of weeks, anyway."

"Well, that's better than nothing," Cliff responded, with his sick little smile.

We had rounded Angel Island, and were beating up through Raccoon Straights with a herd of other small craft.

"Can you drop me at Tiburon?" Cliff asked.

"Sure, don't you like sailing?

"Oh, it's okay. Just that I had Andy pick me up on a street corner near where I live. It would probably be better if I returned some other way," he answered. "I'll catch the ferry back to the City."

We sailed into Tiburon, lowered the sails, and coasted to the marina's guest dock. Cliff hopped onto the dock before we could even tie up. He gave a curt little wave, and walked off toward town.

Raising the sails, we headed back for my marina. Wisps of fog drifted under the Golden Gate Bridge as we crossed back to the San Francisco side. It was beautiful, and with the good breeze we moved right along.

"So what do you think," I asked.

"I don't know. Something doesn't seem to fit right. First he doesn't seem to know anything about it, and then he does. Mmmm. Maybe he just wanted to see how much you knew."

"How'd you meet him?"

"I had been working on a series of drug-related killings about six years back. Even then he was working undercover. He had been tracking the movement of drugs through the state. I almost blew his cover when I picked him up. I just turned him loose, but I should have charged him with something so he would look like a legitimate hood."

They had run into each other over the years on other cases. "It's not the kind of thing where you are buddy-buddy. You don't socialize in the off hours."

"I've worked with him a few times so I thought if anyone knew if organized crime was involved, he would. He's a strange one, though," Andy observed.

During the remainder of the trip we talked of lighter things, like how the Giants were going to get out of their slump. "I can't wait for football, though," Andy said. "The 49ers were really great last year."

It was 5:30 p.m. when we tied up at my dock.

"Want me to have an officer stick around here?" Andy asked.

"Oh, good heavens, no," I said. "If they've been watching at all, they know you've been with me, and they have to believe that we've talked about all of this.

I did give him the names of the two toughs, though, before he left.

I was hosing the salt off the boat, when Andy came back on the dock.

"I just talked with the office," Andy said. "We're pretty sure it was murder. The ME found needle marks behind his ear, and indications that his wrists and ankles had been bound. I just wanted you to know." With that he turned and left.

I called the office, but the paper had already been put to bed, and the presses were running.

I heated a frozen dinner, and after eating I headed back to the Clarion. Max was still there and I filled him in on all that had happened.

Chapter 8

Thursday P.M.

————— ≫◈≪ —————

Back at the Clarion, I told Max of what the medical examiner discovered, and that I would have a new lead for the story. It definitely appeared that Simon was murdered.

He asked a few questions when I told him that Simon's death had been meant to look like an accident. After answering Max's questions, Max went into his deep thought process, chewing the stub of his cigar to shreds. Finally he scribbled something on a piece of paper and handed it to me.

"Let's use this as the headline," he said. "We'll play it above the fold on page one, with a photograph. Then we'll jump it to the inside. It's too late for the Avenues Edition, but we can make it on the Down Town Edition"

Back at my desk I started writing:

CITY OFFICIAL'S DEATH; MANSLAUGHTER OR MURDER SAY AUTHORITIES

By David Montgomery

SF CITY HALL – Simon Blare, a key official in the City's massive wastewater construction project, was found dead in a sewer early Thursday morning, and may have been murdered.

San Francisco Coroner Kenneth Chong showed that Blare's death may have been made to look accidental. Tests currently being made are believed to show that Blare was actually murdered.

Blare has been missing for five days before his body was found Thursday, but the coroner's office believes he may actually have been dead only two days.

Police have not established a motive for the killing, but will be interviewing all those who were in contact with Blare the Monday he disappeared

Blare's body was found by two...

* * *

I blended this lead into the story I had already written and made a few additions to the body of the text. After I sent the copy to Max, I sat back at my desk and planned the steps to be taken tomorrow.

I decided to spend some time at Bates and Broadman. Alexis had said any help in coding the data would speed up the process. I tried not to let the fact I was intrigued by the woman cloud my judgment of priorities. I also outlined the information I needed to gather for a follow-up story tomorrow. I had just started to clean up my desk in preparation to go home when my phone rang. It was the receptionist.

"There's a young lady in the lobby who wants to see you. Her name is Margaret Worthington," the receptionist said.

"Tell her I'm working on deadline," I lied. "It will be twenty or thirty minutes, if she wants to wait."

My desk was now neat and orderly. I killed some time by reading the evening newspaper, a competitor. After about thirty minutes I thought she might have left, so I headed for the lobby.

She hadn't

"Hello, Margaret. What can I do for you?" I asked.

"Oh, I'm so glad you're here," she said nervously. Her gestures were random, and over exaggerated. "Can we go somewhere…where we can talk?"

"Sure. Want to come into Editorial, or the conference room?"

"Well," she said awkwardly, and looked outside the front door. "Is there somewhere we could get a drink?"

"Of course," I said with more accommodation than I felt. "There's Ole's just down the block." Then to the receptionist I said, "Tell Max…er…Mr. Delacroix, that Miss Worthington and I stepped down to Ole's for a few minutes, and I'll be right back." It was a kind of insurance that someone knew where I was going. Margaret had seemed very nervous, and I didn't know what she had going on.

Ole's had originally been a working man's bar. But as this part of the city sprouted high-rise office buildings and condo complexes, Ole's character changed. Most of the clientele were now office workers, junior executives and newspaper people, mostly from the Clarion.

During our half-block walk, she didn't talk much, mostly just looked at me, and smiled nervously. She did say that she enjoyed dinner with me at the banquet; and that she was terribly sorry for making such an ass of herself.

The after-work trade at Ole's isn't large on Monday evenings. We found a booth at the back, pretty well away from everyone else, and ordered drinks.

"Okay, so what's on your mind besides the fact that you enjoyed dinner, and are sorry that you made an ass out of yourself?"

"I know I'm bothering you. I'm sorry. You probably don't even like me, and I would understand," she blurted out, tears welling up in her eyes. "I just don't know where to turn."

A tear rolled down each cheek. "I don't…I don't have… any friends…I mean that I can talk with…or at least would…or could understand. They wouldn't even know what I was talking about."

"So talk." I said bluntly. "It's your nickel."

I didn't feel very nice just then. And I really didn't want to encourage the nearly adolescent confidences I was certain she wanted to reveal. However, she stuck with it and I later appreciated it.

"As you've already gathered, I'm a pretty spoiled brat. And I'm not laying the blame on my parents, but they have pretty well raised me to be somebody's society wife. I've been to the best schools, and all that. But practically speaking, I couldn't hold a job. Honestly, I'm not sure I … even know what one is."

"I'm not pleased about this, and I suppose my battiness is a form of rebellion. But you see, when I was twelve, my brother was killed in Vietnam. After that my parents focused all their attention on me…I mean really babying me. In the process they let me get away with the most outrageous behavior."

"The only time they really insist on anything, is to accompany them to various social functions. They hope I'll meet some eligible bachelor, who will make an honorable offer, and take me off their hands.

"I understand that they were trying to make up for their sense of loss, by giving me what they couldn't give my brother, so I got a double dose of spoiling, okay"

I nodded that I understood what she was saying.

"I'm telling you all this," she said, "not as an excuse, but so you know that I have no practical way to deal with what is happening. I love them both so much I don't want to see them hurt."

She was coming across far better then she had Saturday night. She was beginning to appear as a genuine human being, with some understanding.

"My father is quite well off, and never needed to take this position as Chief Administrator. I think he took the position out an altruistic belief," she said. "He feels that the people of the City have been very good to him in business. And when this position came along, he felt it was a way to put something back into the City.

"After he was appointed, everything went very well. There were exciting events, parties...all sorts of good things for the first two years...actually up until about six months ago when they started construction on the new sewer," she said.

She said how her father, who had previously enjoyed his work, began coming home upset, or depressed...and now he has been receiving strange phone calls...and Floyd Hunt has been pressuring him to make some sort of decision. "But I don't know what is about."

"He is really trying to direct my father's decisions," she said.

"You know, I hate to say it because he is my father, but he is a good administrator." She said. "But now I am beginning to feel that he is out of his element with this sewer thing. He is not a trained engineer, and they throw this technical jargon at him, almost as if to deliberately confuse him."

"I...I'm afraid," she said, giving me a pleading look.

I had been slouching back in the seat during her discourse. I leaned forward, reached across the table and put my hands over hers.

"It's alright to be afraid," I said. "But it is important to understand what one is afraid of."

"Well, it is hard to define," she said. "I have this ominous feeling, like something is hanging over my father's…like… like he is being set up for something."

"I don't trust Mr. Hunt," she said. "I have this feeling, like he is part of some evil force which could destroy Daddy, on a whim. I know it isn't rational, but last night made it so strong."

"What happened last night?" I asked.

"It was nearly ten o'clock, I guess, and Mr. Hunt came to the house. He and Daddy went into Daddy's office. After a few minutes I could hear Mr. Hunt shouting at Daddy." She related.

"It was something about Daddy having to approve a contract…one that he said Daddy had already agreed to approve. Then they must have been talking about costs, because I heard Daddy shout back that he would not approve anything until he was convinced that there would be no more cost over-runs.

"Daddy told Mr. Hunt that he was tired of his lying, that it was destroying all their credibility. Then their voices lowered for a few moments. But then Daddy was shouting that he would not be blackmailed into doing anything he did not think was right. He ordered Mr. Hunt out of the house." She stopped, as if she was afraid to go on.

"And then what?" I gently prodded her to continue.

"No," she said softly, and looked directly at me. "Before the library door opened, I heard Mr. Hunt say something about Mr. Blare, and what happened to him. As Mr. Hunt left, Daddy was screaming at him that he would not be threatened.

"I tried to talk with Daddy, but he just went back into his office and closed the door. He would not talk with me or with Mother at all.

"Oh, David, I'm so frightened. Not for me, but for Daddy. Mr. Blare died, didn't he?" she asked.

"He was killed," I answered softly.

"Oh, my God!"

"Look, Margaret. I'm sure your father will be alright," I soothed. I really hoped she would not get hysterical now, not in Ole's

"Margaret. Do you think you could get him to talk with me?" I asked.

"I…I don't know. Daddy is kind of funny. He has always held things inside. He never cried, or said very much; even when Buzz, my brother, died. I think he feels it is a sign of weakness to show emotion, or talk about problems.

"Is he in any danger?" she asked.

"Probably not in any physical danger," I answered. "But I am sure that the danger will be reduced if he is willing to talk with me. It is important that you arrange a meeting for me as soon as possible…even this evening, if you can."

It isn't going to be easy," she said. "Besides his natural reluctance to talk about things, he'd be afraid you'd use his own words to make him look bad."

"I don't write like that," I said. I thought for a moment of how it would be the most convincing. "Look. Within a week, or two, I will be writing one or more articles about the sewer project. At that time, I will be talking with everyone connected with the project…even your father. At that time, I would be asking about things I have already found out. He would be in a defensive position because he would have to prove that he did not know about bad stuff that is going on.

"But, if instead, he works with me, before I have to come to him, it would look more like he wanted to get the problems solved," I said, wanting to build some logic for her to use with her father. "And I know that the public perception of someone who appears to be forthright is that he is an honest person."

"He should know by now that I do not slant the stories I write," I said.

She nodded her understanding.

I had just told Margaret that I would be at my boat in about forty-five minutes, when Max walked into Ole's. He looked around, saw us, but went to the bar rather than disturb our conversation. I waved him to come over.

"Max Delacroix, I'd like you to meet Margaret Worthington. She is going to try and arrange an exclusive interview with her father about the sewer construction, for us." I said as an introduction.

I told him we were about to leave, otherwise we'd stay and have a drink with him. I knew he had come in specifically to see if I was there, and was all right.

"That's okay," Max said. "Oh darn. I just remembered something I have to do before I left the office. Okay if I walk back with you two?"

"Of course," I answered, and the three of us walked the half block to the Clarion.

I saw Margaret to her car, while Max waited in the clarion doorway. After she was gone, Max and I held a little conference. I thanked him for checking on me, and told him what Margaret had told me.

"Tread lightly," Max cautioned. "If he is involved, he could be trying to find out what we know. On the other hand, he actually could have been duped. He may just be realizing how serious this is. Either way, he could be using her to find a way out for himself."

I nodded in agreement. We both felt that if he was innocent, he was in no physical danger. We also agreed that Lieutenant Sullivan should be told that Worthington may have been threatened by Hunt through a reference to Simon Blare.

I finally reached Andy at home. He was catching up on some family time. His wife, Helen, didn't sound very pleased to hear from me. But she let me talk to Andy after I promised that my message would not take Andy out this evening.

Briefly, I told Andy about the threat to Worthington, and suggested that Hunt might know a lot more about Simon's death than we had suspected.

Andy told me that his report he turned over to City Hall concluded that Simon's death was not accidental, and was probably murder. He said he would have someone keep an eye on Hunt.

After I finished my conversation with Andy, I headed for home. I was still hungry, even though I had eaten earlier, but decided an omelet could tease my taste buds. For a change I chopped some vegetables into the pan. When I sat down to eat, I found it had turned out better than I had expected, and that I was really hungry.

It was an hour before the phone rang. It was Margaret. She said her father had seemed interested, but had gone out.

"Do you think he is in any danger?" Margaret asked.

"No, I don't think he is in any physical danger," I reassured her. We talked a bit longer and I found that she really could be a pleasant person.

"David," she said, "I want to thank you so very much for listening to me. You are about the only person who listens and takes me seriously…I mean for me, not for who my father is. You don't seem to care about who people are or who they are related to. You just take people as they are. I like that."

I thanked her, and suggested that she might want to consider doing something on her own…something to set her apart from her parents, like get a job, or volunteer work.

"That's one way to get people to respond to you, for your own qualities." I said. "Call me when your father gets home, if he is still interested in talking with me."

I hung up, and settled down with the last of the sewer documents. It was after midnight when I finished, and settled into bed.

Sometime in the night I dreamt the telephone was ringing and ringing. But when I awoke, all was quiet so I slipped back into a comfortable oblivion

Chapter 9

Friday

I awoke early, and rolled right out of the bunk. There were no foghorns this morning. When I opened the hatch and caught my breath at the freshness of the air. I could still see some stars, but they were fading in the false dawn. I showered, dressed and fixed a good breakfast. It was going to be a long day.

It was about 90 miles to Sacramento. I hoped that, with a little luck, I could be back in the city by early afternoon. With breakfast over and the dishes done, I was on my way. My route lay across the Oakland/San Francisco Bay Bridge. When I came off the bridge on the Oakland side, the sun was just peeping over the Oakland hills. San Francisco bound traffic was already backing up at the toll plaza. I really felt good that I didn't have to make that commute every day.

It was not a bad drive to Sacramento on Interstate 80. But after Fairfield, the scenery got monotonous – a straight flat highway between flat fields with straight, even rows of crops.

I rolled into downtown Sacramento a little after 8 a.m. and found a place to park near the Capital. It was a pay meter, but allowed up to 3 hours. Since it was unlikely that the state employees would be at work yet, I got a cup of coffee at a coffee bar. There were three guys in suits, conspirally plotting the day's work. I figured they were probably lobbyists.

At precisely 9 a.m. I walked into the Secretary of State's Business Division office. A bright-eyed young receptionist asked if she might help me. I told her I needed to research some corporation records.

"Just a moment," she said, "let me get one of our analysts to help you." Almost like a puppet on a string, a fresh-faced young man popped out of the inner office door. I showed him my press identification and a letter of request. He invited me inside. As we walked down a long corridor, I explained what I was looking for.

"Oh, that's no trouble. We can get hard copies of that information for you. How many corporations do you need?" he asked.

"Twelve, to start," I replied. "We'll see where it leads from there."

"Oh, well, let me explain our procedure. Maybe there is a shorter approach," he said. "Everything is on microfilm. To produce a hard copy …paper copy…takes about four hours. The cost is $1.50 each. If you have more referencing, rather than delay you for the hard copies, maybe I should just let you look at the microfilm yourself. Then when you are done, we can make the hard copies of only the ones you need…all at once."

I thanked him for his suggestion. He seated me at a microfilm viewer, and showed me the organization of the microfilm library. I was like a kid in a candy store.

The first five corporations went like a breeze. The corporate owners were all individuals, usually people with enough capital to start a business, or multiple individuals who shared ownership...some of whom I had met, and others whose names were familiar in the San Francisco business world. I made notes of all the information.

The sixth one was Sorensen Construction Corporation. It was one of the firms doing the excavation for the project. Besides Al Sorensen, the ownership listed two corporations as co-owners. Both corporations were registered with the state. One was Materials Suppliers, Inc. and the other was Truck Leasing, Inc.

As I backtracked, I found that Truck Leasing, Inc. was a wholly owned corporation of McKee Corporation, a Delaware corporation. The owners of McKee were listed as Lawrence Languitini, Joseph Petroni, McKelig Corporation of Delaware and McKraskie Corporation of Illinois.

The other corporate owner of Sorensen Construction Corporation, Material Suppliers, Inc., showed Al Sorensen, McKelig Corporation (the Delaware corporation which owned part of McKee Corporation) and McKee Corporation directly. It was so inter-related I had to draw a diagram to help sort it out.

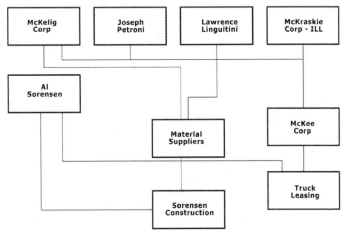

It was interesting to note that Lawrence Linguitini, president of McKee Corp, was also the registered representative of McKelig Corporation of Delaware. I tracked through the remaining six corporations on my list, and found that three other corporations were intertwined with McKee, Material Suppliers or Truck Leasing. One other firm on my list had, what appeared to be, unusual relationships with multiple out-of-state corporations; but not with the McKee tangle.

After I had made notes of all the corporations, I flagged down the college grad and gave him my list of corporations on which I wanted the printouts of the full documentation.

"I won't be able to wait for them today. Do you suppose, if I paid the postage, you could see that they were mailed to my office this afternoon?" I asked.

"Of course, I'd be delighted," he answered. Then, after looking at the list, "Say, are you working on an expose?"

"Not really. Why do you ask?"

"A federal agent was in last week. He pulled all the documentation on this McKee Corporation," he said. "Oh, maybe I shouldn't have said anything."

"Don't worry. It was probably a routine inquiry," I reassured him, struggling to hide my excitement. "Besides, what you just told me I couldn't use in a story."

"You must have an exciting job, being able to write about all the things going on."

"Well, really it is about as exciting as what you saw me doing this morning." I said. "Most of my work is doing exactly what I was doing...well maybe today was a little more exciting because I got to drive all the way to Sacramento to do it."

He was still chuckling as I left. It was before noon when I pointed my bug toward the City. It had been a very profitable morning. I felt so good that I took time to stop for a large, juicy hamburger at a truck stop along I-80.

When I reached the Clarion, I reported immediately to Max. He was ecstatic over what I had found. We now had many pieces to our puzzle, and some very strong suspicions. However, so far we did not know how they fit together with the other information.

We discussed the possibility of breaking a story now on the inter-relationships of the companies working on the sewer construction. However, we decided against it. The timing was not right. It was premature, since all we could show was that there were relationships, and suggest that there might be something wrong. We were confident that none of the other media had these relationships so we would not be likely to get scooped.

We decided to go for the whole story, whatever that was, to lay out for the public exactly how the City was being defrauded. So back to the clip files I went, to find every City project on which these companies had worked. I was so absorbed in this research that I nearly forgot to call Mary Smaller to tell her when I'd pick her up. We made arrangements for me to pick her up at City Hall for our date.

By the time I left to pick up Mary, I had researched through four years of city government clips. There were 15 projects, which included at least one of the companies related to McKee Corp. All of the projects had suspicious cost overruns.

I had just signed out at the reception desk on my way out when Mrs. Richman stopped me.

"Oh, thank goodness I caught you before you left. Tomorrow, Saturday evening, there is a rather large dinner party for the Downtown Business Association, their annual event. I would appreciate it very much if you could attend."

"Well, I…"

"You don't have other plans, do you?"

"Ah…well…no," I answered reluctantly. I desperately wished I could lie in these kinds of circumstances.

"Good. Normally Max, Mr. Delacroix represents Editorial at these functions. Unfortunately, he is going to be out of town for the weekend. I would like you to stand in for him. Please feel free to bring a guest. We have a whole table, and two places are allocated for Editorial."

"Well, alright." I said, feeling reluctant.

"Many people dress formally, but a dark suit will do quite nicely," She added. "Oh, yes, it is at the Fairmont Hotel, in the Main Ballroom. Dinner is at eight o'clock," she added. I will sooooo look forward to seeing you there."

"Yes…of course," I nearly stammered. "It does sound like an…ah…interesting evening."

I was stunned. Lucky Max. He had escaped. Social events like this are definitely not my kind of entertainment. As a rule, I hate them. However, then again, it would add to my education of the city, I rationalized. These would be the business movers and shakers, and who knows…it could just be interesting.

Mary was waiting on the City Hall steps when I arrived.

"Waiting long?" I asked as she got into the car.

"Not at all. I had just come out when you pulled up. Your timing was perfect. Your car isn't as disreputable as you said on the phone."

"It does run most of the time. So, what would you like to eat? How are you on seafood? On the other hand, would you prefer Mexican? Of course we could have Middle Eastern, French, Chinese, or Italian…all of the above… or none of the above? However, your answer will not be accepted until we have a drink", I said breezily.

She laughed. Her laugh was easy and was melodious. I pulled away from the curb and headed for a cocktail lounge near Fisherman's Wharf. It was a great place to watch the sun set and see any ship traffic on the Bay.

I collared a table right by the windows and seated her where she would have the best view of the sunset's changing colors. We ordered drinks. Hers was a bourbon and water, a nice clean drink.

"My daddy always told me the sweet drinks make you sick. 'Stick with good old bourbon and branch water, he said, and you'll always be fine.

It turns out her father was a nuclear scientist, employed by MIT. After World War II, he had gone to school at the University of California on the GI Bill. He had been in awe of the power of the atomic bombs we dropped on Japan, but he felt there were many other uses for this energy... peaceful uses.

"Of course it took him eight years, just to get his BA because he had to support a family," she said. "But he did it and more. Who'd have thought an Okie with an eighth grade education could become a full professor." She described other pieces of her background and family.

Gradually I turned the conversation around to her job, and what it was like to work for Hunt. "What's it like working in City Hall?" I asked. "I kind of imagine it is a little like being in a fish bowl."

"Oh, not at all...not in our office, anyway. I don't see many outsiders...mostly just contractors and engineering consultants, those who need to work with the Engineering Department," she said. "Even that contact is limited because most of that work is done by other people."

"How'd you wind up working for the City, anyhow?"

She explained that when she had gotten married, they moved to San Francisco, because his work was here.

"He was one of those old fashioned type, who felt wives should not work. After a year of staying home...and not getting pregnant...I got bored."

"So, I decided to get a job, in spite of what he said. I really expected to get pregnant as soon as I started working. If that happened, I would have quit.

"I looked at what I could do, which wasn't very much. I have a BA in anthropology, which qualifies me for nothing very much, and is virtually useless in the business world. You need to be working on a doctorate to even get a research assistant job. I think Dad sent me to college to find a husband, but all I got was this worthless degree. She laughed her musical laugh.

The only skill she had, when measured against the job market, was typing..."and even that wasn't so great...just adequate for a college term paper."

After several unsatisfactory job placements, she decided to take the City's Civil service examination. "I made a sufficiently high score to get hired a few months later." She added to her skills by taking shorthand and computer skills at the community college.

"I think my refusal to be bored, as well as a desire to pull my own weight, contributed to my divorce," she said. "I really felt like I was nothing, and every level of achievement meant something. Poor Doug, my ex-husband, he really wanted a dependent butterfly to show off to his friends, a trophy. Since I refused to be that type of person, it ended our marriage."

As she described her marriage, I marveled at the different kinds of trips people try to lay on each other. However, I had to bring us back to City Hall.

"I guess Mr. Hunt relies pretty heavily on you?" I questioned. We were now well into our second drink.

"He's a strange one." She answered. "There are some complicated things he encourages me to handle...like compiling the bidding specifications. Yet some of the very simple, routine, daily operations he does himself."

"I don't understand," I said, rather absently to hide my interest in Hunt's office operations.

"Oh, like simply cross checking the numbers on the daily progress reports from each of the projects. Anyone could run a calculator to verify the totals. However, either he or his assistant insists on doing it. You'd think their time was more important than that."

"That does seem strange," I agreed.

"By the way, he was very upset by the story you wrote. Did he really tell the police to hold up on the investigation of Simon's disappearance?"

"Well, he did admit telling the police to sit on it," I said. Then I shifted the conversation back to neutral territory by calling attention to the vivid sunset colors. We watched the colors gradually fade, and talked about the things the City had to offer.

"All right...time for the quiz. What kind of food is it going to be? A...B...C...D...or E" I asked.

"The seafood sounds good, but I haven't had real Italian food for a long time," she answered. "I think it's under "E" or other, because you only mentioned it at the end of your list. But it really sounds good."

"Italian...real Italian...then that is what it will be. My Lady, I have just the place for you. It can't get any more authentic. The owners are Italian from Italy."

I paid the bar tab, and we drove toward the Marina. Just off Lombard Street's motel row, near the grocery store that Lange and I frequent, is a restaurant, which I think serves the best, original, home-cooked Italian meals. Lange and I had eaten there just a few nights ago. Most of the better-known Italian restaurants are in the North Beach area. But this one, maybe because it was off the beaten track, had maintained a homier, less commercial atmosphere.

Mamma and Papa Conte, the owners had come from Italy 50 years ago. Jobs were hard to come by when they arrived. So, having a little money they started a boarding house away from the Honky-Tonk area of the City, renting a huge house, and let out rooms to boarders. Dinner came with the price of a room.

Their reputation for excellent food had grown until there might be twice as many at the dinner table as the number of room guests. Eventually they opened a separate restaurant. The boarding house is long gone.

Mamma and Papa are still at the restaurant most evenings, but the sons do most of the work, using the old-time recipes.

In the car, on the way to the restaurant, I put my hand on Mary's hand. She did not withdraw her hand; rather she gave it a squeeze. As we walked from the car toward the restaurant, we held hands. At the corner, waiting for the light to change, she pressed her shoulder against my arm.

At the restaurant, Mama seated us and Papa brought a carafe of house red wine and two glasses. They do not take orders here. Whatever they were serving for that meal is what they placed in front of you, family style. There was always more than you could possibly eat. I have known the Conte family from the first week I was in San Francisco, and being frustrated with trying to find an apartment. It was their son, Tony who first suggested combining my two desires...a place to live and a sail boat.

Papa sat down across the table from us, and poured wine into our glasses. "So David, it has been such a long time, what, two nights? Who is this lovely young lady?" After I introduced Mary, Mama came by the table and put her hand on her husband's shoulder. "Papa, I'm sure they have other things they want to talk about."

Tonight's dinner was very thinly sliced beef in a savory sauce, pasta; and a delicious vegetable that I thought might be Swiss chard, and salad. And for desert, we had flan.

Through our dinner conversation I learned that Hunt's primary circle of friends were a few members of the construction industry. Mary said that he spoke frequently with a Lawrence Linguitini, the president of McKee Corporation. It the same Lawrence Linguitini I uncovered earlier in the day.

"I never met the man. He doesn't come in to the office, only calls," Mary said, "but I would know his voice anywhere. It is very distinctive. They talk almost every day.

You know, I've been rattling on about myself, and I really don't know very much about you. But I feel like I've known you for ages," She said. "I assume you live in the City, but you've never really said."

"Yes, kind of…I'm kind of both in the City and outside the City. I live on a 36-foot sailboat on the Bay. It is tied up in the Marina Yacht Harbor, nearby, ready to go for a sail at a moment's notice."

She was fascinated with the idea of living on a boat, and insisted that I show it to her before I take her home. I told her a little of my background. As I was talking I felt her leg move against mine, under the table. It was all most pleasant, however, I felt guilty. I had intended to provide a relaxing environment, one in which she was comfortable talking. The alcohol and my patient listening had worked…maybe a little too well. It was certainly not my intent to seduce her.

Dinner over, we left the restaurant, with the promise to Mama and Papa to be back soon. As we walked to the car, she appeared to twist her ankle. I put my arm around her to steady her. Looking up from her foot, I found her looking at me intently. Her eyes drew me closer. I covered her lips with mine.

There was an immediate response. Her lips parted, and I felt her tongue on my lips, probing into my mouth. At the same time she shifted her weight onto her twisted ankle, and pressed her body against me. There was an immediate stirring in my groin. If it was her intent to arouse me, she was certainly succeeding.

After a few moments, we broke apart. We had missed a full change of the lights.

"Animal," I said teasingly. "I don't know if it is safe to take you home with me."

She turned her face down, and didn't respond.

"Hey," I said, putting my hand under her chin to turn her face toward me. "I am teasing." I kissed her again, pulling her close to me. She put her arms around me, drawing us even closer. It was a car horn, belling us, which brought us up for air. By then I didn't know how many light changes had occurred.

"Wow, look at us. Here we are, like a couple of teenage kids, necking on a street corner." I joked. This time she laughed her musical laugh. "Let's at least go where the whole world isn't watching."

We drove to the marina, a few blocks away. I led her to my boat.

"Oh, it doesn't look as large as I expected," she said.

"It's deceiving in the dark," I responded. "Come on aboard, and I'll show you around."

I gave her a hand onto the deck.

I opened the hatch, helped her into the cabin and flipped on the lights.

"Oh! This is nice," she exclaimed. "And it's really quite roomy."

She stood, uncertain of where to move. I motioned her to the dinette, and opened a bottle of wine, and poured two glasses. She took one and drank half of it almost like a glass of water. She looked at me nervously. It appeared as if she was unsure of what she wanted. As if before we got to the boat she felt secure to be provocative, but once here was unsure that this was what she wanted. I refilled her glass and sat down across from her. I really felt guilty about the pretext for this date, and if she wasn't so appealing, I probably would have avoided the earlier contact.

To give us both time to determine where we were, emotionally, I showed her the boat. I showed her how the space was used efficiently. That there was a forward berth, how the table converted to another double berth, how the galley worked, and my little stateroom under the cockpit, that was large enough for a queen-sized berth. "It is certainly roomy enough, but making the bed in these cramped quarters is no easy task."

"Look," I started. "I won't touch you, if you don't want. I feel guilty that I…"

She put her fingertips on my lips. Her eyes were moist, almost teary.

"Please…don't talk…I know," she said, placing her arms around me, and pressing her breast against my chest, and her lips on mine. Her passion was as close to the surface as were her tears.

I felt her hands working the buttons of my clothes, and I found my hands opening the buttons on the back of her high-necked dress, with growing impatience. Her dress and bra fell away. I stepped out of my clothes, and we stood naked, kissing each other, locked in an embrace. The touch of her smooth, white skin nearly drove me wild. I reached down and lifted her in my arms, held her close for a moment, then carried her to my bunk.

I began by caressing her, kissing her breasts and stroking inside of her thighs. Then she impatiently pulled me on top of her. She was like a woman possessed. She guided me into her, and literally devoured me.

It was over almost right away, and she turned away from me. We lay quietly for a few minutes. I stroked her back and arm.

"Lay still," I whispered. "I'll be right back."

I slipped out of the bunk, refilled our wine glasses and brought them back to the bunk.

As I slid back into the bunk, I realized she was crying. Gently I turned her toward me, and pulled her close against me, her head on my shoulder.

"I'm sorry…you must feel…that I've…I've used you," I said slowly. "I shouldn't have let things happen this way. I'm sorry."

"Oh…that's…not it." She said, sobbing. After a moment she stopped crying, and began giggling.

"It is so ironic," she said. "You apologized for using me, when actually I was using you."

"I don't understand."

"Well, I live with two other women, and I'm stuck in a job where all I ever meet are married men. Those who aren't married, aren't worth dating. It's horrible. I haven't met anyone I could or wanted to date in almost two years. And then you came along. I'm a frustrated woman.

"I knew you asked me out to find out about Mr. Hunt. So…when I told you 'yes', I was determined you would pay for your inquisitiveness with…ah…personal service." She laughed, then got all weepy again.

"Now, I'm so ashamed," she cried. "I've never done anything like this before. It is so against everything I've ever been taught…like being a whore, but different."

"Shhhh," I comforted, stroking her hair. "I wouldn't have asked you out if I didn't like you, and wanted to get to know you better. I'm not a total sociopath. I really like talking with you…being with you. Whatever you've said about Floyd Hunt, I could have found out another way. I like you, and like being with you."

I said it sincerely, because I meant it. I didn't have any expectations for the evening. But I have found her witty, charming, and a lot of fun.

"It just may be that we both started this evening with the wrong motivations," I said, and kissed her wet eyes. "But now that we've settled that score, let's just enjoy each other for ourselves."

She kissed me – a long lingering kiss. It brought new stirring of passion in both of us. For a long time we just caressed each other, building new heights of excitement and desire. Finally, we made love...long lingering love... the proper way.

Later, we fell asleep in each other's arms.

Chapter 10

Saturday

It was already past 7 a.m. when I awoke to the smell of coffee and the sound of bacon sizzling. I rolled out of the bunk, and looked for my shorts.

Mary was standing at the little galley counter, wearing my old striped robe, a cup of coffee in one hand and a spatula in the other. She was turning the bacon.

"You're really quite well organized," she said when she saw me. "I was able to find everything quite easily. Coffee?"

"Please," I said. I felt foolish, standing there stark naked. She poured a cup of coffee, and handed it to me. My shorts must have gotten lost in the tangle of clothes on the cabin sole.

"Thanks."

"You're nothing like my ex-husband," she said. "He couldn't find anything, even if he was wearing it."

"Oh?"

"Well, it's gratifying to find out there are men who don't have to be looked after, like a child."

I found a pair of shorts in a locker, and put them on while she was talking. I felt a little less foolish. I don't know why I had felt self-conscious after having been intimate with this lovely creature last night.

"Well, there are a number of us who are pretty self-reliant. I think I've survived. Even when I was married, she wasn't with me very much of the time," I said. "Of course if she had been, maybe I wouldn't have lost so much of my laundry across half the countries of the world."

She laughed her melodious laugh. It was so delightful to hear her laugh.

"But don't you suppose some people pretend dependency?" I tentatively asked.

"I'm not sure I follow you."

"Well, most men, I think," I spoke carefully, for I sensed vulnerability in this woman, "have found the most satisfying relationship with a woman, to be the one with their mothers, who fed them, did their laundry, and bandaged their skinned knees. Maybe they try to parrot that when they marry."

"I've never thought about it like that," she said. "That could be."

"Myself, I find any kind of artificial crutches too difficult to tolerate in a relationship. So, I'm just plain, blunt David Montgomery."

"But enough of relationship philosophy," I said. "I like my eggs over easy, and my bacon not too crisp." The switch broke the seriousness, and she laughed again.

"You make very good coffee, and you sure look better in that robe than I do," I added. She blew me a kiss.

We ate breakfast, and talked about general interests. I found out she likes classic jazz, as I did. Her favorite color is an earthy red, and more …all the kinds of things two people usually discover about each other as they get acquainted. It seems only a little odd that we had shared the more intimate part of a relationship before getting to know each other at a more superficial level first.

It was refreshing. We had stripped away any need for posturing or game playing. Our conversation was completely honest, likes and dislikes were openly expressed.

It appeared she was searching for something that I doubt she had yet defined. She had led a sheltered childhood, and was still carrying some of that innocence. She felt a need to make a contribution to the world, and so volunteered at the SPCA. Even though she had been married for two years, she was still new to emotional adulthood, trying relatively safe experiments so she could know first-hand the kind of lifestyle she wanted to develop. Her fresh honesty all contributed to her being a wonderfully, delightful person.

Breakfast finished and another cup of coffee, she began picking up the plates.

"No you don't," I said, with mock firmness. "No guest ever does dishes on this boat unless we are under sail." I quickly washed the dishes while she finished her coffee. When I was done with the dishes, I sat back down beside her.

I kissed her. As we kissed, she drew herself to me. The robe was mostly open and I put my hand inside to feel the smoothness of her skin. I kissed her neck and moved my hand to her breast. The nipples hardened as her excitement grew.

Gently I led her back to the bunk, where we made rich, full, satisfying love.

The morning had flown. It was as if there were just the two of us, alone on a deserted island; instead of being tied to a dock in the middle of a busy city marina. It was a little startling to see all the activity when we emerged from the boat to take her home.

"You don't have to take me all the way home," she said as we got into the bug. "Just drop me at the subway. Really, I don't mind."

"Nonsense. After such a beautiful night and morning, I am not going to let you just get whisked away on a subway. You can't get rid of me that easily."

At first, with the outer world intruding on us, there was little conversation. Then gradually we started talking about the different characteristics of San Francisco area and the East Bay, on opposite sides of the Bay. It was a pleasant drive over the Bay Bridge and through the Oakland hills, and down the valley toward Concord.

"I think Mr. Hunt would just shit, if he knew his secretary had just gone to bed with the reporter who is investigating him," she said completely unexpectedly. It was a startling thought, and I burst out laughing.

"Before we get into that," I said, "how would you like to spend next weekend with me on the boat? If it is nice we'll sail, and anchor out some place, like maybe Angel Island, and if it is not nice, we'll just hang around the marina, or walk through the neighborhoods," I suggested.

"You don't have to do that," she said, reverting to an earlier self-effacing attitude.

"I know I don't have to … but I want to. I'm asking for myself, not for the investigative reporter," I urged.

"Oh, David, it really sounds nice, and I'd love to. Unfortunately, my parents are coming into town, Saturday, and will be here for about a week," she said, sounding genuinely sad that she couldn't join me.

"Okay, rain check. We'll do it another weekend." I wasn't sure if she really was busy, or just gave herself an out.

I pulled up at her apartment; one of the large East Bay complexes…three swimming pools, tennis courts, gym, and more.

"And you don't meet any men here?" I couldn't help asking.

"Oh, yes. It is just that they are so…macho acting, like any woman should be falling all over herself to be with them. I'm really turned off. They even talk about the other women they've laid…right in front of us.

"Real class, right?" I asked, jokingly.

"I'm starting to look for another place," she said. "But it is hard to find anything I can afford on my own. I'd love to live in the City, but it seems so expensive, even considering the lower cost of commuting.

She smiled at me, leaned over and kissed me warmly, then got out of the car.

"Thank you, David, for such a wonderful night. You're really very sweet." She said as she closed the car door.

"Mary," I said through the open car window, "I think you are an extraordinary lady. So, remember, you have a rain check for the next weekend, or any other weekend you are available. I'll talk to you later."

As I drove away I figured she probably wouldn't go out with me for a while. She had tried something new, and even though I thought it turned out well, she scared herself. She had to answer some questions from within before she would be fully comfortable with me. And I had some serious questions to examine, as well. In the back of my head I knew this was the kind of woman I could become totally involved with…even marriage. If it became very serious between us, I would have some hard decisions to make. This was not the kind of woman that I could, or would want to have the loose freedom, that I have today. Also, the boat was very comfortable for one person, but it would be very cramped for two of us. And I liked my life style, and the ease of coming and going. But still, there was something about this woman that tugged at me.

As I headed back to San Francisco I suddenly remembered I had an event to attend this evening. It was an event for which "…a dark suit will do quite nicely." Only, I did not have a dark suit. My dress up consisted of a corduroy jacket and one of two pair of slacks. My everyday attire was wash pants and semi-dress shirt, or turtle-neck sweater. The corduroy jacket and slacks would just not cut it, which meant I had to rent a tuxedo.

When I reached the City, I drove to a men's store I liked. While waiting for a sales person, I looked at the formal wear book. At first, I thought it was looking at the wrong book. There were peach ones, chartreuse ones, baby blue ones, lavender and beige ones...so many different colors and styles to choose from, it was a little overwhelming. Twenty minutes later, after trying on a full set for fit, I was on my way back to the boat with a basic black tuxedo and all the parts that went with it.

I cleaned the boat, and then spent the remainder of the afternoon reading the rest of the sewer documentation. I found that the project was not as simple as just building super large sewer ducts. Because of the City's terrain and diverse soil compositions, even the method of construction was complicated. For example, in the hills they would have to blast out rocks while in the Marina area, if they used the usual pile-driving and big ditch technique, the soft earth would collapse, bringing down buildings. So in this area they had to use a burrowing technique that left a wall as the burrowing device moved forward.

And once it was all completed, the different parts had to work together in a balancing process so the sewage would be adequately treated in the new sewage processing plants. Computers with real space age technology would control the flow balancing.

As I dressed for the evening, I let my mind wander over what I had just read. I had this mental image of the whole system in operation. It was an image. . . like a malevolent science fiction machine; a giant machine which was almost alive; with big tentacles under the streets, sucking up waste;

operating without human intervention. And every once in a while, someone was sucked into it and disappeared... forever...like...Simon.

Then, like a flash, something inside my brain clicked. I knew where Simon was going when he left his home last Monday night. He was going to check something in the sewer system. And I knew where. In more than 100 miles of sewer tunnels, he would have started where the water was running from the out-fall.

Of course! Why it would be Lands' End, where he saw the water coming out of the out fall, where his body was found. If I had the sewer map I had given to Roger Bates, I would have checked right then. In addition, if my attendance at this function tonight weren't a command appearance, I would have stripped this monkey suit off, pulled on pair of jeans and gone out prying up manhole covers.

With that on my mind, I reluctantly got into my car for the trip to the Fairmont Hotel.

Parking on Nob Hill near the hotel is difficult at any time of day or night. The hotel has parking and there is an underground city lot, but they both cost money, so most people crowd the few legal spaces, and the many not so legal spaces. However, with my beat-up bug I was able to find a tiny space only a block from the hotel. It took five hitches to squeeze into the bumper-to-bumper row of cars. The fact that there were "No Parking" signs up and down the block did not bother me. None of the other cars had tickets, so I was sure I would be safe. Besides, the "Press" sticker in my front window has previously prevented tickets.

Dinner was in the Main Ballroom with no-host cocktails being served in the room next door. I sauntered into the cocktail room. I felt like what a fish out of water might feel like...very exposed. Everyone was in his or her finery. They all looked so much more at ease than I felt, even with my rented tux. I did not see one person I knew. Wading through the crowd, I reached the bar and waited my turn. I ordered a double scotch on the rocks, and paid for it. Now I felt a little better. At least I looked like everyone else, with something in my hand.

I drifted around the room, stopping here or there to listen to bits of conversation, which caught my attention. Finally at the end of the room, I saw a face I recognized. It was Brian J. Worthington, III, the City's Chief Administrator, the man at whose party I drank too much. He was visiting with three couples when I walked up.

"Ah, Mr. Montgomery, if my memory serves me correctly," he said.

"Yes, Mr. Worthington. I just wanted to tell you what an enjoyable evening it was last week. Thank you very much."

"Oh, you're most welcome. By the way, have you met these people? Mr. Montgomery is with the Clarion," he said by way of an introduction, and named the couples standing there. He returned to conversation he had been having about how the city is trying to encourage business growth.

Just then, a tall, slender young woman joined our group. It was Margaret. She had a drink in each hand.

"Here, Dad," she said, and handed Worthington one of the glasses.

"Margaret, you know these people," indicating the three couples, "but I'd like you to meet Mr. Montgomery."

"Oh, we've met," she said, flashing a smile at me. "It was his paper's picnic on Angel Island that I went to last Sunday. And he lives on a boat." She continued on, impervious to the previous on-going conversation.

"David, are you alone? My parents insisted I come to this thing. At the last minute my date got sick. I really think he didn't want to come to this stuffy thing. They're probably only going to play old fogey music, as well. I wish I had thought of getting sick," she rattled on.

"Margaret!"

"Oh, Daddy, you knew I didn't want to come. But I promise I won't embarrass you."

The others laughed politely. Everyone could feel her frustration.

"I am alone, Margaret." And I have two seats at the Clarion table. If it is alright with your father, I'd be delighted to escort you here at the dinner," I said. I could almost hear Worthington breath a sigh of relief.

"Of course, of course," he answered quickly.

"Margaret?" I turned and made a mock bow toward her, which nearly flustered her, but she recovered quickly.

"And to think, I was about to suffer a fate worse than death...boredom," she said.

"You can do me a great favor, besides," I said. "You know I've only been in the City a few months. I'm sure you can help me by telling me who all these people are."

"You mean I don't get off Scott free?" she retorted. "Darn."

"Well, we'll make it painless," I said. Seeing that her glass was nearly empty, I added, "But for starters, let's get another drink."

As we headed for the bar, I heard one of the women say to her husband, "See, chivalry isn't dead."

We got another drink, then drifted with the crowd toward the Ballroom. At the door we almost bumped into Floyd Hunt, who was trying to buck the flow to get into the cocktail room.

"Oh, Mr. Hunt. Have you met Mr. Montgomery?" Margaret asked.

Before he could answer, I spoke out. "Hello, Mr. Hunt. So good to see you again."

"Oh...ah...Hello Montgomery. Hello Margaret. Is your father inside?" he asked. During the brief interchange his face had drained of color, then turned a purplish shade.

"Why, yes." She answered, pointing in her father's direction. Without another word Hunt pushed his way inside. But rather than going toward Worthington, he headed for the bar.

"My, he is certainly strange," Margaret said. "Usually, in public, he is so much more courteous."

"I wouldn't worry, Margaret. I think he has a lot on his mind, right now. I just wrote an article which is very critical of his actions regarding the Simon Blare's disappearance. I think he must be very upset to see me with his boss's daughter.

As we worked our way into the Ballroom, Margaret said Hunt had worked for her father for the past four years, but her father had never seemed very comfortable around him.

"Daddy actually distrusts the man. He was the one Daddy was shouting at the other night"

"If your father is so uncomfortable around him, why did he hire Hunt?"

"Oh, Daddy never hired him," she answered. "He's kind of like family. You know, you don't have much choice about your relatives. You inherit them. Well, Mr. Hunt was already City Engineer when Daddy was appointed."

In the Ballroom we checked in with a young lady stationed at a table. She directed us to the Clarion table. It was located at one corner of the dance floor, and excellent location. The Clarion's sales manager and assistant publisher and their wives were already seated at the table. I steered Margaret to the side of the table nearest the dance floor. After making introductions, we sat.

Mrs. Richman and an elderly gentleman arrived at the table a few minutes later. The circulation manager and his wife followed, almost immediately.

At the arrival of Mrs. Richman, everyone was reintroduced. Mrs. Richman presided over the polite conversation until dinner was served. Dinner was remarkable good, considering the hotel was serving a thousand people for just this one event. Who knew what else was happening in the hotel this evening. It always amazed me how a large hotel can orchestrate such a large event and have the meal turn out on time, and edible.

Fortunately the after dinner speeches were reasonably short. The president of the City's business association welcomed everyone. He was followed by the Mayor, who pledged support for the City's business community. A State Senator spoke about how San Francisco was a pivot point for the state's economy, and that the State had a larger economy than many countries. After that, there were a few short comments by other people before the stage was turned over to the band.

During the speeches, Margaret kept up a whispered commentary about the speakers, or other people we could see in the audience. She honored my request fully, and I received a cram course on who's who in San Francisco. At the end of the speeches, she excused herself and, with a couple of other ladies from our table, went to the powder room.

I was sitting, watching all the people, when I felt a hand on my shoulder. It was Mrs. Richman. I started to rise, but she kept her hand on my shoulder and said, "Please stay seated. I've asked the waiter to take drink orders when the ladies return. It has all been taken care of. I will be leaving now, but I wanted to tell you how delighted I am that you and Miss Worthington could be here tonight. Miss Worthington was a very good choice.

I thanked her, and decided against telling her it was happen-stance that Margaret was at the Clarion table. Let her think whatever she chooses to think about my ability to make social contacts.

Margaret and the other ladies returned to the table, talking about how the powder room was a crowded mess. "Oh, I'm sorry I missed Mrs. Richman's departure. She seems like such a grand lady."

We danced a few dances, but Margaret had been right about the music. It seemed pretty 'old fogey' to me, too. So, I suggested we go someplace a little more lively.

"I thought you'd never ask. I've already told Daddy I would be leaving, and had a ride home. He and mother will just stay here and talk for hours. It's all so dull."

We did the scene. We stopped at three different clubs, then wound up at Earthquake McGoon's for the jazz. It was past 2 a.m. and I was exhausted.

"Ready to go?" I asked. "I'll take you home."

"Yeah, let's go."

But once in the car she had other ideas.

"Let's go to your place. Do you have any stuff?"

"Stuff?" I answered with a question, knowing where she was headed.

"Yeah, stuff…pot or coke…you know."

"No," I laughed. "Scotch, bourbon, wine, maybe some beer, coffee and tea makes up my total drug list."

"I thought you media people all had a little stuff around?"

"Actually," I chuckled, "most of us newspaper people are pretty stuffy, but we don't use 'Stuff'. We couldn't do our jobs if we were even a little high."

She was quiet for a bit as we drove toward her house.

"Well, at least show me where you live."

Since it wasn't much out of the way to swing by the marina, I decided to humor her. I stopped the car so it faced my dock.

"What in the world are you doing?" she asked. "I thought you were going to show me where you live."

"You wanted to see where I live. It is over there…the fifth boat on this side of the dock. You were on it when we went to Angel Island."

"You're kidding. I didn't know you lived on it. Well, let's go take another look at it." She opened her door.

"Not tonight, Margaret. It's nearly 3 a.m., and I'm going to take you home.

"You mean you're not going to take me to bed? I thought all newspaper men wanted to bed women every chance they could."

"Margaret," I said as I started the car, "one of the things you need to learn in life is that you can't type-cast people. Just as sure as you do, they'll disappoint you by going and doing something you didn't expect."

"And maybe," I continued," just maybe, someday I will take you to bed…but not this morning."

We drove the rest of the way to her parents' home in silence. I parked in their driveway, and escorted her to the front door.

"Good night, Margaret. Thank you very much for your assistance with my education," I said sincerely. "Now I can put faces with some of the names I hear."

I started to turn and she put her hand on my arm to stop me.

"David," she said, "I'm sorry. I was a real ass."

"Oh, don't be silly. See ya, huh?" I responded.

"Promise?" she asked plaintively. "You will, won't you."

"Do my best," I said lightly. "And get your father to meet with me.

I turned and left. Margaret watched from the doorway as I pulled away. I was so tired. All I could think of was my bunk.

At the boat, I stripped and plunged into my bunk, glad that tonight I wasn't sharing it with anyone. "Poor little rich girl,' I thought as I drifted off to sleep.

Chapter 11

Sunday

———————≫◆≪———————

I probably would still have been sleeping for another hour if it weren't for the noise and hollering outside. Then through my fog I heard Lang's voice, forceful, but not shouting.

"Look, I was in my slip and the boat was tied up. The engine was not running. You hit me. Why do you think I am at fault? I want your driver's license, and insurance certificate. I assume you have insurance."

I could hear another voice, a little further away. It was a winey voice with a little snarl in it, but I could not make out what was said.

"No, it is not just a little nick. It appears that you have punctured a hole in my hull. And if you could see the front of your boat, you would not think it was so minor, either."

With that I thought I should probably get up. I slipped on some jeans and went on deck. I couldn't see anything, so I stepped onto the pier, and walked to the end. There was a small cruiser dead in the water behind Lange's boat. The bow of his boat was pretty-well stove-in. When I saw the amount of damage I thought I should call it in. Because it was in the marina, I dialed 911, for the police. Watching the people on this other boat, their unsteady actions suggested to me that they had been drinking.

No one seemed in danger, so I dialed the police report line "I want to report a boating accident in the Brickyard Marina."

"A moored boat was hit by another cruiser."

"No. There does not appear that there were any injuries."

"From the actions, there might have been some drinking."

"No. I am a bystander. I live on the boat in the next slip." I gave her my name and slip number.

The operator said she would send a squad car, but that she was also notifying the Coast Guard. I gave her the slip number where Lang's boat was tied.

The Coast Guard cruiser showed up before the police. Their cruiser was the size of Lange's boat, and dwarfed the offending cruiser. The commanding Lieutenant immediately asked for identification from the offending skipper. The small boat driver hesitated for a few moments, as if debating on the necessity. One of the women said something and he slowly pulled his wallet from a hip pocket. He fished something from the wallet and handed it to the Lieutenant.

"Ain't you goanna get his license," blared the small boat driver.

"Not necessary," said the Lieutenant. "I already have him on file."

The small boat driver smirked before the Lieutenant continued, "He is a captain in the Coast Guard Auxiliary."

"Have you been drinking, Sir?" The Lieutenant asked.

"I might have had a beer... or two."

"Do you mind taking a Breathalyzer test?"

There was a conference in the boat between the driver, another man and a woman.

"I didn't think I had to do that"

"Drunk boating is very much like drunk driving," responded the Lieutenant. As they had been talking the other coastguard person tied the smaller cruiser to the end of the pier.

During the discussion the police arrived and two officers had come down the pier to join the conversation.

"Yes, Sir. It carries very similar penalties to drunk driving," One policeman agreed. "Now if you would be so kind as to step out of your boat here, we can continue this conversation on more or less dry land. The small boat driver climbed onto the pier without any problems. The officers watched him closely to see if there was any unsteady movement, but he seemed in full control of his movements.

The Coast Guard Lieutenant handed the drivers' license to the police officer. "This is more of a land side incident, so if you don't mind I'll let you handle it. We'll forward our report."

The police officer that took the license nodded in acceptance.

After interrogating the small boat driver, and taking a statement from Lange, the police officer wrote a ticket, citing the small boat driver for reckless boat handling and not operating it in a safe manner.

"You understand this is like reckless driving in a car, and you will have to appear in court. You will not be able to just pay a fine and not appear," said the officer. "The judge will set the fine, probably based upon the damage level."

"The gentleman here, indicating Lange, will submit his repair bill, and you will need to do the same," continued the officer. "I would guess that insurance will cover most of the damage repair, except the fine." Lange had been leaning on the rail listening to the police officer.

The man nodded in understanding.

The small boat driver and one policeman climbed into the smaller boat and headed back to the launching ramp.

when the police officer was finished, the Coast Guard Lieutenant called to Lange.

"Can we tow you anywhere. I know there is no repair shop near this marina."

"Thanks, but I'll take it over to Alameda. That is where I've had other work done. They know the boat."

"It's no problem to tow you. You don't know what internal damage may have been done...motor mounts loosened, water lines damaged. I'd feel better if we towed you"

"I don't want to put you guys out."

"No problem."

The Coast Guard crew unfastened the lines, and walked Lang's boat out of the slip. With three lines to secure the boat to the Coast Guard cutter, they eased away from the slip. I hollered to Lange that I would be over shortly to bring him back.

I disconnected the live-aboard lines, the telephone, electricity and water line, and started the diesel to motor out of the marina. By the time I came to the end of the breakwater, I had the sails up, flapping wildly until I killed the engine and set the sails.

There was a brisk wind out of the North, across the Bay and I fairly flew. I held it tight to the wind so that the lee rail was nearly in the water. One of the things I liked about my boat is that it has a wide beam and would be almost impossible to tip it over. By the time it heels far enough to risk getting wet, the wind starts spilling from the sail.

It took about 30 minutes to reach the entrance to the Alameda Estuary. I shortened sail and restarted the engine. Entering the Estuary, I passed the Coast Guard Cutter on its way out.

"You must have been flying," hollered the Lieutenant.

"I had a good wind," I shouted back.

I dropped the sails. The boat yards were about half-way down the estuary and I saw Lange standing on the dock, waiting for me. He had called the owner, so there was someone there to meet him when he arrived. They would call him later with the evaluation and estimate. It's nice when you know people.

Lange was aboard before I could even tie up. He had two suitcases and a duffle bag that he stowed in the cabin.

"My guess is that it will take about 10 days to check it all out and repair the damage." He said. "Meanwhile, I called that bed 'n breakfast across from Marina Greens. She has a room and was delighted that it would be for at least a week, though I will miss the comfort of my own accommodations."

"What's new about Simon," Lange queried.

"The funeral is Thursday. They had to push it out for an aunt and uncle and some cousins to get to town. There is one from out of the country and others from back East.

"I did bring the papers on those companies. They are in my suitcase," he said "There are only three that are suspect. Two have ties to suspect ownership, and one is not a real company. There is one more I have questions about. I'll give them all to you later."

I didn't push the boat as hard as I did coming over. I did not know how long it has been since Lange had been sailing.

"My, this is exhilarating," he exclaimed. "I had forgotten how enjoyable it is to sail. But you can get more out of her, can't you?"

With that I pulled the main sheet tighter, pulling the sail closer to the center of the boat. We instantly heeled more sharply.

"Ah, that's more like it." Lange responded.

It was low tide, and with the glasses you could see the start of the sewage outfall as it ran into the bay.

Noticing the outfall, Lange queried sarcastically, "Did they expect Simon's body to just be flushed out into the bay?"

We sailed around the back side of Alcatraz Island before heading for our marina.

Once back in the slip, Lange helped me get it back in live-aboard shape, and washed down the deck and fittings.

"It's the little things that keep it ready to go at a moment's notice."

I asked him if he wanted a lift to the bed-n-breakfast, but he declined. "I just called a cab," he said, and left with an insult to my VW.

Chapter 12

Monday

M onday morning, the fog was back, lying on the Bay like a heavy wet blanket, muffling sounds, and deadening the clinking of rigging. Even the thuds of joggers' feet were less distinct, over-ridden by the soft splats of water dripping from the rigging. And the fishing boats, normally heard bustling for the open sea, could have been a world away. Even the squabble of gulls fighting over a morsel of food was less pronounced.

The greyness of the morning seemed to set my mood. For a time I just lay in bed and let my mind wander idly, retracing all that had happened over the past week. Finally, I rolled out of my berth to shower and dress.

Maybe a good breakfast will brighten my mood, I thought. So I cooked turkey bacon and eggs. Then toasted an English muffin and even broke out the jam. After a second cup of coffee, I felt I like I was almost human, much more congenial and ready to face the day. I gathered my notes, an armload of sewage documentation and my camera. Even though it was just a little past 7 a.m., I headed for the office.

Once there, and settled at my computer, I wrote more about the discovery of Simon's body. I had just placed it in the copy box, outside Max's office, when he came strolling in.

"I hope you had a very wonderful weekend," I said sarcastically. "You left me stuck with that business association banquet."

"Interesting?"

"Not really, but the evening got better after we left."

"We?"

"Remember Margaret, at the picnic?"

"Oh, yeah, that blond that hit just about every ball I pitched."

"That one." Then I changed the subject.

"From what I've learned, Hunt, or his assistant, are the only ones to see the daily activity and progress reports. I also know that he speaks frequently with Linguitini. Since any skimming or graft would have to have help from the inside, it rather points to Hunt and his assistant.

"Simon had also said Hunt was the only one who got to see the overall picture." I explained.

"Well, the scenario hangs together," he said "There are still a lot of loose ends, but only in two areas: how the rip-off actually takes place, and to substantiate Barbara's role."

"Ahhh, By the way, for your information, Barbara is, according to my informant, having some sort of relationship with Dan Kirkman," Max sounded reluctant to mention it, but with Barbara's possible involvement he seemed to need to say it.

"Apparently it has been kept very discreet...well out of gossip range," he said. "If this gets out, it would ruin Dan. I like the guy...hell of a good TV journalist...best on the West Coast."

"How would it ruin him" I asked. "Other people have affairs. When it is over, they go back and patch things up, or get a divorce."

"Not if your father-in-law is a big wheel and major stockholder in the network." Max answered. "Kirkman would be out so fast he wouldn't have time to get up from his desk. And he would be blackballed in the industry. Daddy is about the nastiest person I've had the misfortune to encounter."

I told him I understood the sensitivity of the situation. Having fully briefed Max, I told him I was going to spend the day between Dr. Lawrence at the University and our engineering company, Bates and Broadman. He already had all the photos he needed to run with my story, so I felt comfortable being out of the office the rest of the day, after staff meeting.

"Max, the story is good as it stands, unless something new turns up. I'll call in, but otherwise I'll see you tomorrow."

After the staff meeting, I called Andy.

"The tentative autopsy is inconclusive, Andy reported. "According to the coroner's preliminary report, Blare died of asphyxiation . . . from sewer gas. Sewer gas is very lethal, they say, and it affects the nervous system.

"The lab boys didn't pick up much, either. He may, or may not, have been moved after death, they say." Andy reported. "We still have some unanswered questions, like the flashlight, but with the autopsy report, the department is pressing for an accidental finding."

"Could the pressure be coming from Hunt?"

"Don't know, but I'll find out," he responded. "But Dave, I want you to know, off the record, this doesn't feel like an accidental death."

I told him I appreciated his comment, and asked if I could come by later and go through Simon's personal effects.

"Sure. Let's make it after lunch…say about 1:30 or so." He agreed.

I hung up and headed for Dr. Lawrence's office at San Francisco State. The University is located on the ocean side of the City, and always has a breeze off the Pacific. It does not have the spacious lawns of many California colleges, because of having to put so many building on site. Nevertheless, it does have a view of the Pacific from many locations.

Dr. Lawrence greeted me very sadly in his office.

"Simon's death is a great loss...to the profession and most particularly for me," he said. "He had such a brilliant mind. Tell me, how did he die?"

"Well...the preliminary autopsy report...said sewer gas." I said hesitantly I did not want to upset him more than he already appeared to be. I also did not want to give information, which could be sensitive.

"Really?" Dr. Lawrence asked. His voice sounded incredulous. "Tell me about it."

I decided his loyalty to Simon placed him on my side, so I explained what Andy had told me over the phone. I described what I had seen, and the conditions I experienced in the tunnel, and where the body was located. I even told him about the lantern.

"That's very strange," he murmured, thoughtfully. "When do they say he died?"

"The preliminary report estimated the time of death early Tuesday morning," I said "But that may be because it was when he was reported missing. What is it you find so strange?"

"Well, to begin with, from what you described of the location, it would be almost impossible to have a concentration of sewer gas...one of the methane series... sufficiently concentrated to kill a person. He was rummaging in a pile of rolled charts and diagrams on a worktable while he talked.

"Oh, don't doubt for a second that sewer gas is lethal in a high enough concentration. But this is usually only found in very confined areas." He continued. "And of course there is the flashlight. That would not normally burn more than four or five hours continuously…and probably much less, because of the corrosive atmosphere."

"Ah, here it is," he said, extracting a rolled chart. He unrolled it, and clipped it over a whiteboard hanging on the wall. It was a map of the sewer line of the area around Veterans Hospital.

"Now this is where you said you entered the sewer," he said as a statement, pointing to a mark on the diagram. "Here is the hospital parking lot. You walked maybe a hundred feet to this junction." He pointed out my route on the diagram.

"And you said Simon's body was found right here, against this baffle wall." He added

I nodded when he looked at me for confirmation.

"Well, if you notice, it is only about 200 feet to the opening for Lands' End outfall. That's an eighteen-inch opening. That means there is a goodly amount of air here." He paused, pointing to the location of the baffle, and was still for a moment, apparently lost in thought.

"I don't think it was possible for him to have died there." He burst out. "There was way too much air for a concentration of sewer gas – high enough to kill a person -- to be present at this location. Besides, it is heavier than air, and would most likely be more concentrated closer to the floor of the tunnel. But even there it would be pretty diluted."

"Would you be willing to explain that to the police?" I asked.

"Of course I would. Only I can't leave just at this moment. A colleague, Dr. Arthur Sherman of Columbia, is here on a guest lecture exchange. He is presently in class, but will be out shortly, and then we can go," said Dr. Lawrence.

"He is, by the way, much more of an expert in this kind of matter, than I," he said. "He was a medical doctor before deciding to enter the precise field of engineering."

"Oh, that's fine," I said. "Lieutenant Sullivan, the homicide detective won't be available before 1:30 this afternoon."

"Excellent. You and Arthur and I can have lunch together," he said more brightly than he had appeared earlier. "In the meantime, how much have you learned?"

I related to him the different materials I had read, and the gist of what I had learned. He quizzed me on several technical areas. To my surprise, I found that I could answer most of his questions.

"Excellent!" he exclaimed. "You have a very receptive mind."

"I just have a lot of questions, for which I seek answers," I said

"Ah," he responded, "but that is the very essence of learning. In seeking, you assimilate more information than the bare facts you seek. This information you must sift… and discriminate to match it to the criteria for the facts you seek.

"And in this process, people learn," he continued. "The tidbit of information which does not fit the criteria, still has a value, and is retained. By remembering this tidbit, it may be applied in the future without the effort of research. That is the essence of learning."

"Oh, but here I am, lecturing…and we're not even in a classroom." He chuckled.

I laughed and complimented him on his theory of learning. At that moment there was a knock at the door and, without waiting, it opened.

In the doorway stood a tall, gaunt older man, I judged to be in his late sixties or early seventies. He wore a pin-stripe suit, which hung loosely. This accentuated his height and thinness. He had a heavy shock of unruly white hair, and bushy white eyebrows, giving me the image of a shaggy white palm tree.

"Oh, Arthur. I'd like you to meet that nice young journalist I've been speaking of; David Montgomery, Dr. Arthur Sherman.

"I'm delighted to meet you," he said solemnly. His voice was a deep monotone. I felt like I was meeting a characterization of a mortician. "I understand you are working on a project which may be turning out to be rather unpleasant.

"That is very true," I said. "However, it is a pleasure to meet you."

"Well, now, Arthur. David. Shall we go to the faculty lounge for a bite of lunch?" asked Dr. Lawrence. "Perhaps after lunch, since you have the afternoon free, you might like to join David and me for a trip to police headquarters."

On the walk from the Engineering Building to the faculty lounge, Dr. Lawrence explained what had just turned up about Simon's death. Dr. Sherman agreed. "And if I can be of any assistance I would be most pleased. This is, of course, a page out of my earlier life."

At the entrance to the faculty lounge, Dr. Sherman stopped abruptly. He stared at a newspaper in a distribution box. It was the early street edition of the Evening Exchange.

"Who is that woman?" he asked, pointing at a photograph on the front page."

"That is Barbara Blare, the wife of Simon Blare, the one we were just talking about." I answered. "That looks like an earlier photo of her. Her hair style is different now… shorter."

"Most odd," he mumbled. "Terribly odd." He seemed, for a moment, to be lost in another world. Then he turned to enter the faculty lounge.

I bought a copy of the newspaper, and brought it into the lounge with me. Both Dr. Lawrence and I had noticed his strange behavior over seeing Barbara's picture. Once seated at a table, I was about to pursue his reaction when Dr. Lawrence spoke out.

"Arthur, do you know that woman?" He asked.

"Probably not," he responded slowly, studying the photograph in the paper I had laid on the table between us. "It just looks so very much like someone I once met…under rather unusual circumstances."

"Where was that?" I asked, pushing the paper closer so he could get a better look at the photograph.

At that moment, we were interrupted by the waitress, who wanted to know if we were ready to order. We took a hasty glance at the menu, and ordered.

"Well, Arthur, you've aroused our curiosity. Are you going to tell us, or let us dangle impatiently forever?" Dr. Lawrence probed.

"There really is not very much to tell. Nothing ever really happened. It was more the circumstance of it, which was so very odd." Dr. Sherman answered.

"It was, perhaps, four years ago. There was this International Engineering Conference in Las Vegas. You remember, Augie. You had a broken leg and were unable to attend."

"Yes, of course." Dr. Lawrence answered. "That was in May…just over four years ago."

"Well, I had been consulting for a number of communities…You understand," he said as an aside to me, "that most college professors consult on the side to supplement the pittance we are paid by colleges and universities. What we learn from consulting we can bring back to the classroom...a little like the science professors who do their research on campus."

I nodded my understanding.

"Well, these communities were looking for innovative designs for sewage processing...to get better solids separation and fluid processing. So I was providing some modest advice on the feasibility of their designs. I was subsequently asked to speak at the conference and to moderate one of the workshops," Dr. Sherman related.

"When I got to Las Vegas, to my surprise I found that all my expenses would be covered. It started when I checked in at the hotel. Well, I knew it wasn't the Association that was doing this. I was given an envelope, and in was five hundred dollars, a return airline ticket and a note. The note said that everything had been taken care of, and thanks for my assistance."

"I thought this was a mistake and it was for someone else. But no, the clerk assured me that it was for me."

"And sure enough, the hotel bill was pre-paid. I could go anywhere and everything was already paid for. Even my pipe tobacco, which is an odd Swedish brand, was provided.

"Anyway, I hadn't been in my room five minutes when there was a knock at the door. I opened it, and standing there was this woman" pointing to the picture..."or someone that looked like her" he said.

"She said she had been retained to...ah...see to my every comfort." Dr. Sherman said.

"Well...I...ah...of course told her I was quite comfortable. I remember that she laughed and came right on into the room. She went to the bar and fixed us both a drink. It was quite extraordinary. She knew exactly what I drank.

"I never did…ah…use all her services, but she literally haunted me throughout the entire five-day conference… outside of the sessions. Everywhere I turned, she was there. If I ate by myself, she would join me.

"She was quite pleasant to talk with. I remember, the first morning at breakfast, I told her she should tell the person who retained her, that he was wasting his money.

"I thought she was going to cry. She explained that she had been retained for the duration of the conference. If I didn't want her services, then please let her appear to try. Her employer, she said, would otherwise become quite angry. I felt sorry for her. And we did go to a show or two together.

"Quite by happenstance, I happened to meet her employer, though I didn't know it at the time.

"I had to change my return airline reservations so I could attend a meeting in Los Angeles, before returning home. I was at the front desk, inquiring where I might exchange my airline ticket. The clerk was no help at all, and we were both getting exasperated, when this gentleman stepped up asked if he might be of assistance. He took care of all the arrangements, and I assumed he was with the hotel.

The young woman told me later that he was her employer. She had been afraid I was complaining about her, and then realized I could not have known him.

It wasn't until I returned to the East Coast that I found out my benefactor represented a firm I had recommended for a contract to one of my clients," said Dr. Sherman.

"Do you remember the name of the firm?" I asked.

"Not precisely. I do remember it as being something like a Scotch sir-name. Ah…Mc…McCle…No…McKelick… McKelig. That's it! McKelig Corporation."

"Do you remember the man's name, or what he looked like?"

"I'm sure I can't recall that," said Dr. Sherman. "But I do remember I envied his hair. Mine is so unruly, somewhat like a thatched roof. His was just turning grey, slightly wavy, and every hair in place. He combed it straight back from his forehead. Oh, I wish mine would behave so well."

"Do you recall anything else about him?"

"No…as I recall he was of rather average size and build. Oh! In spite of his grooming, I had the impression he might have been a laborer at one time…the hands, you know, heavy, broad across the knuckles.

"Oh yes, one other thing. He had an Italian name, something like Lasagna. His voice was…it was…well, kind of gravelly. It is amazing to me how much I do remember, but I am sure this makes no sense at all."

"Oh, Dr. Sherman, you've no idea how much this might help. Maybe it doesn't fit right now, but it could give us just the background information we need," I said. Already my mind was making comparisons of the characteristics he had just described to a specific person I had met.

Throughout the remainder of lunch, we talked about the circumstances of Simon's death. Dr. Sherman agreed that it was highly unlikely Simon had died where he was found.

It was not the best lunchtime conversation, but both professors were dealing with it very academically. While they talked, my mind kept running back over all the little pieces of the puzzle, trying to find places for all of them. Cliff had a gravelly voice, but he worked for the State Attorney General.

"There are certain things the coroner should look at very carefully in the blood analysis," Dr. Sherman said, drawing me back into the conversation.

"I was the assistant coroner in New York for twenty years, and we frequently pulled bodies out of sewers. Some of the deaths were even accidental. Some were not. The blood analysis is one of the most critical elements in determining which is which...even when other evidence is not available.

We finished lunch and went to my car. A VW Bug is not a very large car, and the two professors were at least six feet tall. When they saw the car, Dr. Sherman immediately volunteered for the back seat. Dr. Lawrence would not hear of it and it almost became a shoving match. Finally, I interceded, saying that Dr. Lawrence was an out of town guest, and should probably have the front seat. Dr. Lawrence immediately folded into the back seat, smiling with glee. Even with more room in the front seat, Dr. Sherman needed to make two approaches to insert his lanky frame into my Bug.

I drove the two professors to police headquarters. I checked them through police security and escorted them to Andy's office. We were early. He was just finishing lunch at his desk.

"Boy, did you miss a good lunch," I teased.

"Aw, shut up. When this is all over, you owe Helen and me a night on the town." He retorted. "City Hall wants my report yesterday. And while I am sure it isn't accidental. However, I can't prove it is homicide."

"You might be able to make that determination, if you listen to these two gentlemen." I said, and introduced them to Andy. I made sure he was aware of their qualifications.

Andy handed me a small plastic tray with Simon's personal effects while he and the professors got acquainted. On the tray were his wallet with eighty-three dollars, three credit cards, his California driver's license, a parking ticket, photos of his parents and of Barbara, and other identifying papers. Also on the tray was a small manila envelope containing seventy-two cents, a small pocketknife, a book of matches, a wristwatch, two pens, a pencil, and a set of keys. There were six keys: one looked like an automobile key, a mailbox key and the other four were door keys.

All of a sudden, I remembered. There was something missing.

"Excuse me, Andy," I interrupted. "But is everything here? I mean, were the pockets of his rain coat checked?"

Andy straightened up. He looked at me intently, waiting for me to continue.

"When Simon left the house Monday evening, he was wearing a rain coat," I said. "He stuck a flash light in one pocket. The lantern found beside him would not fit into anyone's pocket.

Andy immediately flipped through his notes. After a moment he found the page he was looking for, and read intently. When he was done, he looked from one to the other of us before he spoke. "When Blare was found, he was not wearing a rain coat," he said flatly.

"There," I said excitedly, "that proves something funny is going on. Where are the raincoat and the other flashlight? Also, these gentlemen can tell you why Simon could not have died at the location where he was found."

First Dr. Lawrence explained why it would be almost impossible for there to be a concentration of sewer gas in that particular location. Dr. Sherman agreed with Dr. Lawrence and further explained the properties of sewer gas. He then asked to see the detailed analysis of the coroner's report.

"I have only the findings, not the analysis," Andy said. He had been taking notes while the professors had been talking.

Dr. Sherman quickly reviewed the findings. When he was finished, he asked if he could speak with the pathologist who had performed the autopsy.

Andy called the coroner's office. After a brief conversation, he hung up. "They were not pleased, but since I am authorizing it, they could not argue," Andy said.

With that, the four of us made the walk through the halls, now more crowded than Sunday morning, to the adjacent building that housed the coroner's office, laboratory, and the body lockers.

Dr. Kenneth Chong, the coroner, greeted us himself. He had been the senior pathologist at the City's hospital before he was appointed coroner a year ago.

"Dr. Sherman, so good to see you again," said Dr. Chong. "You probably don't remember me, but I was in one of your classes on forensic medicine in New York a number of years ago. I believe you were assistant coroner there then. It was your class which helped me decide to specialize in pathology."

"Why, Dr. Chong, of course I remember you," rumbled Dr. Sherman. "You were one of the best analysts of all the students in the course. And I always remember the bright ones."

"I would be most pleased to have you look at the analysis of this case, although it is not my own." Dr. Chong said. "Unfortunately, becoming coroner has taken me out of the lab and made me an administrator. Here is a draft of the analysis."

Dr. Sherman immediately began reading. He turned the eight or ten pages rapidly. When he neared the end, he stopped. He lifted his head, and stared thoughtfully at the ceiling.

We all stood expectantly, waiting for what he would say. After a moment, he looked at Dr. Chong, and smiled.

"Dr. Chong, this is excellent documentation. The analysis is quite logical," Dr. Sherman said. "If I may trouble you, I would like to see the body and the photographs taken prior to the autopsy."

"Why, of course, Dr. Sherman," said Dr. Chong.

We trooped into an examining room, all five of us. An attendant wheeled Simon's body in on a gurney. Dr. Sherman flipped rapidly through the photographs, stopping occasionally, as if looking for something specific. He then removed his coat, rolled up his shirt sleeves, washed his hands, and donned a pair of latex gloves.

With the assistance of, a magnifying glass and the young pathologist who had performed the autopsy, he conducted an inch-by-inch examination of Simon's body – even under his fingernails and toenails.

"Ah," said Dr. Sherman, softly, as he inspected an area behind Simon's right ear. "Doctor?" he queried, and looked at Dr. Chong. "Would you like to take a look at this and tell me what you see?'

Dr. Chong bent over the body, minutely inspecting the area indicated. After a moment, he straightened.

"Doctor, it appears that there might be a bruise on the skull area behind the right ear. Also, right at the base of the ear there appears to be a mark, similar to a needle mark," pronounced Dr. Chong, as he looked at the young pathologist.

"May we have a tissue and blood analysis from this area?" Dr. Sherman asked.

"Why most certainly," replied Dr. Chong, who motioned to the pathologist to perform the task.

While the young pathologist extracted the sample, Dr. Sherman continued his minute inspection. He returned to the areas of the wrists and ankles.

"Doctor," he said, still bent over the body, "would you be so kind as to inspect the area immediately below the watch band marks?" Dr. Sherman asked. "Is that an indentation nearly circling the wrist, or are my old eyes playing tricks on me?"

Dr. Chong bent over the body and almost immediately straightened. Red faced he agreed that there was, indeed and indentation in the tissue of the wrist. "I see we will need to have some staff training on the powers of observation."

"Would you be so kind as to check the other wrist and both ankles?"

While the pathologist was completing the inspection, Dr. Sherman turned to us and said, "Gentlemen, I submit that when the additional information is factored into this excellent analysis, the conclusion of the report will change substantially."

"I believe this man was knocked unconscious, drugged, bound, and left where he would be sure to succumb to sewer gas." He continued, "I also believe that in the fragment of tissue taken from behind the right ear, you will find traces of a drug similar to curare – almost indistinguishable now, because of the normal toxic wastes produced in the blood at death."

"As you re-evaluate the data in the light of the new findings, I believe you may find that the time of death was probably not more than forty-eight hours before he was found." Dr. Sherman concluded his lecture.

"Kenny," Dr. Sherman said, and placed his arm around Dr. Chong's shoulders, "I remember only too well the days of the coroner's office – totally over worked, underpaid, harassed—I know, too well, I know. I have no doubt that had you performed the autopsy yourself, you would have seen what we have just discovered.

"And, by the way, I can be available to give training classes," he added.

"My advantage on this," Kenny, "is that I have seen too much of this kind of death. That is why, after twenty years in the coroner's office, I left medicine completely. I became an engineer."

Dr. Chong nodded his head appreciatively. Andy just shook his head in astonishment. Dr. Lawrence beamed. The young pathologist busied himself with cleaning up, and tried to be invisible.

I motioned Andy out into the hall. He lit a cigarette, and we talked about what I could use in the update to my story for tomorrow's paper. I did not want to blow the evidence for him, but I needed to be able to use as much as I possibly could.

In exchange for the few concessions he made, I told him a little about Dr. Sherman's experience in Las Vegas. I mentioned that he was struck by the woman's similarity to Barbara. Although it was risky, I thought I would bounce a question off Andy.

"Andy, do you know, off hand, if Cliff has ever done any work in Las Vegas?" While it could have been coincidental, Dr. Sherman's description of the woman's employer and his voice made me think immediately of Cliff.

"I don't know, but I could ask him."

"No, no, don't ask him," I responded a little too quickly. It aroused Andy's curiosity.

"Why do you ask? You don't think…"

"Oh. No." I interrupted. "It's probably nothing. However, when Dr. Sherman described the woman's employer, it made me think of Cliff. I'm sure there's no connection. There must be thousands of guys in the western states who look a little like Cliff."

Andy nodded, and seemed to buy my explanation.

When Dr. Sherman had cleaned up, I took the two professors back to the university.

"I don't know how to thank you, Dr. Sherman and Dr. Lawrence," I said as I dropped them off by the Engineering building.

"Oh, please," said Dr. Sherman. "Except for the circumstances, I rather enjoyed finding out I still had my touch. Besides, I've always felt a little tarnished from my Las Vegas experience. This may have been an opportunity to… mmm…well, clean off the tarnish. I only hope the police catch these people.

It was 3:30 p.m. I decided I still had a little time to drop by Bates and Broadman before returning to the office to write a new lead for my story on Simon's death.

Chapter 13

Monday PM

---◆◆◆---

I did not stay long at Bates and Broadman. Alexis had just completed designing the parameters for the computer analysis. The next job, a big one she said, was to code all the elements of the sewer construction so they could be read into the computer as a data file.

"It is only then that we can start the actual analysis," she said.

I found it remarkable how utterly intriguing this woman was. She was not pretty, or beautiful, as usually defined – her features were severe and irregular, her shape angular – but she was stunning.

Perhaps it was that she seemed very reserved that she gave the impression that she was untouchable, but not snobbish. I felt that any man wanting to break through her shield would have a major challenge.

Back at the Clarion, I told Max of what the professors uncovered, and that I would have a new lead for the story. It definitely appeared that Simon was murdered.

He asked a few questions when I told him that Simon's death had been meant to look like an accident. After answering Max's questions, Max went into his deep thought process, chewing the stub of his cigar to shreds. Finally he scribbled something on a piece of paper and handed it to me.

"Let's use this as the headline," he said. "We'll play it above the fold on page one, with a photograph. Then we'll jump it to the inside."

Back at my desk I started writing:

CITY OFFICIAL'S DEATH; MANSLAUGHTER OR MURDER

By David Montgomery

SF CITY HALL – Simon Blare, a key official in the City's massive wastewater construction project, was found dead in a sewer early Thursday, and may have been murdered.

Aided by a visiting New York ex-assistant coroner, San Francisco Coroner Kenneth Chong showed that Blare's death may have been made to look accidental. Tests currently being made are believed to show that Blare was actually murdered.

Blare has been missing for five days before his body was found Sunday, but the coroner's office believes he may actually have been dead only two days.

Dr. Arthur Sherman of New York, who assisted the coroner, described this death as a "style of killing" he had seen frequently during his 20 years as assistant New York Coroner.

Police have not established a motive for the killing, but will be interviewing all those who were in contact with Blare the Monday he disappeared.

Blare's body was found by two…

*   *   *

I blended this lead into the story I had already written and made a few additions to the body of the text. After I sent the copy to Max, I sat back at my desk and planned the steps to be taken tomorrow.

I decided to spend some time at Bates and Broadman. Alexis had said any help in coding the data would speed up the process. I outlined the information I needed to gather for a follow-up story tomorrow. I had just started to clean up my desk in preparation to go home when my phone rang. It was the receptionist.

"There's a young lady in the lobby who wants to see you. Her name is Margaret Worthington," the receptionist said.

"Tell her I'm working on deadline," I lied. "It will be twenty of thirty minutes, if she wants to wait."

My desk was now neat and orderly. I killed some time by reading the evening newspaper. After about thirty minutes I thought she might have left, so I headed for the lobby.

She hadn't

"Hello, Margaret. What can I do for you?" I asked.

"Oh, I'm so glad you're here," she said nervously. Her gestures were random, and over exaggerated. "Can we go somewhere…where we can talk?"

"Sure. Want to come into Editorial, or the conference room?"

"Well," she said awkwardly, and looked outside the front door. "Is there somewhere we could get a drink?"

"Of course," I said with more accommodation than I felt. "There's Ole's just down the block." Then to the receptionist I said, "Tell Max…er…Mr. Delacroix, that Miss Worthington and I stepped down to Ole's for a few minutes, and I'll be right back." It was a kind of insurance that someone knew where I was going. Margaret had seemed very nervous, and I didn't know what was going on.

Ole's had originally been a working man's bar. But as this part of the city sprouted high-rise office buildings and condo complexes, Ole's character changed. Most of the clientele were now office workers, junior executives and newspaper people, mostly from the Clarion.

During our half-block walk, she didn't talk much, mostly just looked at me, and smiled nervously. She did say that she enjoyed dinner with me at the banquet; and that she was terribly sorry for making such an ass of herself.

The after-work trade at Ole's isn't large on Monday evenings. We found a booth at the back, pretty well away from everyone else, and ordered drinks.

"Okay, so what's on your mind besides the fact that you enjoyed dinner, and are sorry that you made an ass out of yourself?"

"I know I'm bothering you. I'm sorry. You probably don't even like me, and I would understand," she blurted out, tears welling up in her eyes. "I just don't know where to turn."

A tear rolled down each cheek. "I don't…I don't have… any friends…I mean that I can talk with…or at least would…or could understand. They wouldn't even know what I was talking about."

"So talk." I said bluntly. "It's your nickel."

I didn't feel very nice just then. And I really didn't want to encourage the nearly adolescent confidences I was certain she wanted to reveal. However, she stuck with it and I later appreciated it.

"As you've already gathered, I'm a pretty spoiled brat. And I'm not laying the blame on my parents, but they have pretty well raised me to be somebody's society wife. I've been to the best schools, and all that. But practically speaking, I couldn't hold a job. Honestly, I'm not sure I … even know what one is."

"I'm not pleased about this, and I suppose my battiness is a form of rebellion. But you see, when I was twelve, my brother was killed in Vietnam. After that my parents focused all their attention on me…I mean really babying me. In the process they let me get away with the most outrageous behavior."

"The only time they really insist on anything, is to accompany them to various social functions. I think they hope I'll meet some eligible bachelor, who will make an honorable offer, and take me off their hands.

"I understand that they were trying to make up for their sense of loss, by giving me what they couldn't give my brother, so I got a double dose of spoiling, okay"

I nodded that I understood what she was saying.

"I'm telling you all this," she said, "not as an excuse, but so you know that I have no practical way to deal with what is happening. I love them both so much I don't want to see them hurt."

She was coming across far better then she had Saturday night. She was beginning to appear as a genuine human being, with some understanding.

"My father is quite well off, and never needed to take this position as Chief Administrator. I think he took the position out an altruistic belief," she said. "He feels that the people of the City have been very good to him in business. And when this position came along, he felt it was a way to put something back into the City.

"After he was appointed, everything went very well. There were exciting events, parties…all sorts of good things for the first two years…actually up until about six months ago when they started construction on the new sewer," she said.

She said how her father, who had previously enjoyed his work, began coming home upset, or depressed…and now he has been receiving strange phone calls…and Floyd Hunt has been pressuring him to make some sort of decision. "But I don't know what is about."

"He is really trying to direct my father's decisions," she said.

"You know, I hate to say it because he is my father, but he is a good administrator." She said. "But now I am beginning to feel that he is out of his element with this sewer thing. He is not a trained engineer, and they throw this technical jargon at him, almost as if to deliberately confuse him."

"I…I'm afraid," she said, giving me a pleading look.

I had been slouching back in the seat during her discourse. I leaned forward, reached across the table and put my hands over hers.

"It's alright to be afraid," I said. "But it is important to understand what one is afraid of."

"Well, it is hard to define," she said. "I have this ominous feeling, like something is hanging over my father's…like… like he is being set up for something."

"I don't trust Mr. Hunt," she said. "I have this feeling, like he is part of some evil force which could destroy Daddy, on a whim. I know it isn't rational, but last night made it so strong."

"What happened last night?" I asked.

"It was nearly ten o'clock, I guess, and Mr. Hunt came to the house. He and Daddy went into Daddy's office. After a few minutes I could hear Mr. Hunt shouting at Daddy." She related.

"It was something about Daddy having to approve a contract…one that he said Daddy had already agreed to approve. Then they must have been talking about costs, because I heard Daddy shout back that he would not approve anything until he was convinced that there would be no more cost over-runs.

"Daddy told Mr. Hunt that he was tired of his lying, that it was destroying all their credibility. Then their voices lowered for a few moments. But then Daddy was shouting that he would not be blackmailed into doing anything he did not think was right. He ordered Mr. Hunt out of the house." She stopped, as if she was afraid to go on.

"And then what?" I gently prodded her to continue.

"No," she said softly, and looked directly at me. "Before the library door opened, I heard Mr. Hunt say something about Mr. Blare, and what happened to him. As Mr. Hunt left, Daddy was screaming at him that he would not be threatened.

"I tried to talk with Daddy, but he just went back into his office and closed the door. He would not talk with me or with Mother at all.

"Oh, David, I'm so frightened. Not for me, but for Daddy. Mr. Blare died, didn't he?" she asked.

"He was killed," I answered softly.

"Oh, my God!"

"Look, Margaret. I'm sure your father will be alright," I soothed. I really hoped she would not get hysterical now, not in Ole's

"Margaret. Do you think you could get him to talk with me?" I asked.

"I…I don't know. Daddy is kind of funny. He has always held things inside. He never cried, or said very much; even when Buzz, my brother, died. I think he feels it is a sign of weakness to show emotion, or talk about problems.

"Is he in any danger?" she asked.

"Probably not in any physical danger," I answered. "But I am sure that the danger will be reduced if he is willing to talk with me. It is important that you arrange a meeting for me as soon as possible…even this evening, if you can."

It isn't going to be easy," she said. "Besides his natural reluctance to talk about things, he'd be afraid you'd use his own words to make him look bad."

"I don't write like that," I said. I thought for a moment of how it would be the most convincing. "Look. Within a week I will be writing one or more articles about the sewer project. At that time, I will be talking with everyone connected with the project…even your father. At that time, I would be asking about things I have already found out. He would be in a defensive position because he would have to prove that he did not know about bad stuff that is going on.

"But, if instead, he works with me, before I have to come to him, it would look more like he wanted to get the problems solved," I said, wanting to build some logic for her to use with her father. "And I know that the public perception of someone who appears to be forthright is that he is an honest person."

"He should know by now that I do not slant the stories I write," I said.

She nodded her understanding.

I had just told Margaret that I would be at my boat in about forty-five minutes, when Max walked into Ole's. He looked around, saw us, but went to the bar rather than disturb our conversation. I waved him to come over.

"Max Delacroix, I'd like you to meet Margaret Worthington. She is going to try and arrange an exclusive interview with her father about the sewer construction, for us." I said as an introduction.

I told him we were about to leave, otherwise we'd stay and have a drink with him. I knew he had come in specifically to see if I was there, and was all right.

"That's okay," Max said. "Oh darn. I just remembered something I had to do before I left the office. Okay if I walk back with you two?"

"Of course," I answered, and the three of us walked the half block to the Clarion.

I saw Margaret to her car, while Max waited in the clarion doorway. After she was gone, Max and I held a little conference. I thanked him for checking on me, and told him what Margaret had told me.

"Tread lightly," Max cautioned. "If he is involved, he could be trying to find out what we know. On the other hand, he actually could have been duped. He may just be realizing how serious this is. Either way, he could be using her to find a way out for himself."

I nodded in agreement. We both felt that if he was innocent, he was in no physical danger. We also agreed that Lieutenant Sullivan should be told that Worthington may have been threatened by Hunt through a reference to Simon Blare.

"Tread lightly," Max said. "If he's involved, he could be trying to find out what we know. On the other hand, he actually could have been duped. He may just be realizing how serious this is. Either way, he could be using her to find a way out for himself."

I finally reached Andy at home. He was catching up on some family time. His wife, Helen, didn't sound very pleased to hear from me. But she let me talk to Andy after I promised that my message would not take Andy out this evening.

Briefly, I told Andy about the threat to Worthington, and suggested that Hunt might know a lot more about Simon's death than we had suspected.

Andy told me that his report he turned over to City Hall concluded that Simon's death was not accidental, and was probably murder. He said he would have someone keep an eye on Hunt.

After I finished my conversation with Andy, I headed for home. I was not hungry, but decided an omelet could tease my taste buds. For a change I chopped some vegetables into the pan. When I sat down to eat, I found it had turned out better than I had expected, and that I was really hungry.

It was an hour before the phone rang. It was Margaret. She said her father had seemed interested, but had gone out.

"Do you think he is in any danger?" Margaret asked.

"No, I don't think he is in any physical danger," I reassured her. We talked a bit longer and I found that she really could be a pleasant person.

"David," she said, "I want to thank you so very much for listening to me. You are about the only person who listens and takes me seriously…I mean for me, not for who my father is. You don't seem to care about who people are or who they are related to. You just take people as they are. I like that."

I thanked her, and suggested that she might want to consider doing something on her own…something to set her apart from her parents, like get a job, or do volunteer work.

"That's one way to get people to respond to you, for your own qualities." I said. "Call me when your father gets home, if he is still interested in talking with me."

I hung up, and settled down with the last of the sewer documents. It was after midnight when I finished.

Chapter 14

Tuesday

———⟫⟡⟪———

I had scheduled this day to work with Bates and Broadman, so immediately after staff meeting I headed for their offices.

This time, when I stepped off the elevator, the receptionist greeted me like a long lost friend—even though I had just seen her yesterday.

"Oh, Mr. Montgomery, I read your article about that poor Mr. Blare," she said. "You really tell it like it is."

I smiled pleasantly at her.

"You must have such an exciting life," she said, as she lifted the telephone receiver to announce me.

"Oh, I do," I said, chuckling to myself. However, about this time, I was wishing it that it was not quite so exciting. "It is just one thing after another, but I thrive on it," I teased.

She giggled like a schoolgirl, as she told Mr. Bates' secretary I was in the lobby.

But it was Alexis Treller who came to collect me, and escort me into the offices. She was as professionally dressed as she had been the day before, with a fuller A-line skirt and a tailored blouse. In heels, she was nearly my height. Her height and slenderness accented her angular features.

I followed her into her office. Her office, like her style of clothing, was simple in decoration, almost austere. The furniture was a light frame construction, similar to a Scandinavian design, and consisted of a desk, a worktable, two bookcases, matching chairs and a settee. There were a couple of hanging plants in front of the floor to ceiling windows. The room had a light an airy feeling, almost like a garden. The only contrast to the room's natural simplicity was the keyboard, computer video display on a stand adjacent to the desk.

She motioned me to a chair, and seated herself behind the desk. She pulled a chart from the worktable, and spread it out on her desk.

"This is where we are, Mr. Montgomery," she said, pointing to the fourth step on the chart. "As you know, we were building a standardized coding structure for all the data. As we sit here, right now, it is being fed into the computer."

"You may have just created a marketable product," I commented. "I'm sure other engineering firms could use something like this." I paused. "By the way, Miss Treller, please call me David. And may I call you Alexis"

"Why certainly," she answered. Then as the complete professional, she changed the subject back to the job at hand. "Now, there are certain items for which we have been unable to establish a standardized code. Perhaps you can help us with those."

I nodded, not exactly sure what would be expected of me. I could use a computer, which I did for all my stories, but how to make it do something other than operate as a word-processing program, I was almost at a loss.

"By the way, Dr. Lawrence will be in about noon to review the design criteria we used," she continued. "By that time we should be able to see some preliminary analysis."

219

"Dr. Lawrence will be much better at helping you establish the codes you need," I excused myself. "He is really much more familiar with engineering projects than I am, because of a close association and friendship with Mr. Blare I'm sure he will put a lot of effort into this. They were very close."

"Thank you for telling me that. Dr. Lawrence will then be even more valuable in the assessment." She said. "This model will reflect performance, as well as costs of construction, and with Dr. Lawrence' help, even the probable cost of operation," she explained.

"Wow," I marveled. "I didn't know you could do so much."

"We have to, these days, with the cost of energy and the environmental impacts from construction." She said.

I was amazed. This woman talked like a computer. I wondered if she might not be a product of the engineering firm – a humanoid in attractive packaging.

"Alexis, I kind of understand what you have been doing, but I am people oriented, mostly because of my craft," I said. "And while I have been exposed to computers and various technologies, it is necessary for me to explain it all in every day terms – understood by ordinary, non-computer, people," I started, giving her a warm understanding smile.

"As we go along, would you mind helping me?"

"Oh, of course not. I don't mind at all," she answered, displaying the first warmth I had seen from her.

"Thank you. I appreciate that. Also, would you mind telling me a little about yourself? I find I work better if I have established a little people-to-people rapport," I said.

"Why, Mr....er, David. Are you...suggesting that I... that I am rather detached...a little like a computer?" She appeared a little bit flustered.

"Well … I would not have said it quite like that." I've really blown it, I thought. "What I probably should have said," smiling so I hoped she would think it was said as a friend, and not criticism. "is that you are very professional, and rather reserved…or formal. And I wanted you to know that it was alright to relax the formality with me."

She started to say something, but I raised my hand to interrupt her so I could finish my thought.

"I also wanted you to know that I won't make a pass at you," and laughed.

She laughed. It was a deep rich laugh.

"David, you must be a mind reader," she said. "I'm a woman in a man's world. The ultra-professionalism and formality are two very good defenses. Most men think I'm terribly cold and impersonal, and they probably would feel very little ego gratification from such a cold person."

"And are you?"

"Perhaps some," she said, with a sound that could have been a sigh. "I grew up in a world of rough and tumble men…oil riggers, engineers, and geologists. Many of them chased everything that wore a skirt.

"My mother ran off when I was three, and my father dragged me through every new oil field in the entire Southwestern Unites States," she explained, her voice edged with what sounded like pain, or bitterness. "I guess I've seen the worst side of the so-called men's world."

Her early education had been at camp tables, oilrigs and an occasional boomtown school. However, she had graduated from MIT at the top of her class.

"Math and science came easily for me, probably because I had already learned the application," she said.

Working with Alexis was a real pleasure. She made sure I understood each step of the process to get to the analysis they would be producing.

Dr. Lawrence arrived shortly before noon, and dug right in to the project. He reviewed the approach Alexis had selected for the computer model, and answered questions about the uuencoded entries.

We ordered sandwiches in, and ate as we worked.

Dr. Lawrence provided some design modifications to be factored into the computer analysis, and praised Alexis for the completeness of the model.

"The design is excellent, and I believe you have constructed an outstanding model," he said. "I may want you to come and lecture at some of my advanced design classes, if your employer will let you. You could make this into a package and market it to other engineering companies… or maybe you do not want the competition. But it is that good."

By the end of the day, we had been able to extract a preliminary assessment of the original design from the computer. It appeared that the construction of the project, as currently designed, would cost more than $4 billion, without including the current inflation factors, such as for cement, increasing at 10 percent a month.

"That's incredible," Alexis said. "It's over three times the City's published estimates. Of course we haven't run any of the optimization programs, or by overlapping subprojects. And we haven't included any of Dr. Lawrence's modifications into the costs yet. But still…"

"I can't imagine either of those would bring the costs down very much," observed Dr. Lawrence.

"How can there be such a drastic difference between the City's estimate and these figures?" I asked.

"Right up front, I really don't know," she answered. "You didn't expect that from the lady computer did you?"

I shook my head, and grinned.

"Okay, I'm going to recheck our work. But I'm fairly certain that we are right on target." She said seriously. "There could be several reasons for the discrepancy…anticipated changes which are not in the documentation…shortcuts not identified in the design…use of non-standard materials… misrepresentation…I'm just not sure." She said. "I think we'll get some clues as we refine the analysis," she said.

"I can guess at two reasons," I said. "Work not performed and substandard work.

"However, what you are telling me is that this sewer system could not be built according to the current design, using standard construction specifications, for the estimated $1.46 billion," I asked. I needed to confirm the significance of the preliminary computer findings.

"Bluntly, correct," Alexis answered.

After bidding Alexis and Dr. Lawrence good-bye, I went back to the paper, picked up my messages and mail, and went to my desk. There was a message from Andy, one from Barbara, and two from Margaret. My mail included the hard copy documents from the Secretary of State, and the new sewer map from the City Engineering Department.

There was a note from Mrs. Richman clipped to the map. "I assume this is for you, since I don't have a son. P.S. I paid the bill from my personal account so I won't blow your cover, 'son'." I laughed when I read it. She was a good sport and had real class.

I called Margaret first. She told me that her father would see me at 9:00 p.m. this evening. It was nearly seven, so I did not have a lot of time.

"He seems very worried about something," she added.

"Did he say what?" I asked.

"No, he still refuses to talk about anything to do with his work."

I said goodbye and hung up. Next, I called Barbara. A woman answered, but it was not Barbara. I explained who I was, and that Barbara had called earlier. The woman was the next-door neighbor.

"Barbara is at the funeral home right now. Mr. Blare's funeral is tomorrow at 2 p.m. at the funeral home," she said. "I didn't know him well, but he seemed like such a nice young man. Oh, I almost forgot, the family and friends are invited to the house after the funeral. I'll tell Barbara you called."

My last call was to Andy. I didn't bother trying police headquarters. I called his home.

"Mrs. Sullivan, this is David Montgomery. I'm terribly sorry to bother Andy at home, but like last night, I won't drag him out."

Without a word, she handed the phone to Andy.

"You called?" I asked cheerfully.

"Yes, I wanted to tell you we did put a tail on Hunt. But I think his friend must have tipped him off…or he suspected we were watching. He is playing it very cautiously. Today he obeyed all the traffic laws, like a saint. Very unusual. Normally he gets at least two moving violations a month that his friend in the department takes care of for him."

I thanked him, and told him about my meeting with Worthington, tonight.

"We may be very close to being able to give you the motive for Simon's death." I said. "The preliminary analysis indicates that the City may have misstated the cost of the project. "The computer analysis suggests that the real costs are closer to three times more than the City has estimated. It probably means that preselected companies bid low on the contract, then will up the ante once they start the project.

"We are too far away to notify Cliff, yet," I said. I added the latter because I still had some work to do in this area.

"I'll talk with you tomorrow and let you know where we are going with this."

Steve had already written a follow-up article for tomorrow's paper, so I could concentrate on tomorrow's activities.

I told Max we probably would have the whole story for the Thursday's paper. "If it goes like I think it will, we can wrap it all up Wednesday."

It was almost 8 p.m. when I left the Clarion. I stopped at a quick order restaurant to grab a bite to eat on my way to Worthington's house. I didn't want the embarrassment of my stomach rumbling while we were talking.

Worthington's house was in an area of fine old homes near San Francisco's old U.S. Army Presidio, now a City multiuse area and green belt. Since I arrived a little early, I cruised the area. I didn't expect any problems, but thought I should be prepared. The streets around the area appeared clear of suspicious cars. There were very few cars parked on the streets in this neighborhood. All of the houses were single-family houses with garages – very large garages.

I parked in Worthington's double-wide driveway. The house was a two-story, a Tudor style home, probably with five, or more, bedrooms. The outside was a mix of stone and stucco, screened with mature, neatly trimmed shrubbery. I walked the curved walk to the front door and rang the bell. Before the doorbell had completed playing its tune, Margaret opened the door.

"Oh, I'm so glad you're here," she greeted me. "He's so moody. I've never seen him like this."

I suggested that once she shows me in, that she should excuse herself.

"Oh, but if it is something terrible, I want to be there… to give him support, moral support," she said.

"You'll be able to do that after I leave," I said. "I think he will feel more like talking without you there. Right now, it would be harder for him to be open with me, if you were there."

She nodded, and turned into the foyer. I followed her down an impressive hallway to the library. I was not prepared for the magnificence of the room. It was lined with floor-to-ceiling bookcases, and appeared to contain many fine old volumes, probably even some first editions. A round, stained-glass window was positioned above the French doors at one end of the room. Worthington was seated at an antique writing desk in front of a fireplace that I could have stood in.

"Daddy, you remember David Montgomery, don't you?" She said by way of an introduction.

"Why, of course. Come on in, David. How are you?" he asked, indicating a club chair near the writing table.

"I'm fine, Sir" I answered.

"Thank you for escorting Margaret the other evening. She has spoken of little else," he said, with a half-hearted smile.

"Oh, Daddy! You are too much. Now, if you excuse me, I have a few things to do," she said, and backed out of the room. She closed the door, but I was certain she was just outside. Her knowledge of Hunt's conversation with her father told me she had been eavesdropping quite a bit lately.

"Mr. Worthington, I'll come right to the point." I said, making sure he knew this would be a serious conversation.

"The new sewer construction project comes under your jurisdiction, I believe," I said. He nodded. "It is in serious trouble. The current estimate covers only about one-third of what it will actually cost. You did not have anything to do with the City's estimates, did you?

"No, I personally am not qualified to provide such estimates. I relied on the Engineering department of Public Works."

"I didn't think you were involved there, but you do supervise the people there, correct?"

"Yes." He answered tentatively.

"Well, some of these people are setting up a method to steal a lot of money from the City. Do you have any relationship with Mr. Hunt?"

"God No!" he exclaimed. "We've recently had words over the cost over-runs on these projects. You are saying it will cost three times as much as the estimates. Oh, God! Something's very wrong."

"That is what Simon Blare was checking when he was killed" I said.

"Killed?"

"Yes. The police are pretty sure he was murdered," I said. "Probably murdered by people connected with the project, because he knew too much. The murderer tried to make it look like an accident, but there is enough evidence to show that it was not an accident."

"There is a conspiracy to defraud the City of millions of dollars through the different construction projects connected with the program. I am about ready to expose this conspiracy. When this comes out, how you appear depends upon what you do this evening...right now." I said. "You could appear as if you were involved...or at the very best, as if you knew but did nothing."

He looked at me in astonishment.

"However, it could appear that you were helping to uncover the situation." I added.

"I...I knew, you know instinctively, that something was not right with all the requests to approve cost overruns," he said. "But...but...right now Floyd Hunt is demanding that

I approve over a million dollars in cost overruns. But I didn't approve them."

"Mr. Worthington, I'm new to the City," I said, "but from what I've heard you are a very highly regarded person. You have some fine accomplishments to show for the short time you have been Chief Administrator."

"This is one isolated problem," I said. "Granted, it is a large one. However, it is not insurmountable. If you tell me what you know, I can probably help you."

"Would you care for a drink?" He asked, now more willing to look at a solution. "I think I could certainly use one."

I nodded. He went to a cabinet, and poured two drinks. I took one sip from mine and set on the small table beside the chair.

"When I took this position over a year ago, I suppose I was caught up with the prestige and glamour. I really believed that everyone in the 11 departments I supervise were loyal, trustworthy, and honest. I really was not prepared to deal with the way this bureaucracy works.

"I also assumed that everyone knew his or her job, and was doing their jobs. And, most of the employees are honest and hard working

"I suppose I really was at fault for failing to look more deeply... to see what was really happening in the departments. When I started to probe, I found that promotional training programs were non-existent. However, Civil Service promoted anyway, based on longevity in the job and a test that had little relationship to the job.

"And that is just one aspect of the problem. Since I deal with only summary information, for the most part, that leaves the door open for other things to happen, such as those you are now pointing out.

"Yes, in that respect, I am very much at fault. But I would never steal from the City," he explained. "I am working to correct the things I have found wrong."

"I began to realize three months ago that things with Engineering and Public Works were not going the way I thought they should…I had been misinformed. Most of the variations were in the construction projects.

He had started to keep closer tabs on all the project activities, and had taken the time to speak with people in the City departments. However, he was finding that he had been completely circumvented in many areas, and had a hard time finding out what was really happening within these departments.

"In reality, my presence kept the political heat off the department managers. They could do pretty much what they wanted to do, within reason." He said. "I think they just viewed me as a figure head. That had probably been the situation with my predecessor, and maybe even his…"

"I just don't know," he said and paused. "There are eleven departments, two thirds of all City employees are under my jurisdiction, yet I can't even fire anyone, unless they commit a crime. It is just impossible to keep track of everything going on…twenty-two thousand employees, with the managers trying to carve out their own individual fiefdoms." He paused, and took a large swallow of his drink.

"Have you thought of appointing a sewer tsar, someone whose only function is to make the sewer project work properly?" I asked. "He would have to be a tough one, someone who could intimidate people like Hunt, because he wouldn't have the power to fire anyone on the City staff… just make them so uncomfortable they'd quit."

"Now there's an idea. Floyd Hunt would just about croak." He said, smiling with a little chuckle.

"You'd have to get someone who has done this sort of thing before. I am sure there is somebody in the US who has the experience and knowledge. However, I would not advertise it, and it would have to be a contract position, not civil service." I suggested. "Talk with people in Chicago and New York. I'm sure you know some of them."

"It would certainly take the heat off the day-to-day operations so I could look deeper."

"Okay, we have your downstream problem solved. Now about the immediate needs." I said. "We need to make sure that we take care of the apparent malfeasance with the separate projects. I don't think you want any tar from that brush." I said.

Bringing him back to the immediate problem just blew the enthusiasm out of him, and I could see the color drain from his face.

"Yes, we have to get from here to there," I said. "Tell me more about what has been happening?"

"All the contractors are selected through a sealed bid process, but I believe someone inside the department was feeding information to them...or perhaps even doctoring the numbers." He said.

"Any idea who that might be?" I asked.

"Oh, I suspect there is a link between Floyd Hunt and these companies. They show up consistently performing City contracts...and there are always cost overruns." He said. "What has been happening recently is that these companies are all requesting overrun authorization. The rate of overruns could likely triple the cost of the project, as you identified earlier."

"Hunt now tells me the companies will refuse to do any more work, unless the overruns are authorized...yet these are the very estimates to which they bid and contracted." He added. "I'm sure my daughter was alarmed by the argument

I had with Hunt Sunday night. That is probably why she wanted me to talk with you."

"Hunt said he has records that show I have been doing this routinely, and that if I don't authorize the overruns, he will make them public...the inference being that I am in cahoots with these companies.

"I told him that I won't be blackmailed. That is when he brought up Simon Blare's death, hinting that Simon was not cooperative. But he is shrewd. He never really made a direct threat."

"So what do you want to do?" I asked.

"I'm not sure. Last night I went to City Hall, and went through Hunt's office. But of course there was nothing incriminating there." He said. "I just don't know what to do."

"Okay...But what if, you were to call for help from the State; the Attorney General; saying you suspect fraud, but don't have the reliable resources to investigate for yourself?"

He gave me a puzzled look.

"That is part of the Attorney General's job...to support the various jurisdictions in the state when they need help. I would not want to alienate the City's District Attorney, so maybe you write a similar letter to him. After all, the District Attorney is supposed to go after crime."

"Oh... yes... I see. I would not be suspect if I'm the one calling for an investigation," he said, more brightly. "Especially if it is done before any of this comes to the public's attention."

"Okay," I said. "But we must act quickly. Why don't you draft two letters right now? I will make copies, for you and for me, and I will post them tonight."

"Tonight?"

"Yes. Right now." I said. "I have a chart of the interrelationships of these companies that I will send over to your office in the morning. Then I want you to call a press conference for 1 p.m. tomorrow. You can distribute copies of your letters to the Attorney General and District Attorney, and the chart I will send you."

He gave me a puzzled look.

"You don't have to be publically disgraced," I said. "One person can't possibly be everything to everyone, or know everything. I think most of the public knows that, and I think they will understand. You inherited a can of worms, and you are doing something about it."

"Okay, now write those letters." I urged. "If you write them, and I mail them, they won't go through your secretary and become gossip before lunch."

He pulled out two pieces of personal stationery, and began writing. He finished one, and handed it to me.

"That is perfect. It is simple and direct. An appeal he can't ignore."

It was to the Attorney General. It was well written, describing the possible fraud against the City. He asked for assistance by an investigation, and pledged his full support. At the end he noted that he was sending a similar letter to the City's District Attorney, but was concerned about the level of support he would receive from the DA.

The second letter was almost identical. However, in this letter he did not refer to his request to the Attorney General. When I handed them back, he folded them and place them in envelopes, put a stamp on each and handed them to me. He had not sealed the envelopes so that I could make copies.

"All right. I will make copies and have them delivered to you at your office tomorrow, along with the chart of companies. At your press conference, you don't need to say very much. You can use as your rationale the interrelationships, and the cost overruns. That is really all that we know for sure."

"But what if Hunt shows up, or they contact him after the press conference? He'll just say it is all my doing, and I am trying to cover my involvement.

"But all he has is your authorization for some cost overruns. Right?"

Worthington nodded.

"You don't have to worry about Hunt. Hunt won't be there."

For the first time this evening I saw Worthington smile.

It was sad to see how Hunt had intimidated Worthington, who had previously been an outstandingly successful executive. Maybe it is the nature of bureaucracies to funnel people into a particular mold. Lord knows, I have seen this pattern before, taking a strong, creative person and pressing them into a mold, as if they were in a strait jacket, where they can only function as the bureaucracy allows.

"So at the press conference, you are only going to show the interrelationship chart and copies of your letters to the AG and DA, and anything you may have on the cost overruns," I said. "You aren't saying anything about Hunt."

"And if you are as open with the rest of the press as you have been with me, you will receive fair treatment." I said.

"We are ready to break the story right now, but I think we can hold off until Thursday morning. You will have all the documentation you need by then." I added.

"You're going to run that story whether or not I go along with this," he said, incredulously. It had just dawned on him that I knew a lot more about the situation than I had indicated.

"That's right," I said. "You can either appear like a hero, who is trying to set things right...or like you got caught with your hand in the cookie jar."

"You'd do this for me?" He asked, and then his face showed apprehension. "So what...what do you want, from me?"

"Only your cooperation, in helping to solve these problems," I answered. "I'm here because I believe you are an honest man. I think that even if you knew what was happening, you could not have stopped it...not single handedly. I don't think anyone could have stopped the infiltration by these crooks."

"Mr. Montgomery, thank you so very much. You'll never know what you've done for me," he said.

"You should thank your daughter." I said. "It was her interest in your well-being which brought us together tonight."

He showed me to the door. As I turned to say good night, I caught a flash of movement in the hall. I guessed that Margaret had never been very far from the library door.

I stood on the doorstep for a moment to adjust my eyes to the dark. It was after 11 p.m., and there was the typical San Francisco foggy mist in the air. I stuck my key in the car door, and sensed a movement of a shadow by the shrubbery next door. I instinctively turned to meet it, dropping into a defensive crouch I had been taught in the Army, my back to the car.

"Whoa, easy fella," said Andy as he stepped out of the shadows. You are so many steps ahead of me; I thought I ought to protect the most knowledgeable lead I have."

The sudden release of adrenalin left me almost trembling.

"Can you give me a lift?" He asked. "I had them drop me off. I didn't want a tell-tail unmarked police car sitting on the street...though it would have been a lot more comfortable than standing in the bushes."

"I think your goons are on the prowl, and I half expected them to show up. I think they did drive by a little while ago, but they didn't stop.

"Sure, I'll give you a lift." I answered, as my heart rate returned to normal.

He spoke into a police communications device that he had in his pocket, to let his backup know he was leaving the scene for the night.

"I have to stop and make some copies before I take you home," I said

As we got into the car he said, "Darn, Montgomery, when are you going to get a car that a man can fit into,"

We headed for an all-night market on Geary Boulevard, which had a copy machine. On the way, I filled him in on some of what Worthington had said...particularly his suspicions of Hunt.

Andy told me that the police lab report, as well as the coroner's final report, definitely established that Simon had died in some other location.

At the market I made two copies of the letters, and dropped the originals into the post box outside. I let Andy read the copy of the letter to the D.A. When he finished, he let out a low whistle.

"You really think it is Hunt, don't you?" Andy asked, as we headed for his house in the Sunset/

"Let's put it this way," I said. "We now know there some sort of collusion going on with the sewer construction. It can only happen if there is some help from inside Public Works. Hunt and his assistant are the only people who see the daily stats and activity reports," I continued. "That places the suspicion on Hunt and his assistant as prime suspects for the inside contact. But that doesn't make them the prime suspects in Simon's death. However, they are not ruled out, either."

"Simon was the only other person in the department who was in a position to see anywhere near as much of the project as Hunt. But he didn't have access to the original daily reports. I think what he saw was the doctored reports, so when he saw water, or sewage, coming from the Lands' End outfall he knew the reports he saw were not accurate."

"If Simon could not be bought, there was only one other way to handle him, from the conspirators' point of view… which they did

"I don't think it makes Hunt the murderer, but it certainly places him in the middle, as an accomplice."

Andy agreed with my logic, and said they were watching Hunt very closely.

"While I agree with your logic, everything we have so far is completely circumstantial…and some of it is still pretty sketchy, Andy said. "We are going to have to have a lot more before we can pick up Hunt…even just for questioning."

"I think that by tomorrow evening we'll have more evidence," I said guardedly. "With this I think we can rule out any involvement by Worthington."

"What do you mean by that?" Andy asked.

"I'm convinced that Worthington really wasn't involved. That he didn't…"

"No! I mean about evidence by tomorrow evening." Andy interrupted. "Are you up to something I ought to know about?"

"Oh no." I answered, innocently. "I meant that the crime is one that must be solved through logic. I think we can rule out Worthington. This means there are other areas on which we can concentrate, and I think that information will prove to be more fruitful."

I hoped Andy did not think I was on to something. I did not want him to alert Cliff. That was the unknown area that

I had to find out more about. If Andy notified him with my suspicions, it could blow everything completely.

I dropped Andy at his house, and made it back to the boat a few minutes after midnight.

My cell phone rang just after I had put the light out.

"David, I don't know how to thank you," Margaret said.

"Just stop feeling sorry for yourself, get off your ass and go do something productive," I said lightly, and blew her a kiss before I hung up.

Chapter 15

Wednesday

I awoke even before the gulls started squabbling over edibles deposited on the sea wall during the night. It was still quite dark.

I was excited. I knew that with any kind of luck I would have the full story for tomorrow's paper. That was what I couldn't tell Andy last night.

After a quick shower, I dresses and ate breakfast. Then I started dialing the telephone. I had made a lot of contacts over the years, and was starting to collect on some IOUs and create some new ones. My nineteen phone calls were all across the United States. I needed to get the name and phone number of a particular person who held a special government position. I finally got the name and number I wanted.

Using my cell phone I called an old friend from my days in the military. He was a master at electronics surveillance, and was still in the army, working surreptitiously out of a downtown San Francisco building. I explained what I was working on, and said I needed a house thoroughly bugged. He readily agreed after I explained why. Normally he would not have been so willing, but his father and uncle

238

had refused to pay protection to organized crime. They were brutally killed as an example to the rest of the neighborhood.

Finally, I dialed the number that had taken me nineteen calls to locate. It was to a person I had never met. He was one of the top men in the U.S. Justice Department west of the Mississippi, I prayed that he was in.

On the fourth ring he answered the telephone.

I told him who I was and the name of the mutual friend who had given me his number. I told him the whole story – everything. I gave him my suspicions about Cliff and the circumstances, which had led to my suspicions. For more than twenty minutes, I talked and he just listened, only occasionally interjecting a question.

"So you see, I need some help this afternoon," I concluded. "It goes beyond local jurisdiction, and I don't feel I can go to the state."

"Yes, we are **very** interested," the voice said from the other end of the line. He emphasized the word very.

He asked a few questions, which I answered as completely as I could. He asked for my telephone number, and said he would call right back.

After ten minutes I began to fidget. At fifteen minutes I started to worry. At nineteen minutes the telephone rang.

"Your suspicions are correct," said the federal voice at the other end of the line. "The state is not involved. We've been looking at ways to get evidence on this one. He asked for the address and timing. I told him about my surveillance friend. He said he would see that it was covered legally so the evidence would be admissible in court.

"You realize, this whole thing could be nothing," I said.

"They all could be nothing, and sometimes they are, but if we don't proceed on the basis that they are real, we would never get any of them. Your information supports what we already have."

We hung up. I felt good as I walked into the office fifteen minutes later.

"My goodness, you've been early almost every day for two weeks," the receptionist commented as I signed in.

"I can assure you," I said cheerfully, "I am not going to make a habit of it, even though your pretty face does brighten the day."

"Oh, go on with you," she laughed. "I'm sixty, and I've seen some of the young ladies you run around with."

"Ah, but if I appeared more mature, you might take me more seriously, is that it" I quipped, as I headed for the coffee machine. I heard her laughter behind me.

At my desk, I wrote the company interrelationship story, which would be the keystone for Worthington's defense. The story would be a supporting one for the main story I planned to write later.

I made a copy of the corporate documentation from the Secretary of State, a copy of my story, a copy of the interrelationship chart and copies of Worthington's two letters. I put them all in an envelope with Worthington's name on it.

I put the story and the envelope for Worthington on Max's desk. On top, I placed a note. In the note I told Max that this story would be a sidebar to a major story I would have for tomorrow's paper. I asked him to save a large space on the front page for our breaking story.

In the note, I also told Max I would call later and explain why I was absent from the staff meeting.

On the way out I blew a kiss to the receptionist, and I heard her giggle as the door closed behind me.

It was a few minutes before 8 a.m. when I stepped off the elevator on the twenty-second floor, at Bates and Broadman. The receptionist was not at her desk yet, but the door to the inner office was unlocked. I went in. I found Rodger Bates at his desk.

"I see you're also an early riser," I said from the doorway.

He jerked, startled to see me.

"Ah...well...ah, Mr. Montgomery. Come in. What can I do for you?"

"I need a little information. I'll be brief, and let you get back to work," I said, settling into the chair in front of his desk without an invitation.

"I know some of the scam going on with the City construction projects. I'd like you to fill me in on how you think the bidding process is rigged. That is why you don't bid on any, isn't it?"

"Well...yes." He answered. He paused for several seconds, and just stared at me. I just stared back. "Let's see...where to start?"

He described how the engineering specifications released from the City's Engineering Department were legitimate.

"But if we used them, our bid would certainly be higher than the one accepted," he said.

"You see, as I figure it, there has to be two sets of specifications...one which would meet all the normal engineering standards...and a second set for the bidder they want to win." He explained.

"So do you think the second set doesn't meet the proper engineering standards?" I asked.

"I'm almost certain that's the case," he answered. "On projects where there are outside inspectors, say like this sewer project, the projects inevitably have cost overruns. In these cases the total cost comes out to be what any legitimate firm would bid. I believe the standards are not really being met in most of the City's projects."

"But isn't that dangerous?"

"Of course. However, the untrained eye wouldn't see much difference between eight and nine inches of concrete, or that the rebar is lighter than called for, once it is inside the cement. Once in place, no one is likely to dig it up and look. And only if there is an excep*tional* amount of stress would a collapse be likely to occur," he explained.

How many other firms know this is going on?" I asked.

"Probably only a couple of firms in the city." He said.

"Why didn't you just blow the whistle on this?

"A couple of us discussed it. We felt that if we make any challenges, they would be viewed as only sour grapes. You know, our bids were higher so we didn't get the job, and raised a stink."

"You see those firms which go ahead and continually submit bids for every project eventually receive a contract or two. But they are continually under pressure to shave costs, scale down the project…anything to cut costs.

"They are not told to cheat, but the implication is there. There is the constant feeling that if they don't play ball there will be no next contract. The pressure is on to cheat. Of course, the payment authorization is submitted for the full amount, but the difference goes to the collector…some goon who comes by the day after each payment is made.

"That just wasn't the kind of work I cared to do," he said. "I even complained to the State Attorney General's office, but there has been no change in the City's bidding procedure. Some investigator came by and asked a lot questions," he said. "But nothing ever came of it. So, we decided to pursue work in other areas, and have been able to find enough work along the West Coast to keep us very busy."

"Do you think the work on this project is sub-standard?"

"I'm certain it is below standard. But there is no way to determine without a proper on-site engineering evaluation."

"If you had the opportunity to perform such an evaluation, would you be willing to do it?" I asked. "I mean for pay, of course."

"Oh, most assuredly," he answered. "I'd do it just for the firm's direct costs."

"You may get the chance. And, if you don't mind, I'd like to use that offer in one of the articles I'm doing," I said.

A frown crossed his face.

"Oh, I'll be very careful how I use it," I added. "I wouldn't embarrass you."

He nodded in agreement. I heard his secretary in the outer office as the rest of the staff arrived for work.

"Would you mind if I used a computer that I can email an article to the paper?" I asked.

"Whatever you need, just tell Gladys," he said. "I'll tell her to take good care of you. I do appreciate what you are doing. You are helping all of us who want to be proud of the work we do."

I thanked him for his assistance, and joined Gladys in the outer office. She showed me to an empty office that had a computer already set up.

As soon as I had written and emailed the article to the paper, I left to find Alexis. She was in the lunchroom getting a cup of coffee.

"There you are. I've been looking all over for you. It is already late and we have work to do," I said, pretending to be very serious. It startled her. I continued, "Don't worry, I didn't tell Mr. Bates you were late. You really are going to have to watch those heavy dates." I was having a hard time keeping a straight face.

"You…you…" she said, and made a face at me as she picked up her coffee.

"Hold that pose! I want to remember it …an emotional expression from the lady computer." I joked. "If you wait a moment, I'll get a cup of coffee and join you."

"If I didn't think it would go to your head, I'd tell you I had a perfectly dull evening." She said, as we walked down the hall. "But since you head is too large for any known hate size, I won't tell you that."

We spent the morning pushing numbers through the computer. However, no matter what we tried, the lowest costs we could generate were about twice the size of the City's estimate…and that was by cutting down the size of the system.

We even took the objectives the new system had to meet, and using them as the criteria, created a new, minimum cost dummy design. That design accrued a billion dollars more than the City's estimate. This was even with the optimum conditions, without allowing for any construction difficulties, or accounting for the City's hilly terrain.

"Okay," I said to Alexis when we were done, "can you think of anything which would affect the cost more than a few million dollars that we haven't already tested for?"

"Well, there are some variables we haven't tested for," she answered. "But they would only increase the project costs. The only way you could possibly lower the costs, is to simply not do some of the work."

"Like what?"

"Well, for example," she explained" the plan calls for the construction of several temporary bypass lines to be used during the construction of the main storage sewers. Now if those lines weren't built, the cost would be somewhat lower."

"But what would happen to the normal sewage flow, if they weren't built?" I asked.

"If they plugged the sewer, the sewage would probably just overflow through one of the overflow points into the Bay or ocean," she answered.

I turned to the new engineering map we had hung on the wall. She pointed out several different locations where bypass sewer lines had been indicated.

"You mean, if the bypass for the project in Lincoln Park was not built, and sewer was plugged here, the sewage would overflow out this discharge pipe at Lands' End?" I asked, indicating the different points on the map. I was getting excited.

"Exactly," she answered, watching my excitement build.

"Well, that must have been what happened. The Sunday before Simon disappeared, we were sailing, and he saw water…or sewage overflowing here at Lands' End. I'll bet that the Lincoln Park project is now far enough along to let the sewage flow through. I'll bet that if checked, we'd find that the flow volume at the Ocean Side treatment plant was low during the construction period.

"He must have discovered that the bypass was never build, and was killed for it," I concluded.

"Your theory is certainly possible," Alexis agreed. "It makes a lot of sense that this was how they could reduce the costs. But then, how would they be ripping off the City?"

"By billing for the project that wasn't done, and adding cost overruns." I answered.

"That makes sense. If all the work records were cleared at one place, it would be easy enough to phony-up the work records," she said. "When I called you from Hunt's office, I was checking work records, but I didn't find any originals, and they looked like they were all done by the same hand."

"Alexis, you're a genius," I said as I grabbed my notes in preparation to leave. "One of these weekends I'll take you sailing, if you would like. You've been a tremendous help."

"Yes, I might join you, if I can't find anything more interesting to do," and then totally out of character, giggled.

I ran out of the door. I had a lot to do before this afternoon.

Back at the office I told Max about the probability that the sewer bypass near Lincoln Park had not been built, and that the sewer has just been blocked, causing the outflow that Simon and I had seen. 'You might have someone check on the treatment volume during the period the Lincoln bypass was supposed to be operating."

"I'm excited, Max. Very excited. With any kind of luck we'll have the whole story for Thursday's paper. Hold a hole, a big hole in the front page for me. I'll be in around deadline."

"That's pushing the press run," Max said. "We don't do that."

"Max, this will be one of our biggest stories we've ever had. The competition will have part of it tomorrow morning. We ought to be able to bend the rules just this once."

"Well, we might, just this once. I'll clear it with Mrs. Richman," Max said. "It will cost us a couple of hours of printers' time, though, and that's a lot of money for us. Is it worth it?"

"I think it is," I replied.

Chapter 16

The Funeral and Later

———⟫◆⟪———

It was now 1:00 p.m. and I was hungry, having been up before 5:00 a.m. with only an early breakfast. So I stopped at the sandwich shop next door, and then popped into my car for the trip to the funeral home. As I pulled away from the curb, munching on my sandwich, I saw a dark blue car pull away from the curb behind me. Tempted though I was to give them a hard time, I knew I'd meet up with them later this afternoon.

As I parked at the mortuary where Simon's funeral would take place, I saw the blue car go on by. It had followed me all the way from the paper to here, turn by turn. The lot was nearly empty, and I thought maybe I was the first one here.

Walking into the mortuary, I felt uncomfortable. I have always been uncomfortable in mortuaries. I suppose that feeling had been amplified by my experiences in Vietnam, with all the death and destruction around me. For a bit I stood outside until a few other people entered. Finally I suppressed my feelings and entered.

"The Blare memorial service is in the Chapel of Peace," a solemn young man directed me. There was, as is customary, a guest book in the lobby by the door to the chapel. I signed it and entered the chapel.

I walked directly to the family area at the front of the chapel and screened off from the rest of the chapel. Barbara was there, as were Dr. Lawrence and Dr. Sherman, and a few aunts, uncles and cousins. I turned to Barbara and started to express my sympathy and she broke into sobs. I held her hands for a moment.

"Oh David, it is so good of you to be here." She said. Damn but that woman is a good actress, I thought. Barbara introduced me to the rest of the people. Before I turned to leave, Dr Lawrence rose and whispered to me, "…it is indeed the same young lady."

On my way to a seat at the back of the chapel, I saw that it was filling quickly. As I was approach the back of the chapel, Mary Smaller entered the chapel. I walked up to her and took her hand.

"After you pay your respects, will you please sit with me?" I asked. "These things really get me, and I'd like a friendly face nearby."

She gave me a funny look, and then nodded. I didn't exactly lie. Funerals do upset me, especially for people I knew. But when I saw her, I realized she could help me appear more authentic in what I was intending to do later.

She was crying silently when she returned from paying her respects to the family. As she sat, I took her hand.

"He was really one of the nicest people in the whole department," she whispered. "He was important, but always took time to be pleasant to everyone. He acted just like he was anyone."

I squeezed her hand, and nodded. I had trouble swallowing the lump in my own throat.

The service was simple and very short, for which I was very thankful. I felt relief that no one had given a long or emotional eulogy. As they wheeled the casket out, I put my arm around Mary.

"I really must go to the cemetery for the burial," I whispered. "Will you ride with me?"

"I was going back to work," she said. "But I know they won't mind. Besides, Mr. Hunt won't be back to work today…so why not?"

I was very sincere when I thanked her.

Our conversation was rather subdued as we followed in the procession to the cemetery. We each seemed willing to avoid the subject of our night together. We did not speak of the engineering department, either.

The burial was, I suppose, like most burials – a few prayers and readings were said over the body before it was lowered into the grave. People stood around, talking quietly – some remembered other burials – some commented on what the widow wore – and a few whispered rumors about Simon, and how he died. The widow invited everyone back to her house for a few refreshments. Then they solemnly shook hands with, or hugged, members of the family before departing, relieved that they were not the ones receiving condolences.

We were about to get into the car when Dr. Sherman walked up to me.

"I am absolutely sure it is the same woman," he said softly. "And I don't believe she recognized me."

I just nodded in response.

Mary gave me a quizzical look at his comment, but I ignored it.

"Would you mind terribly if we stopped by the Blares' house before I take you downtown? I asked. "I told Barbara I would stop by the house for at least a moment."

"Don't you think it would be a little out of place for me to go?" I knew Simon, but I've only met Barbara once, and I don't know any of his other relatives."

I reassured her that it would not be at all strange for her to stop by for a few minutes.

"Besides, it is comforting for the family to know that Simon was well liked by many people," I said.

We took a longer way to the Blare house, and I drove slowly, my Bug's best speed. I successfully missed a number of stoplights. We even stopped on the pretext that I wanted to buy a package of cigarettes.

"I didn't know you smoked," Mary said, after my return to the car.

"I don't often…sometimes at a party, or when I'm a little upset," I answered.

I could not tell her that the real reason I had been stalling was that I wanted to be about the last person to arrive at the house.

We were successful. The house was packed when we arrived. We mingled with those who wanted to pay their respects more personally – and those who felt better remembering Simon over a drink. The buffet had been set up as a bar, and platters of food spread across the dining table. I got Mary bourbon and water, and a scotch over for me. From here on, I was playing a role. For me, all the lines were cut and dried – I knew them cold. A couple of drinks would even help for effect.

We spoke with many of the people who had known Simon, school friends, engineering friends from the Engineering Society, and Dr. Lawrence. But the person I really wanted Mary to meet did not appear to be here. I was so certain he would be here; I had banked everything on it.

Within an hour, many of the people had left. It was only when we were able to get close enough to Barbara to speak with her that I saw him. Mary had just expressed her sympathy to Barbara, when he brought Barbara a drink.

A sense of relief flooded over me. He was the man I wanted Mary to meet – the man who had been with me on my boat just three days before. There was not a flicker of recognition in his eyes. He was as good an actor as Barbara.

"I'd like you to meet Larry Long, my cousin from Los Angeles," Barbara introduced. She was unaware I had already met him under a different name, and knew of him as yet a different name.

"I'm very pleased to meet you," he said, playing his role perfectly. "I'm only sorry it is under these circumstances."

I hoped my acting was as convincing as his, as I introduced Mary and myself. I had my hand on her arm and felt her stiffen at the sound of his voice. I squeezed harder to keep her from saying what I knew was going through her mind. I hoped I had not bruised her. I was already certain of his identity, but Mary's reaction had absolutely confirmed it.

After a few moments of conversation he excused himself on the pretext of seeing after the guests. But I knew has eyes were on us, from where ever he was. We were soon able to break away from Barbara, and I steered Mary into the kitchen.

"You know him, don't you?" I asked.

"I've never seen him before...but...that voice. I'd know it anywhere."

"I thought you would," I said. I pulled a twenty dollar bill from my pocket and pressed it into her hand. "It is a rather distinctive voice."

"Now I want you to get away from here. Go to Geary Boulevard... at the end of the block...catch a cab." I instructed. "After you catch the cab, stop on the way downtown and call this number...it is Lt. Andy Sullivan. Here is his card. If he isn't at the office, his home number is on the back. Tell him I said for him to get his ass over here right now…immediately"

I explained how to get out of the house from the back, through the passage along the side of the house.

"You son-of-a-bitch!" She said with a smile. You've been using me…but the funny thing is that I don't really mind."

The she kissed me, hard on the mouth. It was a kiss I would have loved to savoir, but I didn't have time.

"Be careful," she said, and stepped out of the kitchen door.

On the way back to the living room, I stopped at the bathroom. I flipped the lock, and closed the door from the outside. I checked it, and found that the lock held fast.

I sauntered into the dining room and poured myself another drink, then into the living room. It was starting to get dark outside. Most of the guest had already departed. I struck up a conversation with the few remaining guests.

Suddenly I felt a presence behind me. I turned. It was Barbara's 'cousin,' Larry Long – or Cliff, as I had first met him.

"Where's your lady friend?" He asked. All hospitality was gone.

Why, I believe she said she was going to the ladies' room." I said. I slurred my speech ever so slightly. He turned and left the room, but was back in a moment.

"The bathroom door is locked, and there is no answer from inside," he said. "Do you suppose there is anything wrong?" His voice did not register any particular concern. It carried an edge of a sharp steel command.

"I don't know. I'd better go and see."

He walked with me. As I left the living room I caught a glimpse of the last guests being ushered out by Barbara. Only Barbara and Floyd Hunt remained in the living room.

I had not seen Floyd before. Obviously, I was delaying some sort of conference.

I entered the hall and found myself facing the two goons at the other end. There was no way to go, but toward them. Cliff was right behind me. They moved forward, and we met right in front of the bathroom door.

"Well, hello. Fancy meeting you here" I said, and smiled innocently at them. They didn't talk, and they did not smile back.

At the door, I put on a little show. I wanted to make sure the last guests had time to leave the house.

"Mary. Honey. Open the door. Are you ill?" I pretended to listen for an answer. "Come on, Hon. Open up. I'll take you home now."

I milked this act for a good couple of minutes before Cliff got impatient.

"Oh, shit," he said. and pushed me aside. He motioned to one of the goons. With one kick, he opened the door.

"God damn it!" shouted Cliff, looking into the empty bathroom. "Where'd she go?"

"Why…I don't know," I said, dumbly. "She said she was going to the bathroom."

He lifted an arm, as if to hit me, but stopped. I almost wished he had tried, for I would have taken him apart, and then suffered the consequences from the goons.

"Alright, what's the game? He asked. He grabbed my arm and pulled me back into the living room, the two goons following behind. I didn't resist. I didn't want him to feel that I going to put up a fight, not just yet. In the living room I pulled my arm from his grasp, and casually seated myself on the sofa.

"Why don't you tell me?" I asked. "Are you asking as Cliff, the Deputy Attorney General…as Larry Long,

Barbara's LA cousin…or as Larry Languitini, West Coast mafia organizer? Which is it?"

Barbara and Hunt stared at me, their mouths practically hanging open in a look of incredulity that I knew that much about him.

"I don't know what you're talking about," he said, feigning innocence.

"Oh, come on. I know most of the story." I said. "But you could help me fill in the blanks."

"To start with, so we can keep the cast of characters straight, your real name is Lawrence Languitini, isn't that correct? Your voice gave you away. It is rather distinctive, you know."

"You're too smart for your own good," Languitini said sparks flashing in his eyes. "You and Simon will soon have something in common."

"That certainly is a direct threat. I don't doubt for a moment that you really mean to kill me now," I said, giving my voice as much bravado as I could.

Hunt's eyes were the size of saucers. I had to keep them occupied so they would not think of where Mary might have gone.

"What's wrong, Floyd. Don't you think your boss would do that? You should know from Simon's death" I said. "By the way, I know all about the scam you've been pulling on the City…pay-offs…altered bid specifications…substandard construction…falsified reports and records…the list goes on and on.

"How'd you find out? Nobody's had access to those records. They're not even stored at…

"Shut up, Floyd!" Languitini shouted.

"Come on, Larry. If you're going to kill me, I'd at least like the satisfaction of knowing how the whole thing went," I said.

"Now, Floyd. I figure you're the one who killed Simon." I said, directing attention back to Hunt.

I heard Barbara gasp. She sank into one of the chairs, sobs shaking her body.

Hunt didn't answer immediately, so I directed the attention to Barbara.

"Barbara, one of the things I don't know," when I said her name she immediately stopped sobbing, "is why you are having an affair with Dan Kirkman."

The sobs resumed.

"Oh, for God's sake, Barbara. Cut the tears." I said sharply. I know you're a good actress. You were also a call girl for Larry in Las Vegas."

The tears stopped abruptly. In case they thought I was just fishing, I spelled out their whole operation. The three of them were spellbound, murmuring agreement with the various key points.

"Now, Barbara. I'm guessing about the Kirkman affair, but I would say it was actually an intelligence probe, which could then be used against him." I said. "I believe Larry needed to know what the press was turning up on the construction scam, and be able to blackmail him, if necessary. Isn't that pretty much how it went?"

"That's right." Barbara said hollowly.

"So, how did you set Simon up," I asked bluntly.

"OH, NO!" she shrieked. "I didn't. He wasn't supposed to die.

"It wasn't murder. It was an accident," Hunt avowed. "See, we were just holding him in an unused sewage reservoir. We didn't realize there would be sewer gas there."

"You son-of-a-bitch," Barbara screaked, coming out of her chair toward Hunt. "You said you found him dead. You said you only moved him to the tunnel so his body would be found."

255

"You God damn liar. How much else did you lie about? She stood right in front of him screaming with rage.

"SHUT UP!" Shouted Languitini. He pulled a .38 pistol from under his jacket. The goons moved toward her.

"Barbara, as I was asking," I said just loud enough to attract attention. I didn't want the situation to get out of hand. "How did your affair with Kirkman start? Was this something which just happened, or did Larry put you up to it?"

I proceeded as if there had been no interruption. I ignored Larry's finger twitching on the trigger. Barbara regained control, and slowly returned to her chair. She put her head down. It was a moment before she spoke.

"Well...you have to realize...that...I thought I was out...really out of the ...whole nasty business in Vegas, when I married Simon," she said. Her composure had almost completely returned.

"What I didn't realize was that my meeting Simon had been arranged by Larry. He even encouraged me to marry Simon. Later I found out it was so that he could keep track of construction in the San Francisco area.

"We had been married six month. I was starting to believe I was really out of that rotten Vegas scene. Then one day he," she pointed at Linguitini, "showed up on my doorstep."

"Shut up, Barbara," said Languitini.

"I won't shut up," she said, angrily. "You said you'd tell Simon all about my sordid past if I didn't help you with just one little thing.

"Only you never kept your word. There was another... and another...and another. You said you'd leave me alone, but you didn't. The next thing I knew I was set up with Kirkman. I was as badly enmeshed as I had ever been in Las Vegas...even worse.

"I didn't want to do anything with Dan," she said, the tears running down her face. This time I really believed she was not acting.

"Simon was the only good thing that ever happened to me," she said and paused.

"AND NOW YOU'VE KILLED HIM!" she screamed at Languitini, coming out of her chair again.

"Larry," I said, again just loud enough to catch everyone's attention. I wanted the tensions to ease. I hoped to continue things on an even keel. I wanted to avoid another killing – especially mine.

"Larry, why were you afraid of Kirkman? I mean, why pick him to set Barbara up with?"

"He almost got me in Sacramento on some of the pay-offs to a few legislators," he answered. Then he smiled his evil smile, and visibly relaxed. The goons also relaxed.

You've been playing a dual role for a long time, haven't you?" I asked. "An undercover agent for the State Attorney General in one role, and a mafia organizer in the other – that's a pretty fine line, isn't it?

Languitini looked at me and shrugged.

"Just for my own curiosity," I asked, "did you infiltrate the A.G.'s office as member of the eastern organization, or did you turn bad once you were there?"

"Let's just say undercover work offers certain business opportunities," he answered with a sneer. "But it was organized from the beginning."

"I imagine the A.G.'s office did provide some advantages," I said. "I suppose that is how you were able to eliminate all your competition in the drug smuggling."

"Smart ass. Pity you won't have the chance to write about it," he responded. "No one is going to be able to finger me."

"What?" Hunt grunted his eyes wide with apprehension.

"That's right, Floyd," I said. "He's afraid that you're too soft...that you'll break too easily when you're arrested. While you may have wanted to believe you were just going to hold Simon, he would never have allowed you to turn Simon loose...not with all he knew.

I was talking with much more bravado than I felt right then. While I believe he didn't want to kill us right here, he did have an apparent taste for blood. Inside I was praying that I could hold him off long enough for my plans to work.

"And, Barbara," I continued, "you and I know too much to be let loose. He double-crossed you, and he is afraid you will try to get even.

"He also knows that I'd write a story which would expose him to the world. His eastern contacts wouldn't like that at all. We have enough knowledge to send him to the gas chamber so he can't afford to have any of us alive after tonight.

That sick, evil smile had been growing on Languitini's face while I had been talking.

"You understand perfectly, Mr. Montgomery." He said.

"Your only real mistake, Larry," I said, about to set everything into motion, "is in being here. I was counting on the fact that you weren't sure Barbara would keep her mouth shut until you arranged an appropriate accident.

What he doesn't know," I said, turning toward Barbara and Hunt..." about to say the magic words, "is that I have insur...

The front door burst open. I caught a glimpse of Andy's face as two shots were fired almost simultaneously. I saw Andy crumple as he made a low dive for Languitini.

"FREEZE!" Shouted a voice from the hallway to the back of the house at the same instant my shoulder hit Languitini at the knees. His second shot went harmlessly into the ceiling.

In seconds men carrying pistols and shotguns were swarming into the room. Linguitini was disarmed, shoved against the wall, frisked, and handcuffed.

The two goons hadn't even had time to draw a weapon before they were disarmed and handcuffed, as were Hunt and Barbara. It seemed like less than a minute before the five were being led to awaiting cars.

"Mr. Montgomery?' Barked one of the be-suited men, after I picked myself up from the floor. "Agent Charles Smith, FBI. We want to thank you for your assistance and cooperation. Your man will have the tapes for you shortly. Will you be needing a lift downtown to make your statement?"

"I have my own car, but what about him?" I asked, going to Andy.

"He's not badly hit. We've already called an ambulance, said the agent. "I'm sorry this happened, but when he came running up to the door so fast, we couldn't intercede in time.

"It was just plain dumb," said Andy. "Anyone on the street could see the guy holding a gun on you. I figured you were in a real mess. I didn't stop to think. I should have called for backup."

"Thank you, Andy. I really appreciate your concern," I said, feeling a lot of guilt right now. I had almost cost Andy his life.

I sat on the floor beside him. He was hit high on the right side of his chest, almost in the shoulder. He didn't seem in much pain, but shock was starting to set in. He shivered visibly. I took off my jacket, and put it around his shoulders.

"I'm sorry, Andy," I said. "I only wanted you to be here for the credit. I expected those guys to keep you outside.

"I never thought I'd have to shoot at a friend," he said slowly.

"I know," I answered. "You and I have both learned something from this. People aren't always what they appear to be."

"Hell," he said. "I'll be back at work in a week." His bravado was voiced through chattering teeth as a chill wracked his body.

"Why don't you take two weeks? It might help keep Helen from being quite so angry with me" I said, as the medics brought in a gurney. "It might be the only way you'll be able to take advantage of those nights on the town you said you were going to collect from me."

I watched as they loaded him into the ambulance. It left with siren screaming and lights flashing. I drove to the federal building, downtown. The first thing I did was call Max. I told him what happened, and I'd be a little later than I expected...but we had the whole story.

He told me Tim had photos from outside the house of Languitini holding a gun, and of Sullivan crashing through the front door. Tim also had shots of the FBI leading away the conspirators.

"Are you alright?" Max asked.

"Yeah, I'm okay," I answered, wearily. "I'll be there as soon as I make my statement...Less than an hour.

"Don't worry," he said, "we'll hold that front page hole, no matter how long it takes.

My friend from the Presidio brought in two sets of tapes he had recorded. During the funeral, he had placed bugs all over the house.

"I decided not to take any chances," he said. "Both of these are originals. I used duplicate recording devices. I got stuff even you weren't a party to."

We checked one set into the FBI's evidence center. He signed the affidavit that he had used prescribed procedures for the electronic surveillance. The evidence clerk provided the copy of the court authorization for electronic surveillance. The other set I stuck into my pocket.

"I owe you," I said, as he turned to leave.

"No…that's okay," he answered. "I figure we're even. You gave me an opportunity I've waited a long time for. I've always believed in the saying 'Don't get mad, get even'. I feel like I've evened the score a bit.

I reported to the agent in charge. He escorted me to a conference room where several agents and a stenographer were waiting. He introduced me, and indicated a chair for me.

"So that you are aware, behind that glass we have a video machine that will record both image and voice. To double-check ourselves, we have a stenographer as well. This is so you are fully informed. Often we don't tell about the video.

"Okay. So where do you want me to begin," I asked.

"Why don't you start at the beginning," suggested one of the agents.

So I told them the whole story. The stenographer took down every word. I was interrupted only occasionally by one of the agents with a question for clarification.

When I was finished, an agent asked if I had any questions.

"I'm just curious about what is likely to happen to Barbara Blare?" I responded.

"It's hard to tell, yet," said Agent Smith. "She has indicated a willingness to cooperate fully. If she does, I am sure things will go a lot easier for her.

"Won't she be a target, if she does cooperate fully?" I asked.

"We realize that, and will make some arrangements for her."

I was surprised that I felt any sympathy for her, but I was glad that she was cooperating.

"Languitini and Hunt are a different story." Smith added. "We are asking for $500 million bail on charges of conspiracy, fraud, murder, attempted murder, assault; more than 50 charges in all. And almost the same for the two hoods. They are wanted in other states for similar crimes.

"We don't think the state will prosecute as strenuously as we will, so we'll most probably retain jurisdiction on all the charges," he continued. "We have the legal basis because this project is partially federally funded, and because the rackets are involved.

"Thanks for your help, I am sure Languitini and Hunt are not going anywhere for a very long, long time. You've given us the break in this case we've been looking for. I expect we'll have a number of additional indictments for some of the people we are rounding up as we speak," he said.

As I left the building, heading for the Clarion, I passed one of the Morning Herald reporters coming into the building for a routine check.

"Hey, Montgomery. I don't often see you in here. What's going on?"

"Not much," I answered. You can read about it in tomorrow's Clarion."

Epilogue

———⟫◆⟪———

It was a beautiful Friday evening; one of the most beautiful I had seen in a long time. The sun had just dropped behind Marin's coastal hills, but the clouds were still highlighted with vivid hues of lavender and orange. Anchored here in Angel Island Bay, the boat swung easily with the tidal current.

Dinner was cooking, and I felt totally relaxed for the first time in weeks. The clean freshness of the air and the striking beauty of the view were totally absorbing. I earned this weekend, I thought.

It had been nearly 11 p.m. Thursday when I final left the Clarion. On the way out, Mrs. Richman had stopped me to say, "Well done, Mr. Montgomery. Well Done." I had written the main breaking story for Thursday's edition. Then I wrote four follow-up stories, explaining how the scam had worked. Max said he would have one of the other reporters follow-up on any additional arrests, and that I should take off until Monday.

When I got back to the marina, I walked to the Bed and Breakfast across the street, where Lange was staying I rousted Lange to join me in a large breakfast of steak, eggs, pancakes, and all the trimmings. After breakfast, I uncorked the bottles.

"Are we celebrating or commiserating?" Lange asked.

"Some of both," I answered. I tossed him a copy of the Clarion, and told him some of the things, which were not in the story.

Over the years that I was a soldier and a journalist, I have seen some nasty things. However, I have learned to steel myself against the emotional impact, especially since I didn't have a personal involvement. This, however, had affected me more than some of the more gruesome events I had covered. Maybe it was because it happened so close to me – to people I knew. And it happened in a town I now call home.

By noon, we were appropriately drunk – a condition in which I was able to find sleep. When I awoke, it was already Friday.

I stopped by the hospital to check on Andy. He was in great spirits, and was harassing the nurses. The doctors had told him he would probably be able to go home on Saturday.

"A penny for your thoughts," said the lovely lady beside me, bringing me back to the present. "You're awfully quiet."

I was silent a moment longer before I answered.

"I was just taking it all in…the sunset…the quietness… the beauty of our surroundings. I find that these things help me put my insides back in order.

She put her arm around my shoulders and her head against mine.

"It's very hard, sometimes, to make sense out of things… especially when you care." She said. "That's one of the things I like about you. You really care about things, even the little things."

My kitchen timer rang. I kissed her forehead, and rose to complete dinner preparation. I took two stuffed

Cornish game hens from the oven, and placed each on a plate. I added steamed rice and vegetables and a salad I had prepared earlier.

"Dinner is served," I called. I lit the candles. As she slid into the dinette, I poured the wine.

"To beautiful things for beautiful people," I toasted.

"She looked at me across the candles, her large, dark eyes twinkling.

We ate without much conversation. Talking was not necessary when looks can communicate. After dinner, it was still warm enough for us to have our coffee on deck.

Around us were the sounds of evening – night birds of Angel Island, mud hens diving for food, the lapping sound of water on the hull. The reflection of the stars above danced on the ripples of the water around us. There was contentment in just being together, without a need of conversation.

I lay back against the cabin, and rubbed her back gently.

"Ooh, that feels good," she said. After a few minutes she turned toward me, putting one arm around me, she laid her head on my chest.

"You're a very unique person," she said. "You're comfortable to be with. I feel as if I've known you for such a long time."

"I know what you mean," I replied. "I feel the same way. It's a very nice feeling, isn't it?"

She did not answer, but turned her face toward mine. I kissed her softly and gently on the mouth. I felt her lips respond. She moved so that she was in my arms, her breasts against my chest.

As we kissed again, I ran my fingers through her hair, and stroked her cheek and neck. Our kisses were long and lingering. I started to feel warm and flushed as my excitement built. My hands moved down her back across her behind and along her thighs.

Finally she pushed away from me a tiny distance.

"Mr. Montgomery," she said, her beautiful eyes looking intently into mine, "there is the most delightful bunk down below. Would you care to join me there? I have this overwhelming desire to make mad passionate love with you."

"Why, Ms. Smaller, I think that is most marvelous suggestion." I answered. "I'm certainly glad your parents postponed their trip."

"I was also very glad I had cancelled my other date. I just hadn't felt like going through the normal introductory games of a first date. When I called to express my regrets, I had the feeling that she was also relieved."

I remembered this afternoon, lying on the deck, catching a few rays of sun, when I heard this melodic voice.

"Hello, the boat. Is your offer still good?"

She was standing on the dock, an overnight bag in her hand. I knew at that moment that without her it would have been an empty weekend. I looked at her now; she smiled, stood, and slowly went into the cabin. I had been very comfortable lying there with her close beside me. I stretched and slowly stood.

I took a last look at the night and the shadowy outline of Angel Island. I thought of how marvelous the human psyche is. Like the human body, time and loving care provide the essential ingredients for mending wounded parts. I was lucky that I had both right now.

I felt a rush of emotions – sadness that such a bright person as Simon was dead – but thankful that he never knew of the treachery so close to him. I felt sorrow for Barbara who had gotten in too deep, and was too weak to extricate herself. But I also felt glad—glad it was all over—glad I could be out here on the water; alive to enjoy this beautiful evening.

With all these feelings running through me, I closed the hatch, turned out the light and headed for a most beautiful dreamland.

THE END

About the Author

―――――――――❖――――――――――

M arc spent more than 20 years as a journalist. More than five of those years were in San Francisco at the San Francisco Progress Newspaper, with the title of Investigative reporter. The series of articles he wrote about the City's waste-water program were nominated for a Pulitzer Prize. Marc hosted a Public TV information program series about San Francisco City Government. He covered the death of Congressman Leo Ryan of San Mateo and the Murder of San Francisco Mayor George Moscone.

Marc grew up in rural Indiana and attended DePauw University in Indiana. He is a Vietnam Veteran.